ELLERY QUEEN'S STRANGEST CASE

THE FINISHING STROKE
takes him into a dark and remote past where a long-buried secret explodes into murder twenty-five years later. And a killer challenges Queen to a game of wits and almost wins! !

THE FINISHING STROKE
the most baffling mystery ever encountered by Ellery Queen, the one he couldn't solve even though he knew the answer.

"Queen has combined memory and research to create a detailed and delightfully accurate picture of America at the end of the Nineteen Twenties; but, as is proper, the novel's true setting is Cloudcuckooland, its true time Nevernever . . . and how good it is to be there and then!"

—*Anthony Boucher,*
THE NEW YORK TIMES

Other SIGNET Ellery Queen Titles

The
Finishing
Stroke

Ellery Queen

a signet book

Published by
The New American Library

SIGNET TRADEMARK REG. U.S. PAT. OFF. AND FOREIGN COUNTRIES
REGISTERED TRADEMARK—MARCA REGISTRADA
HECHO EN CHICAGO, U.S.A.

SIGNET BOOKS are published by
The New American Library, Inc.,
1301 Avenue of the Americas, New York, New York 10019

FIRST PRINTING, MAY, 1967

PRINTED IN THE UNITED STATES OF AMERICA

CONTENTS

BOOK ONE

BOOK TWO

CAST OF CHARACTERS

BOOK ONE

Maximum Legal Speeds for Automotive Vehicles

In closely built-up districts: 10 miles per hour.
In villages or cities outside congested zones:
   15 miles per hour.
In country or outlying districts:
   20 miles per hour.

—From a New York State Law of 1904

∙∙∙∙∙∙∙∙∙∙∙∙∙∙∙∙∙∙∙∙∙∙∙∙∙∙∙

Chapter I ✠ 25 Years before: January 1905

*In Which a Lady in a Delicate Condition Comes
to Grief Through a Convulsion of Nature
and a Headstrong Husband*

FOR CLAIRE SEBASTIAN the new year began with delight. The baby was splendidly active—"Do you suppose it's a *colt*, John?"—and in the privacy of their hotel bedroom she even permitted her husband to feel the little thing wriggling and kicking against her abdomen. They had laughed together a good deal that week.

It had been John's idea to go into the city for New Year's and a few days "on the town." "I know how you've missed the gay life these past months, shut up here in Rye," John had said to Claire. "I think you have a last fling coming before you settle down to the awful responsibilities of maternity."

Secretly, Claire had thought it risqué to plunge into New York's social whirl in her condition. But it was a sweet recklessness, arrived at after a deliberate turning away from the bulging image in her cheval glass. Let those New York cats stare!

Until Wednesday, January 4th, the fling had been wonderful. John had reserved a suite at the Waldorf and had turned his massive back on Sebastian & Craig for the holiday. "It's

11

your week, my dear," he had assured her. "The publishing business and Arthur Craig can limp along without me for a few days." And he had kissed her with gallantry. Claire had actually blushed, it felt so like a honeymoon. "You're getting to be a regular kissing-bug, John," she had giggled. "Do you suppose we might go dancing to some of that awful ragtime music?" But there John had drawn the line.

Claire had no time to feel the loss. They spent New Year's Eve in the plush home of one of her husband's publisher-friends, among famous literary people. The champagne and the chitchat sparkled, and Claire was even asked her opinion of the season's best sellers—Winston Churchill's *The Crossing*, John Fox Jr.'s *The Little Shepherd of Kingdom Come*, Mrs. Wiggin's *Rebecca of Sunnybrook Farm*—and of modern young authors like Jack London, George Barr McCutcheon, Lincoln Steffens and Joseph C. Lincoln. Claire rarely shared her husband's sophisticated New York life, and it was an altogether glittery evening.

In the mornings John insisted on having her breakfast served in bed while he skimmed through the newspapers, reading the choicer items aloud. It seemed to Claire that the whole world was putting on special events in her baby's honor. She followed the last days of the siege of Port Arthur as if she were personally involved, and when on the morning of January 2nd the papers reported that the Russian general, Stoessel, was surrendering to General Nogi, she was surprised at the grimness in her husband's voice. "We'll have to deal with these chesty Japanese some day, mark my words." Claire thought it rather spoil-sport of him. But she had to laugh when he read her President Roosevelt's suggestion—in an excellent imitation of Teddy's bark—that wife-beaters be given the whipping post.

They dined at Reisenweber's, attended the theater every night, had their late suppers at Delmonico's. On New Year's night they saw Sothern and Marlowe in *Romeo and Juliet*, on Monday night Mrs. Fiske in *Hedda Gabler*, and on Tuesday night—in spite of the heavy snow that had begun to fall in the afternoon—they managed to see David Warfield in *The Music Master*.

In the afternoons Claire went shopping down on Broadway. At Arnold Constable's on 19th Street she dutifully bought some maternity dresses for the last months of her pregnancy; but at Lord & Taylor's on Fifth, and at B. Altman's over on Sixth Avenue, she flung common sense to the cold winds and indulged in an orgy of buying for "after"— taffeta petticoats with foaming froufrou; the new short skirts, of daring shoetop length, that were all the rage; exciting high kid boots with French heels, in cunning pastel colors, for day wear; a supply of "rats," cleverly made of wire, to build out her pompadour; even the new long hatpins, which the saleswoman at Altman's assured Claire were smarter than the customary two short ones; and, of course, gowns galore.

"You're not cross?" she asked her husband anxiously. He merely laughed and kissed her again.

So it was heavenly. Until the storm.

The snowfall through which their cab had struggled Tuesday evening to the theater kept up furiously all night. By morning the city lay still under a white straitjacket, with snow still falling. That day the *Herald,* reporting that the city was paralyzed, said that all transportation into and out of New York had been halted; many trains had had to be evacuated and abandoned in the deep drifts; Long Island was isolated.

The Sebastians spent Wednesday inside the Waldorf. John's holiday mood darkened; when it became evident that they could not use their theater tickets—they were to have seen William Faversham in *Letty* that night—he ordered a bottle of Red Top rye whisky and spent the evening sulkily drinking. Claire began to wish they had stayed unadventurously in Rye.

By Thursday morning the city was beginning to dig out of the snow. John left Claire to toy with her egg. He was gone from their suite a long time. When he returned he said abruptly, "I'm taking you home."

"All right, John," Claire said quietly. "Are the trains running?"

"Not yet, and there's no telling when they'll resume service. It may rain, and that will turn everything to ice and slush. Then we will be in a pickle." He did not mention his real reason for wanting to get her out of the city: the report that Police Commissioner McAdoo, in clamoring for 1500 more men, was worried about the ability of his force to cope with the looting that had broken out on the upper West Side. "The sooner we start, the better."

"But John, how are we going to get home?"

"The way we came."

"The auto?" Claire blanched. "How can we, John? The road—"

"Don't you worry about the Pierce. That machine can go anywhere." The big man actually sounded confident. "Get dressed and packed, my dear. We'll leave at once."

Claire crept out of bed. She knew better than to argue with John Sebastian about his beloved automobiles.

She was terrified. She had never got over her fear of the horseless carriages, although she had always made it a point to pretend enthusiasm. He had sold his 1903 Haynes-Apperson Surrey as too slow. Their current machine was a Pierce Great-Arrow Tonneau Car for which he had paid four thousand dollars. It had a 28-32 horsepower engine, its gearshift lever on the steering column, gas lamps, and a trap door

13

under the front seat for tools. Even this was not modern enough for him. He had just bought one of the famous White racing steamers—the auto known as "Whistling Billy"—which could go faster than a mile a minute. Claire silently thanked God that he had chosen the Pierce for the trip into New York.

She stood waiting on the pavement before the Waldorf while her husband supervised the loading of their luggage and her department store purchases through the rear door of the Great-Arrow's tonneau. Horse-drawn drays and cabs were footing it cautiously by on the partly cleared streets; a policeman on a horse—one of New York's new mounted police, organized only the past September—was trying to untangle a mess of skidding traffic at the intersection of 34th Street and Fifth Avenue. There was not an automobile to be seen.

Claire shivered under her fur hat and heavy Russian pony motor coat. John was whistling "Bedelia," his favorite popular song, as if he had not a worry in the world.

He tucked the fur auto robe about her, adjusted the rubberized storm apron over that, pulled his goggles down over his visored cap—he had had the motor warming up for half an hour—threw a dollar to the bellboys, and they were off.

That day—Thursday, January 5, 1905, the most significant day in Claire Sebastian's thirty-three years—was a nightmare of gasoline reek, frozen horrors along the way and slippery threats of death. Worst of all was John Sebastian's cheeriness. It was as if the great drifts, like swooping white bird-wings arrested in flight, the treacherous ruts, the dirty sky, the vehicles abandoned along the city's streets and the outlying roads, the occasional stiff projecting legs of a dead horse, had all been purposely hurled in Sebastian's path to challenge him to combat. Purple-cheeked and powerful, he fought them hour after hour with the cursing confidence of a man who knows that his strength and will must prevail. The pregnant woman crouched by her husband's side, shivering under her furs, alternately peering with fright through the ice-speckled goggles and pulling the woolen scarf futilely across her numbed face ... half dead with cold and hunger, and altogether demoralized.

The only thing that seemed to bother Sebastian was the pleasures the blizzard had obliterated. He kept shouting profanity at the elements that were causing them to miss tomorrow night's performance of *Aïda* at the Metropolitan, with Mme. Nordica, Scotti, and the new young Italian star, Enrico Caruso, whom the critics were calling "the heir to Jean de Reszke in the affections of America." The opera and the theater were two of Sebastian's many passions—about the

14

only two, Claire thought—that she could wholeheartedly share. Even through her misery, thinking of the evening gown she was to have worn to the Met—pink satin with coral ornaments and black velvet embossing, to be set off by a tiara and a string of pearls—Claire felt a sympathetic regret.

Rain began to fall just as they emerged from the Bronx onto the Boston Post Road. Claire clutched her husband's arm.

"John, we mustn't go on," she shouted over the clatter of the engine. "We'll turn turtle for certain!"

"Where do you suggest we stop?" he roared back. "Now don't worry, Claire, we'll be all right. The Pierce has carried us through in bully style so far, hasn't it? You'll be home before nightfall."

Long before sunset he had to stop and light the lamps. Soon they were creeping along at five miles an hour. Claire could feel the Great-Arrow's wheels slip and slide, clawing for traction on the rapidly icing snow.

Sebastian no longer cursed cheerfully. He no longer spoke at all.

A long time later Claire opened her eyes. The Pierce had stopped before an old livery stable beside a small frame house. Kerosene storm lanterns flickered in the wind. Dully she watched her husband get down from the auto and flounder to the front door of the house. He pounded until the door opened and a man in a torn sweater stared out in amazement.

"I saw your sign back there," Claire heard her husband shout. "I need some gasoline. Do you have any for sale?" She saw the man nod. "And my wife could use a cup of hot coffee and a sandwich."

John had to carry her into the steaming little kitchen. It was filthy and fly-speckled from the previous summer, but Claire thought she had never been in such a blessed place in all her life. She crouched by the beet-red stove sipping scalding coffee that tasted like ambrosia brewed from mud, and felt life creep back into her body.

"Poor baby," she heard herself murmur. "Are you still there?" The absurdity of it made her laugh, and she realized with alarm that she was going to be hysterical. Claire took a deliberate gulp that seared the nonsense in its tracks.

They came back far too soon. John drank some of the coffee rapidly, and she knew it was all to begin again.

"Must we?" she asked, trying to keep the tremor out of her voice; John loathed timid women. "I'd rather stay here than go back into that. It's getting dangerous, John. If you have no regard for your safety or mine, think of the baby's."

"Nothing is going to happen to you or the baby."

15

The man in the torn sweater said, "Your wife's in the family way? I wouldn't take a goat out on that road tonight. This ain't Mrs. Astor's town house, lady, but you're welcome to my bed."

"You're very kind," Claire said in a low voice. She knew it was useless. Opposition, criticism of any kind, only made her husband angrier and more stubborn.

"Are you ready, Claire?"

The livery man exclaimed, "Mister, you're loony."

John Sebastian tossed some money on the kitchen table, took his wife's arm, and propelled her into the night. He bundled her back into the Pierce in silence. But as he climbed in beside her he said gruffly, "You need your own bed tonight. Anyway, I haven't come this far to give up now."

No, Claire thought, that's the important thing with John Sebastian—never to give up, no matter what the cost.

Her fears came back in a rush, and she pressed her hands protectively beneath the robe against her belly.

The accident happened without warning. The rain had turned sleety, covering the slush with a film of ice. The Great-Arrow hesitated at the top of a rise in the road, lurched, and started down a hill out of control.

Every muscle in Claire's body contracted. She braced herself against the floorboard, staring wildly into the dark. The big Pierce picked up speed with sickening swiftness. John Sebastian whirled the helpless steering wheel this way and that, furiously.

Then they went into the skid.

Claire screamed, *"John!"*

It was the last sound Sebastian heard before the crash.

It seemed to him that someone was hammering on his skull with powerful strokes. The pain awakened him to icy darkness. He had been thrown clear; he was lying in a snowbank beside the road. He must have been lying there for some time; there was a moon now, and the rain had stopped. He sat up in the snow and took his head in both hands, but the throbbing did not go away. He staggered to his feet, feeling himself all over. Everything ached, but nothing seemed broken.

I was lucky, John Sebastian thought.

Suddenly he thought, *Claire!* He peered about, stricken.

At first he could not find her. The Pierce was lying on its back like a dead animal, half off the road. It had struck a big tree and turned over. Their luggage, Claire's purchases, were strewn all over the road.

Then he saw her.

She had been hurled out of the auto and it had fallen on her. She was lying almost, but not quite, clear; the heavy

16

machine had her left leg pinned down, and part of her thigh.

She was moaning

"Claire!" he cried, thankfully.

He scrambled over to her, fighting the treacherous footing.

She was unconscious; there was a smear of blood on the ice where the back of her head had struck. Sebastian seized the auto and heaved with all his strength. The fabric was stuck fast to the ice. Rage flooded him. He strained until he felt something tear and give. But then he stopped. He could not lift the machine and pull her out from under at the same time.

"Claire." He stared down at her bluing face, fighting panic.

Then he began to run up the deserted road. Once he slipped, falling heavily. He got up, his right elbow and hip burning, and ran on.

And there, a few hundred feet up the road, miraculously, were a white picket fence decorated with snow, a stand of big ice-covered trees, and behind them a lamplit little house. At the fence stood an iron standard, with a swinging black sign on which some gilt lettering glistened in the moonlight.

Sebastian peered, breathing in long white gasps.

Cornelius F. Hall, the sign said. *M.D.*

A great joy seized him. He wrenched the little gate open, floundered up the walk, and began to punch the doctor's door.

"I'm afaid it's more serious than a broken leg and a head wound, Mr. Sebastian," Dr. Hall said. He was a slow-moving little man of perhaps forty with bristly red hair and tired brown eyes. "I've set the leg and treated the wound, although I won't know the extent of the concussion for some time. But just now that's the least of it."

John Sebastian heard the little doctor dimly. The noise in his head had become a dull roar through which the real world had difficulty making itself heard. He could hardly remember how they had managed to free Claire and carry her to the doctor's house. He had crouched in the chilly parlor before the smoky little fire for over two hours while the doctor and his thin-lipped, untalking wife—a trained nurse, he recalled Dr. Hall's assuring him—worked mysteriously over Claire beyond the closed door. The tea Mrs. Hall had given him had grown cold between his hands.

"The least of what?" he asked stupidly.

The doctor gave him a sharp glance. "Are you sure you're all right, Mr. Sebastian? I'd better look you over now, while I have the chance."

"No. My wife, take care of my wife. Don't stand here jawing, man! What's the matter with her?"

"Her injuries, the shock of the accident, they've induced labor, Mr. Sebastian. She's going to give birth prematurely." Dr. Hall looked unhappy. "Mrs. Hall is getting things ready now. Will you excuse me, please?"

"Wait, wait, I don't follow," the publisher muttered. One of the several Gibson-Collier's drawings on the parlor walls was lopsided; it kept distracting him. "You mean my wife is going to have her baby—now, here?"

"Yes, Mr. Sebastian."

"But she can't. She mustn't!"

Dr. Hall's fair skin reddened. "Man proposes and God disposes, sir. I'm afraid you have no choice."

"I won't permit it!" The blood vessels in Sebastian's temples jumped. "Her own doctor—Rye . . . Where's your telephone?"

"I don't have one, Mr. Sebastian," Dr. Hall said.

"Then an auto—sleigh—anything. What kind of quack are you, anyway? I'll go for him!"

"I have no auto, sir, and my sleigh cracked a runner this afternoon on my way back from a sick-call. My rig is in the barn, but on that ice neither you nor my horse would get fifty yards." The little doctor's voice hardened. "Every moment you delay me is endangering your wife's life, Mr. Sebastian. She's your wife, but I suggest you don't take too long making up your mind."

Sebastian sank into a Morris chair. Dr. Hall stared down at him with some bitterness. The mysterious door opened. Mrs. Hall called urgently to her husband, "Doctor."

Sebastian gaped beyond her. Claire was stretched out on a bed like a corpse, a corpse that whimpered in a doglike way. Mrs. Hall vanished. And there was the door again.

"Hurry, Mr. Sebastian. Do I go ahead, or don't I?"

"Yes," the publisher whispered. "You'll do everything you can, Doctor?"

"You understand, Mr. Sebastian, your wife is in a seriously weakened condition."

"I understand. Go on, man. For God's sake, go to her!"

Ages passed.

At first John Sebastian thought that if the screams did not stop his head would explode. But when they stopped, he found himself praying that they would begin again.

He had no thoughts that made sense. He saw everything through a blur—the droopy rubber plant, the bearded chromo over the mantelpiece, the ball-fringed runner on the upright piano, the stereoscope with its box of views on the table, the green rope portieres masking the dingy hall. Once he got out of the Morris chair to straighten the Gibson girl, who had become intolerable. There were other prints on the

18

walls, Frederic Remington reproductions, orange-colored violent scenes of the old West. But a moment after he turned away he could not have said what they depicted.

And then, like an apparition, there was Dr. Hall again. He had come in with noiseless little steps, sipping hurriedly from a cup of tea and eyeing Sebastian over the rim as he came. Long red smears stained his smock, as if he had had to wipe his hands on it in haste.

The husband stared at the stains, fascinated.

"You have a son, sir. The time was one-o-nine A.M. My congratulations."

"A.M.," Sebastian said in a loud voice. "Which day is this?"

"You can put it down as Friday, January the sixth, since it's past midnight." Dr. Hall sounded hearty, but his tired brown eyes remained alert. "He's a small one, Mr. Sebastian. I judge about four pounds."

"Where are we?" the publisher muttered. "Where is this house?"

"On the outskirts of Mount Kidron, not far from the Pelham Manor line. Four pounds isn't bad for a premature baby, and he's sound as a dollar. Mr. Sebastian, as soon as this is over I really should examine you."

"Mount Kidron." Sebastian tore his glance from the bloody smock. "And my wife?"

Dr. Hall said rapidly, "Under the circumstances, I must be frank. Your wife's condition is critical. In fact ... Well, sir, I'll do all I can."

"Yes," Sebastian said. "Dear God, yes."

"You ought to know, too, sir—she's going to have another child."

The big man said hoarsely, "What? What did you say?"

"You see, the first delivery weakened her to the danger point. A second ..." The little doctor's red hair seemed to be flying off in all directions. But he was only shaking his head. "Now you'd better relax while I see to my patient. Here, drink the rest of this tea."

"But it will kill her!" Sebastian was on his feet, pulling at his collar, eyes distended in an enormous glare.

"Let us hope not, Mr. Sebastian."

"Take him from her! Let him die. Just save her life!"

"In your wife's condition, surgery would be almost certainly fatal. Besides, the child is coming naturally."

"I want to see my wife!"

Dr. Hall looked at John Sebastian with his sad brown eyes.

"Mr. Sebastian," he said clearly, "she doesn't want to see you."

And he was gone again.

Sebastian sagged into the Morris chair, clawing for some

handhold to his old masterful self. He was unconscious of the hot tea slopping onto his thigh from the cup the doctor had placed in his hand.

A twin . . .

Damn him.

"She doesn't want to see you."

Damn him, damn him!

The cup slipped from Sebastian's grasp, shattering on the hearth and sending a long splash into the fire, which hissed with hate.

But he heard only the reproachful echo of his folly, and the guilt-ridden man sat cracking his knuckles in an agony of despair.

Sebastian raised his head. "Well?" he said harshly.

Mrs. Hall remained by the closed door. She was wrapped in her own sexless plainness, her thin lips all but invisible. The hand on the blue china knob was so tense it looked bleached, like an old bone.

Dr. Hall approached the seated man slowly. He had removed his smock; his shirtsleeves were folded back above the elbow. The freckled hands were puckered white, as if he had washed over and over to cleanse them of mortality.

"Well?" Sebastian asked in a higher key.

"Mr. Sebastian." The little doctor paused. "The second child, an identical twin boy, was born at two-seventeen . . ."

"Never mind that! How is my wife?"

Dr. Hall said stiffly, "I'm sorry, sir. She has died."

There was the emptiest silence.

"If you wish to see her—"

Sebastian shook his head twice, violently.

"Well, then, the babies—" the doctor said.

"No." The big man jumped to his feet. His face had settled into stone. "What time is it, please?"

Dr. Hall pulled a nickeled watch from his vest. "Two minutes of four." He cleared his throat. "Mr. Sebastian," he began again.

"If it's your fee you're concerned about, name it and I'll write out a check."

"No, no, sir, it's not that—"

"Have you made out the death certificate?"

"Not yet. Sir—"

"Please do so. I'll see that an undertaker gets here as soon as possible. As for the child, I must ask you and Mrs. Hall to care for him until I can arrange to have him called for. Mrs. Sebastian's doctor will undoubtedly wish to send a trained nurse for the child's removal to Rye."

"The child?" Dr. Hall blinked. "You mean the children, of course."

20

"I said the child," John Sebastian said. "The first-born."

"But, sir—!"

"My wife has given me only one son, Doctor. The second murdered her; he can never be a son of mine. I want nothing to do with him. In fact, it will be extremely difficult for me . . . even the first . . ." He turned away.

Dr. Hall's glance met his wife's across the parlor. "You cannot be serious, Mr. Sebastian."

Sebastian laughed. "Where can I rent or buy a sleigh and a horse?"

"You can turn your back on your own flesh and blood this way, sir? Without a qualm?"

"You don't understand," the publisher said with contempt. "The little monster killed my wife."

The doctor was silent. At the door, Mrs. Hall stirred cautiously.

"Surely you have some plan about the . . . second child," the doctor said at last. "What do you intend to do with him?"

"I'll pay you to keep him here until my attorneys can arrange to place him somewhere or other. If you can't be bothered, of course—"

Mrs. Hall said quickly, "Oh, it wouldn't be a bother."

"No." Her husband's voice was eager. "Perhaps the hand of Providence has been in this after all, Mr. Sebastian. Mrs. Hall and I have never had a child. It's been a source of great unhappiness to us. If Mrs. Sebastian's unfortunate death has really determined you to accept only the son who was born first—"

"Are you trying to say, Doctor, that you and Mrs. Hall would like to have the other one for yourselves?"

"If you will give him to us."

Sebastian waved bitterly. "He's yours. And may he bring you better luck than he did me."

Mrs. Hall uttered a very small cry. Then, like a mouse, she disappeared.

"It would have to be made legal," Dr. Hall said. "So that you can't change your mind. That would be too damnably cruel. You understand me, sir? Papers—you'll have to give us papers."

"You'll get your papers. I'll even set up a trust fund for him. Anything, Doctor, within reason. I'll talk to my attorneys about it at the first opportunity."

"Thank you, Mr. Sebastian. I thank you for Mrs. Hall as well as myself."

"You're entirely welcome." Sebastian's tone was dry. Suddenly he lurched and groped for the back of the Morris chair.

"Mr. Sebastian!" Dr. Hall sprang forward.

"No, no, I'm all right—just dizzy—brain-fag . . ."

21

"You'd better lie down, sir."

"No." The big man took hold of himself. "You haven't answered my question. Where can I procure a sleigh?"

Dr. Hall stared at him. Then he murmured, "Yes, perhaps that would be best. Up the Post Road a mile or so . . ."

The elderly maidservant said in a weepy voice, "Mr. Sebastian, Mr. Muncie is here. You oughtn't to see anybody, sir. If you'd only let us call the doctor—"

Sebastian said from the bed, "Oh, stop gibbering and show Muncie in."

It was January 11, 1905, a Wednesday afternoon. From the four-poster in which he was lying John Sebastian could see the breakers rolling in on the Rye beach, looking as cold as he felt. As cold as Claire . . . if she could feel . . .

"Well, Mr. Sebastian," a hearty voice said.

"Come in, Muncie, have a chair—"

"They tell me you're a sick man, Mr. Sebastian." The lawyer seated himself beside the bed. "They haven't exaggerated. You don't look at all well."

Sebastian looked impatient. "Muncie—"

"I understand that even before the funeral you had attacks of vertigo, and that they've persisted. Apparently, too, you've had lapses of memory these past five days. Why won't you let them call a doctor?"

"I don't need a doctor! Muncie, I want to write a new will."

"Now?" The lawyer looked uneasy.

"Of course now! Don't you understand English?"

"Wouldn't it be more sensible, Mr. Sebastian, to wait until you've fully recovered from the accident?"

Sebastian glared. "Are you suggesting that I'm incompetent?"

"No, no," Muncie said hastily, opening his attaché case. "How do you wish the existing will changed, sir?"

"Retain the bequests to the servants, the employees at Sebastian and Craig as I previously specified, and so forth. But the income from the bulk of my estate—and of my wife's, when the legal folderol is finally cleared up and it comes to me—is to go to my son John." Sebastian half sat up. "You know the son I mean, Muncie?"

"Of course." The lawyer was astonished. "The child in the nursery in charge of that nurse, and a fine lad he seems to be." He coughed. "Wouldn't it be best to leave all this for another day, sir?"

"The child in the nursery," Sebastian muttered. "That's right, Muncie, my son John, my only son. Put it down just that way: 'My only son comma John.' You understand?"

" 'My only son comma John,' " the lawyer murmured.

22

"He is to receive the income until age twenty-five. At twenty-five he inherits the principal. Have you got that?"

"Yes, Mr. Sebastian."

"If I should die before my son reaches his majority, he is to be placed under the guardianship of my business partner and friend, Arthur B. Craig. Craig has already agreed to assume the responsibility. Craig is also to be executor and administrator of the estate, as in the current will. If my son dies before reaching the age of twenty-five, I leave the estate to Craig. That's all, Muncie. Draw it immediately."

"I'll have it for your signature tomorrow, Mr. Sebastian."

"You'll have it for my signature tonight!" Sebastian sank back, exhausted.

Muncie consulted his watch. "I'm not sure . . . Surely the matter is not so urgent, Mr. Sebastian?" He essayed a laugh. "Even if we had the misfortune to lose you at this moment, sir, since your son is your only natural heir he'd inherit anyway—"

Sebastian whispered, "I want it down on paper, over my signature, Muncie, just as I gave it to you." Then he sat up with a shout. "Do you understand, damn you?"

The lawyer fled.

Muncie was back with two of his clerks that night. He read the will to John Sebastian in a sharp, offended voice. The publisher listened eagerly, nodding at every phrase. When the lawyer had concluded, the bedridden man seized a pen and wrote his signature with great care on both copies. Then the clerks signed in witness, and the three men turned to go.

"Thank you, gentlemen," Sebastian said. "Oh, Muncie."

The lawyer turned back.

"Forgive me if I've seemed peremptory. You've been most understanding."

"Perhaps not, Mr. Sebastian, perhaps not," the lawyer said, unbending a little. "However, it's done. Was there something else?"

"Yes. A matter I must really take care of . . . a certain trust fund to be set up . . . certain legal papers drawn . . ."

"Can't that wait until tomorrow, either, sir?" Muncie asked, smiling. "I really must advise you to consult a physician before attempting any further exertions."

"Perhaps you're right," the publisher murmured. "I'll have Dr. Westcott over in the morning. And that matter I spoke of . . . very well, Muncie, another day . . ."

His voice trailed off. The lawyer hesitated, then left.

John Sebastian lay back, content. The murderer was thwarted; there was no mention of him in the will; no one— not Muncie, not Craig, not anyone connected with John

Sebastian, publisher and widower—no one but Dr. and Mrs. Hall knew of that murderous little existence, and those two had reason enough to keep their mouths shut . . .

Sebastian fell asleep.

And in that sleep he died. He was found by the elderly maidservant early the next morning, already in rigor mortis. At the insistence of his friend and business partner, Arthur Benjamin Craig, the coroner's physician performed an autopsy. He found a blood clot on the brain. Sebastian had suffered internal head injuries in being thrown from the capsizing Pierce Great-Arrow. His refusal to seek medical care after the accident had probably killed him. It was conjectured that his rather odd behavior during the last five days of his life was a direct result of his injuries.

John Sebastian was buried in the family plot in the Rye cemetery beside the fresh grave of his wife.

When Dr. Cornelius F. Hall read of Sebastian's death, he said to his wife, "We may be luckier than we know. That fellow was capable of anything."

Mrs. Hall shivered and hurried into the room in which Claire Sebastian had died. It was now a nursery.

Dr. Hall made discreet inquiries and ascertained that Sebastian had died before setting up the trust fund he had promised. When the provisions of the will were published, the little doctor read them closely. There was no provision for a second son; indeed, no mention of a second son's existence. Dr. Hall smiled. So far as he could determine, no one alive suspected that John Sebastian's wife had given birth to more than the single male infant in the Sebastian nursery in Rye.

"Thank God!" the doctor's wife said; and she went about the tasks of her new motherhood with a gaiety that made Dr. Hall hum as he clipclopped along the roads of lower Westchester in his sleigh.

He recorded the births with the town clerk at the Mount Kidron city hall. The doctor was careful to wait until he could bury them among seven others from confinements he had attended in and about Mount Kidron. The town clerk was deaf and half blind; he had entered so many births in his weighty ledger during his forty-five-year tenure of office that their specifications no longer registered in his brain.

"But we're protected," Dr. Hall remarked to Mrs. Hall.

"Against what, Cornelius?"

He shrugged. "One never knows."

All this happened the year Ellery Queen was born, and an even quarter century before he agreed to attend the extraordinary Christmas house party in Alderwood, New York.

BOOK TWO

Chapter II ✠ Tuesday December 24, 1929: Christmas Eve

In Which Ellery Joins a Yuletide House Party in Rural Westchester, and John Sebastian Hints of the Shape of Things to Come

How YOUNG ELLERY was may be judged by the fact that he took his reviews seriously. The sweet ones puffed him to the point of bloat; the sour positively shriveled him. The reviews of *The Roman Hat Mystery* had been, on the whole, nourishing. The touch of acidity in the *Saturday Review of Literature* notice, however, infected him deeply. To be accused of mere competence was galling; to be called a "philovancish bookworm" etched itself into his soul; to be charged with coyness revolted him. There is an innocence and wonder about a young author's first-born; to call it names is to commit a crime against nature. Ellery writhed.

But all that was past. The book had been published in mid-August; the reviews were all in by mid-October; by mid-December, so far as Ellery was concerned, they might never have been. In those days he had the elastic confidence of youth, which might be stretched but never snapped; and

25

he accepted Arthur B. Craig's invitation for the Christmas to New Year's holiday—tendered well before Thanksgiving—without surprise, as if it were his due as an Established Author. It would have pained him to learn that he had been asked more as a "character" than as a literary lion-cub; fortunately, he never learned it.

His only connection with Craig was John Sebastian, Craig's ward and an acquaintance of Ellery's. Young Sebastian maintained a flat in Greenwich Village, and Ellery had run across him in and about the Village at sundry soirees, literary and artistic. A certain brashness in common had drawn them together. Sebastian was a dilettante poet of great charm and, Ellery suspected, some talent; not quite of F. Scott Fitzgerald's lost generation, he was of the piercing-eyed, lank-haired, Byronic model then fashionable in New York's Bohemia. He always spoke of his wealthy guardian with cynical affection and a tone of amused patronage that the young reserve for their more indulgent elders.

Arthur Benjamin Craig was a printer by trade, an artist in the design and production of fine books who had elevated his craft to the status of a profession. Beyond Craig's relationship with young Sebastian, and the fact that his press printed the prestige books put out by the house of Ellery's publisher, Dan Z. Freeman, Ellery knew nothing about him.

Ellery had accepted Craig's invitation on impulse, but it occurred to him belatedly—just before Christmas—that acceptance would leave his father alone over the holiday. He offered to send his regrets, but Inspector Queen would not hear of filial sacrifice.

"There's a new lead on the Arnold Rothstein killing that's going to keep me busy over New Year's," the Inspector had reassured him. "You beat it up to Alderwood and have yourself a time, son. Just go easy on the bathtub gin."

"From what John's said," Ellery grinned, "it's more likely to be vintage champagne and pedigreed Scotch."

The Inspector looked skeptical. He was also worried. "The papers predict a white Christmas. When are you driving up?"

"Tuesday afternoon."

"There are supposed to be snow flurries Monday and a heavy snow Tuesday. Maybe you'd better take the train."

"Old Duesey's never failed me yet." Ellery's Duesenberg was not the patrician Town Cabriolet of the moment. It was a 1924 open model, bruised and battered by 135,000 miles of hard driving, and he felt an affection for it that he would have lavished on an ancient but still serviceable saddle horse. "Besides, Dad, I've bought a set of those new Weed American crosschains. We'll be all right."

As forecast, a heavy snow began to fall early on the

morning of Tuesday, December 24th. By noon, when Ellery set out, the streets were blanketed.

He had had the West 87th Street garage put up the top and the side-curtains, so he was protected from the snow; but not even his old racoon coat and fur earlaps were proof against the wind, a wicked nor'easter that went through the curtains as if they were made of cheesecloth. By the time he reached the parkway at the Westchester county line he felt as if he were encased, like a Siberian mastodon, in a glacier. He had to pull up at a diner in Mount Kidron, where he surreptitiously laced a mug of coffee with brandy from his silver hip-flask. At Mamaroneck and White Plains he stopped again to irradiate the inner man; by the time he had crossed White Plains and was headed northwest on the road to Alderwood, the flask was empty. He reached the town in a pleasant state of neutrality, half ice, half glow.

Alderwood was forty miles from New York, a heavily treed community of small estates with a population of 6000, and an immaculate little business district with loops of snowy Christmas lights across the main street and Santa-bedecked shop windows sparkling with frost. The Craig place, he learned, was on the northern fringe of town, and Ellery found it after a dreamy search that involved a mere two excursions up byroads that led nowhere.

It turned out a huge sprawl of a house, of incredible spread, coming to a giant peak—a two-story-and-attic so broad it looked sat upon. Ellery recognized it as a heroic example of the triangular American Shingle architecture of the '80's. Two great banks of bow window, one above the other, in the darkly weathered shingles of the side wall facing the road gave the building an astonishingly modern look. The entrance was at right angles to the main road, opening from a large open porch supported by fieldstone pillars. The whole monster was thickly nested in shrubs, an Ancient Mariner of a house with a Galway beard. It rode the crest of a wave of snow-covered lawns.

Perhaps it was the glow in which he sat comfortably piloting the Duesenberg up the baronial drive, but Ellery had the queerest feeling that he was driving in state up to the front door of Elizabethan England. In his misty condition he would not have been surprised to find himself greeted by bewigged footmen in ducal livery and a beruffled host in doublet and hose. He could already see whole-tree Yule logs, rush-strewn stone floors, and wolfish dogs tearing at haunches of venison. And plenty of toddies, of course—steaming varieties, served in pewter tankards.

He began to whistle "Greensleeves."

And when he drew up at the porch, there, waiting for him, were the tall, dark and handsome figure of John Sebastian and, at Sebastian's side, a mountain of a man, a sort of cross

27

between President Hoover and Henry the Eighth—huge, square-faced and bearded, smoking a bulldog pipe benignly and smiling in welcome.

"You made it," young Sebastian cried, springing into the snow to seize Ellery's hand. "Don't bother with your car or luggage, Ellery. Arthur, this is Ellery Queen, slayer of dragons and brain extraordinary. His father is a real live police inspector, too."

"And a genial snuff-taker, let's not forget that," Ellery said slurrily. "Mr. Craig, I'm honored, gratified, and glaciated. And crushed," he added, nursing his right hand. Arthur Craig's grip went with his dimensions, undiscouraged by his sixty-three years. His hair and beard were still thickly blond. The dark eyes in the great head were as lively as his ward's, but they were illuminated by a patience and generosity, Ellery thought, that John's—or Henry the Eighth's, for that matter—lacked.

"A veritable father-image," John said solemnly. "That grip has kept me in my place since my knickerbocker days."

"With dubious results, I'm afraid," Craig said in a comfortable rumble. "Mr. Queen, welcome. I don't know why you should feel honored and gratified, but the glaciation we can remedy immediately. Felton, take care of Mr. Queen's bag and car." A muscular houseman in a black suit and bowtie slipped down to the car. "The toddies are on the hob."

And they were served in pewter tankards, too. Nor was Ellery astonished to find himself in a great half-timbered hall of a room, feudal with oak paneling, beamed ceiling, brass-studded settles, a copper-hooded floor-to-ceiling fireplace, with copper and leather and black iron and burning brass everywhere. He went upstairs behind Felton with his friend and an aromatic tankard for company, and he remarked with enthusiasm, "Wonderful place for a Christmas holiday, John. I can almost hear Sir Andrew Aguecheek shouting to Sir Toby, 'Shall we set about some revels?' "

"And old Belch yelling back, 'What shall we do else? Were we not born under Taurus?' "

"I'm Gemini myself."

"To quote a dreary old bore of a lady you're going to meet shortly—by their stars ye shall know them. Honestly!" Sebastian put an arm about Ellery; he seemed boyishly happy. "You ferret, you, I'm glad you could get here. This should be one dilly of a party."

"No murders, please."

"Curses, I'll have to change the agenda! Here's your billet, Ellery. Anything you want, ring Felton. When you've come unstuck, amble downstairs. There's a little package I want to present to you."

"Now? Aren't you being premature?"

28

"Present, sonny-boy—as in introduce. The package is named Rusty Brown, whom I can't conceal from you any longer."

"Rusty Brown? Sounds like a baseball player."

"Heaven forbid. We're very good friends; you know? So hands off, Ellery. *Comprends?*"

"Do I look like a cad?"

"Where my emotional responses to Miss Brown are concerned, anything in plus-fours is a cad until proved otherwise." John Sebastian stuck his head back in. "By the way, don't go wandering on your way downstairs. This old manse has thirty or more rooms in various wings, half of them never used. I had more hideouts here when I was a kid than the James boys. If you should get lost in one of them we mightn't find you till Epiphany. Hurry it up, will you?"

Ellery saw John Sebastian's point with the greatest of ease. Rusty Brown had what Elinor Glyn called "It," along with generous dashes of chic and spirit. She was a lively package with well-rounded corners, little-girl features, a dimple, flame-colored hair coifed in the latest bob, smartly casual clothes and a pair of eye-catching earrings apparently made of welded steel. She looked remarkably like Clara Bow. But her green eyes were direct, and Ellery liked her firm, no-quarter-asked handclasp. She was a talented designer of costume jewelry, textiles, wallpaper and such. No more than twenty-four, her fiancé's age, she had already set up shop on Madison Avenue, and her "Rusty Brown Creations" were beginning to be mentioned in *The New Yorker's* "The Talk of the Town" and sought out by Park Avenue.

"So you're the rising author John's been regaling us with to the point of indigestion," Rusty Brown said. She had a clear voice, with no nonsense about it, like her eyes. "He's even made me read your book."

"That's the kind of gambit I've never learned to resist," Ellery said. "Here goes: Did you like it?"

"I thought it terribly clever."

"Do I detect a worm in the fruit?"

"Well, perhaps too clever." Rusty showed her innocent dimple. "Might I say—precocious?"

"You have to watch this wench, Ellery," John said adoringly. "She draws blood."

"I'm bleeding," Ellery moaned.

"It's no crime to be young, Mr. Queen," Rusty murmured. "The crime is to let it show."

"I'm practically a haemophiliac," Ellery said. "And this is the redoubtable Miss Brown's mother?"

Mrs. Brown was Rusty in a Coney Island mirror, with green eyes turned sly, bad teeth, and red hair lapsed into pinkish gray. There was a Medusa-like intensity about her that vibrated almost audibly. Ellery put her down at once as

29

a Cause Woman, or at any rate a fanatic about something. It turned out that she was a devotee of astrology, a devout communicant of the occult and an amateur medium. Her Christian name was Olivette.

"Your Sign is the Twins, isn't it, Mr. Queen?" Mrs. Brown asked him immediately, with a great deal of breath.

"Why, yes, Mrs. Brown."

"Of course. Gemini governs the intellect, and John says you're *so* intellectual."

"Mother is psychic, although a little advance information now and then helps," Rusty said dryly. "Darling, might I have some more toddy?"

"And this young lady, Mr. Queen," Arthur Craig said, "is my niece Ellen, down from Wellesley for the holidays." His paw was fondling a long, dainty hand. "Ellen, John and The ABC Press are my three reasons for being. I've put my imprint on them all."

"And an exquisite edition this one is, Mr. Craig," Ellery said. "You've raised this alluring female, too?"

"Ellen's father died soon after she was born—he was my only brother. Naturally, Ellen and her mother came to live with me, Marcia being in poor health and unable to raise her baby without help. Then Marcia died, and I had to become Ellen's father *and* mother."

"The only mother in captivity with a beard," Ellen Craig said, tugging at it. "Unique in all other ways, too. Are you going to patronize me, Mr. Queen, for not having my diploma yet?"

"My exclamatory description of you a moment ago was forced out of me by the facts, Miss Craig. When does Wellesley reluctantly let you go?"

"In June."

"I'll be there," quoth Mr. Queen gallantly.

Ellen laughed. She had quite the nicest laugh—amusement in music, feminine and unaffected. She was a tall girl with a pert cock to her fair head and a delicately angular face under broad temples. Ellery decided quickly that Miss Craig was not all on the surface. There was buried treasure here, and he found himself in a mood for digging.

So when Rusty and John wandered off to act as lookouts for the other expected guests, and Craig permitted himself good-humoredly to be dragged off by Mrs. Brown for a horoscope reading, Ellery said, "Do you mind being left in my company, Miss Craig?"

"I'll tell you a secret, Mr. Queen. I've had a hopeless crush on you ever since I read your book."

"Thank heaven you don't think me precocious!" Ellery looked apprehensive. "You're over twenty-one, aren't you?"

Ellen laughed. "I'll be twenty-two in April."

30

"Then let's go find ourselves an abandoned inglenook or something," Mr. Queen said enthusiastically, "and pursue this inquiry further."

The big green Marmon "8" going up Alderwood's main street in the deepening snow was having a hard time of it. The tires were chainless, and the rather erratic driving of the girl at the wheel kept her companion on the edge of his seat.

"For God's sake, Valentina, watch the road!"

"Compose a tone-poem, Marius," the girl said. "I'll get you there in one piece."

"The least you could do, in the name of common sense, is to stop at a garage and have the chains put on."

"Relax, we're almost there."

Valentina Warren was a passionate and volatile girl with a theatrical background of large roles in summer stock and small ones on Broadway. She secretly modeled her appearance and style on Joan Crawford; she had seen *Untamed* five times. To get to Hollywood was Valentina's great crusade; to become a famous movie star was her Holy Grail.

For the drive upcountry she had dressed in the latest in winter sportswear according to *Vogue*—a skiing costume of braided Norwegian trousers, with a forest green broadcloth vest and matching beret. Over this she had draped, cape fashion, a heavy green wool coat with black fox collar and cuffs. Valentina inclined to the color green because, in combination with her airy gold hair and ground-chalk complexion, it gave her what she considered "a Greek tragedy look." One of the few things that made Valentina angry was to be called "a lot of fun." She equated fame with solemnity.

If epic gloom was not in the Warren girl, it filled young Marius Carlo to the brim. He was of mixed Spanish and Italian descent, with a dash of Black Irish, and his soul was as dark and pitted as his skin. He had a positive flair for self-depreciation; romantic and imaginative, painfully aware of his physical shortcomings, he made less of himself than he was. He defended himself with sarcasms.

Carlo was a composer of solid talent if no great originality, with his musical roots in Stravinsky and Hindemith. Recently he had come under the spell of the Austrian modernist Arnold Schönberg, and he had begun to compose prodigiously in the Schönbergian idiom—terse atonal works which no one heard but the adoring clique of Greenwich Village poets, artists and musicians who had attached themselves to him like a fungus. For his daily bread he played the viola in Walter Damrosch's symphony orchestra, heard coast-to-coast each Saturday night at nine over NBC. This was his cross; and when he had been invited to spend the holiday in Alderwood he had seized the opportunity to report himself to

31

the Damrosch business office as stricken with double lobar pneumonia.

"Let them play their goddam Tchaikowsky without me," he had snarled to his friends. Then he had added with characteristic hopefulness, "Maybe they'll fire me."

He had been born with undeveloped arches in both feet, and he still had to wear heavy supports in his shoes. They gave him a labored walk which, when he hurried, turned into a sort of scuttle. "Marius the Crab, that's me," he would say bitterly.

Valentina negotiated the glassy main street of Alderwood safely and headed her Marmon toward the north end of town.

"Marius, do you know what's up?" she asked abruptly.

"What's up where?"

"Up here. What's this house party all about?"

"How should I know? The days when I was in John's confidence are footnotes in the sands of Time."

"Oh, stop being so Oedipean. You know what I mean. John's up to something, but what?"

"Ask him." Marius glowered at the snowy road. "I hope the hooch is good."

"He's been dropping awfully mysterious hints," Valentina said thoughtfully. "About something big coming off around New Year's. I wonder what it is."

The young musician showed his teeth in what might have been a grin. "Maybe you'd be better off not knowing."

"What's that supposed to mean?"

"Slow down, damn it!"

"All *right*. Marius, what do you *know*?"

"Have you seen Rusty the past few weeks?"

The actress was startled. "Not since before Thanksgiving."

"The baggage glows, especially on the fourth finger of the left hand."

"They're engaged?" Valentina cried.

"Friendship ring. *They* say. A little nothing of four carats."

"You think that while we're up here . . ."

"With John anything is possible, even marriage." Marius shrugged. "Kismet. What will be, will be."

"Oh, come off it. I don't believe that."

"You don't?" he said softly.

Her violet eyes flicked over him. Then she looked back to the road. "Not necessarily," she said, just as softly. "Marius, you know . . . you could help me. We could help each other."

He glowered at her. Then he laughed. "You bitch. You've seen it. I didn't think it showed."

"Will you, Marius?"

He did not reply for a moment.

Then he muttered, "Why not?" and sank deeper into his thin balmacaan and muffler.

"It's still coming down," Ellery announced as he and Ellen Craig paused in the hall to stamp the snow off their shoes.

"And getting darker and colder," Ellen called. "What a wonderful beginning for Christmas!"

"Come in by the fire, you two," her uncle said. "Ellen, your hands are frozen."

"But look at the oven in her eyes," John Sebastian grinned. He was tending bar in the temporary absence of Felton, who had driven the Craig Peerless down to the railroad station. "Here, Sis, have a cocktail."

"Gosh, yes!"

"Ellery?"

"Definitely. How many more are coming, John?"

"Four. Another, Marius?"

"Indefinitely," Marius Carlo said.

"I wouldn't worry," Craig said. "Dan Freeman and Roland Payn are driving up together, and that Lincoln All-Weather Cabriolet of Dan's will go anywhere. Sam Dark's just at the other end of Alderwood. And if Mr. Gardiner is coming out by train—"

"I do hope the New York trains have kept running," Rusty said. "We can't have that sweet old man missing the party, can we, darling?"

"I would cut my throat," John said, illustrating with a forefinger. "Drink, Val?"

"Not just now, thank you." Then Valentina said brightly, "What's this about a minister coming, Rusty? Are you two going hick town on us?"

Rusty laughed.

"All in good time, kiddies," John said. "Here, Ellery, let me freshen that."

"Easy, boy—whoa! Mr. Craig, did you say Freeman is coming? Dan Z. Freeman?"

"Yes, Mr. Queen."

" 'I will tell thee wonders,' eh? How did you ever get Freeman to accept a house-party invitation? He's one of the shyest birds I've ever met. You know, he's my publisher."

"I know," Craig smiled.

"Well, two people here will have something in common, then," Marius Carlo mumbled, staring into his glass. "You can complain to Freeman about the promotion he didn't give your book, Queen, and Freeman can tell you all about the sales of the important titles on his list."

"Why, Marius," Ellen said in dismay.

"Don't mind him, Ellery," Rusty said. "Marius has a contempt for everything he thinks isn't art."

"But especially for bad art," Marius said.

"And especially," Ellen snapped, "if it makes money."

"Marius, you shut up!" Valentina said. "He doesn't believe a word of it, Ellery. He's just consumed with jealousy. I thought your book was *merveilleux*."

"And I think we ought to change the subject," Ellery said cheerfully, but as he did so he looked Marius over with interest. "Who is Roland Payn, may I ask, Mr. Craig?"

"My attorney, an old friend." The big man, too, was inspecting the young musician. "And Sam Dark's been our family doctor ever since he came to Alderwood. Ah, Mrs. Brown. We've been waiting for you to join us."

"I've been looking over our horoscope reading, Mr. Craig," Rusty's mother cried, bouncing into the room, "and I do believe I made a wee mistake. The position of Jupiter at your ascendant—"

"I take it I have reason to feel relieved," Craig smiled. "Martini, Mrs. Brown?"

"I'd *adore* one. The juniper has *such* significance, you know. Don't ever cut a juniper bush down in Wales; you'll die in a year."

"Drink some of the gin they're allegedly making from it these days," John said, "and you'll die a lot quicker than that."

Ellery said gravely, "It also cures snakebite and strengthens the optic nerve, Mrs. Brown."

"Really, Mr. Queen?" Rusty's mother exclaimed. "I hadn't known that. John, didn't Rusty say you expect more people?"

"Four, Mother Brown."

"Why, that will make us a party of twelve. How very relieving, John! Imagine if you'd asked *one more person*." She gulped her martini and shuddered, whether from the gin or the horrible thought Ellery could not determine.

"Twelve?" Marius Carlo held out his empty glass. "Don't you count the servants, Madam?"

"The servants?" Mrs. Brown looked blank.

"No one counts the servants. Comes the—"

"—revolution. We know, Marius." Valentina was annoyed with him. She threw her head back and became throaty. "Come on, Johnny, let us in on it. The bi-i-ig secret."

Sebastian laughed. "For one thing, I have a birthday on the fire—January sixth, two weeks from today. I'm hoping you can all stay until then."

"Why?"

"Four reasons." He was enjoying his mystery. "Right after midnight of January fifth, four important events are scheduled to take place in my life." He shook their questions off, grinning. "Wait till the others get here."

34

"But I am," a high-pitched male voice said from the doorway. "Let the festivities begin!"

"Sam." Craig hurried forward with pleasure. "No trouble getting here, I see. Mabel, take Dr. Dark's things." The Craig maid, a strawberry-cheeked Irish girl, ran in to be greeted by the newcomer with a vigorous pinch on the cheek. Mabel giggled, took Dr. Dark's fur hat, greatcoat and galoshes, and disappeared. "Let's see, now, Sam. I don't believe you've met Mrs. Brown . . ."

Dr. Sam Dark was a large fat man, almost as large as Arthur Craig, and even broader. His sandy hair bushed like a busby from his smallish head; he would have looked ridiculous except for his eyes, which were bright with shrewdness. His blue serge suit was unpressed; one cuff button dangled on a long thread. But there was a solidity, a set of dependability, about him that Ellery liked on sight.

"Have you arranged to stay the entire week?" Craig asked when Dr. Dark was seated by the fire with a glass cuddled in his huge hand. "The answer had better be affirmative."

"Hollis and Bernstein are covering for me," the fat doctor nodded. "It's a long time since I've enjoyed a family Christmas. As one old bach to another, Arthur, you've done better than I. Ellen, John, here's to the tourniquet that binds, and let's hear no nonsense about blood being thicker than water!" He drank like Hercules.

"You didn't preside at John's birth, Doctor, did you?" Ellery knew vaguely that there was some interesting story about John Sebastian's origin.

"Lordy, no," Dr. Dark said. "John came to me *post uterum,* you might say."

"Aged six weeks, wasn't I, Dr. Sam?" John said.

"Seven," Craig corrected his ward. "You see, Mr. Queen, John's parents died within a few days of each other, back in Nineteen Five. Claire and John—John's named for his father—were driving back from New York to Rye in a blizzard and smashed their car up near Mount Kidron. The accident brought on this fellow's birth prematurely, and Claire died that night. John died of his injuries less than a week later. Before he went, he appointed me the baby's guardian—there were no close relatives on either side, and no other children; John Junior was their first. A practical nurse, a Mrs. Sapphira, whom John Senior had hired when Claire died, came along with the baby. Devoted soul. She never left us—died in this house only a few years ago. Between Sapphy and me, we managed to drag the young ruffian up."

"With considerable help from me," Dr. Dark objected. "Many a time I had to run over here in the middle of the night because Johnny-boy happened to look crosseyed at Sapphy or Arthur."

"With considerable help from everybody," John said, his

hand on Craig's shoulder. "Sapphy, Dr. Sam, Ellen when she came to live with us—but most of all this bearded character. I'm afraid, Arthur, I haven't been as vocal about it as you've deserved."

"Hear, hear," Marius Carlo said, before Arthur Craig could reply. "At the drop of a tear I shall play 'Hearts and Flowers' on that piano—if it's in tune, which remains to be seen."

"Marius doesn't understand sentiment," Rusty said sweetly, flipping her red bob. "You see, he never had a father *or* a mother. He was spawned on a stagnant pool. Weren't you, dear?"

Marius looked at her, black eyes flaming. Then he shrugged and raised his glass.

"Weren't you and John's father in business together, Mr. Craig?" Valentina asked hastily.

"Yes. Sebastian and Craig, Publishers. I was the production half of the partnership. I knew very little about the editorial end, so with John's death I sold out and went back to my original trade, the printing business."

"You make it sound like a stepdown, Mr. Craig," Ellery said. "I'd rather be able to say I owned The ABC Press than many a publishing house. You didn't sell out to Dan Freeman, did you? No, he'd have been far too young."

Craig nodded. "It changed hands several times after Nineteen Five. Dan bought it in the early 'Twenties. And by George, here he is. And Roland. Come in, come in!"

The publisher and the lawyer made an odd pair.

Dan Z. Freeman was a slight sallow man of forty with a big head further enlarged by a hairline that had retreated to the peak of his skull. He had beautiful, brilliant brown eyes.

The publisher seemed embarrassed by the ordeal of meeting a roomful of strangers. He shook hands with Ellery with the ardor of a drowning man embracing a providential bit of flotsam. Ellery had met him just once, when Freeman had accepted the manuscript of *The Roman Hat Mystery* for publication.

"So nice to see you again, Queen," Freeman kept murmuring, "so very nice." And at the first opportunity he slipped into a chair and effaced himself.

Roland Payn could not have effaced himself if he tried. He was a tall florid man in his early fifties with a shock of handsome white hair and the ready, rather absent, smile of a politician. His rich and easy baritone would have done credit to an actor of the old school. Ellery had heard of him through Inspector Queen, who like to brag that he knew every lawyer in New York. Payn was an extremely cautious, shrewd attorney who, like a gilt-edged stock, attracted only the most conservative clientele. For all his distinguished appearance and pear-shaped tones, he rarely argued a case in court. The bulk of his practice was will and estate work.

"Now that Messrs. Payn and Freeman are here," John announced, "I'm ready to let you all in on the first two of the four cosmic events I mentioned. Mr. Payn, speaking as the Craig family lawyer, how does my status change as of January sixth?"

"That date marking your twenty-fifth birthday," the white-haired attorney said, smiling, "by the terms of the last will of your father, John Sebastian Senior, you come into the principal estate, which has been held in trust for you since Nineteen Five. I'm sure John won't mind my remarking that this will make him a very well-cushioned young man indeed."

"And insufferable, of course," Ellen Craig said, squeezing John's arm. "Imagine John a millionaire!"

"Sickening, ain't it?" John grinned. "And now, Mr. Freeman. Speaking in your professional capacity, what happens on January sixth that I should know?"

The publisher flushed as all eyes went to him. "An event of far greater moment, I'm sure, than the mere acquisition of a fortune. On January sixth The House of Freeman is publishing the first book of verse of a promising young poet—*The Food of Love*, by John Sebastian."

Everyone shouted. Rusty cried. "John, how wonderful! And you never breathed a word to me. Did you know, Mr. Craig?"

Craig's beard waggled. "You don't think anyone could deprive me of the pleasure of doing John's maiden book, Rusty! But Dan and I are a couple of old Trappists." Craig affectionately pawed the publisher's slender shoulder. "We know how to keep our mouths shut."

"John, I'm so happy for you," Valentina murmured. "Congratulations." And she pulled his head down and kissed him.

Rusty Brown smiled.

"I'll take some of that!" Ellen said gaily, and somehow she managed to get between Valentina and John and, after kissing him, to stay there.

John's ears were red. "I wanted it to be a surprise. Isn't it tremendous? I'm still pinching myself."

"And it will sell exactly four hundred and fifty-nine copies," Marius said, waving his empty glass like a baton, "and get a smasher of a review from *The Journal of Veterinary Medicine.*"

But his grating voice was lost in the hubbub; and by the time the last guest had arrived, Marius was tightly asleep in his chair.

The man whose modest valise Felton carried in from the

Peerless was a spare old fellow of great vigor, with barely silvered black hair, childlike blue eyes, a big Yankee nose, and a clerical collar. Arthur Craig introduced him as the Reverend Mr. Andrew Gardiner, recently retired from his Episcopal rectorate in New York. He was actually a friend of the Browns'; Olivette Brown had been a communicant of his church for many years, and he had baptized and confirmed Rusty.

The instant she laid eyes on the old clergyman Valentina Warren grew silent. She curled up on the arm of sleeping Marius Carlo's chair, ruffling his black hair lightly. Her violet glance went often to Rusty's face. She did not look at John at all.

Ellery had been watching her. He murmured to Ellen Craig, "What goes on in that direction, Ellen?"

"Do I look like the counterspy type?" Ellen murmured back. "You'll have to draw your own conclusions, Mr. See-It-All. I gather you do that very well."

"I conclude a triangle."

"I'm *not* helping you with your math, Mr. Queen."

"You know my niece Ellen, I believe," Craig said, coming over with the late arrival. "This is a friend of John's, Mr. Gardiner—Ellery Queen, the author. The Reverend Mr. Gardiner."

Ellery was suprised at the iron in the old man's handshake. "I hear you're retired, Mr. Gardiner. Why in heaven's name would they retire a man with a grip like yours?"

"I'm afraid heaven didn't have much to do with it, Mr. Queen," the minister said, smiling. "It was the Bishop and his gentle reminder that I had passed the compulsory retirement age of seventy-two. Ellen, you're even more radiant than usual."

"My influence, I trust," Ellery said. Ellen flushed slightly, but she seemed pleased.

"In that case," Mr. Gardiner said, twinkling, "having even a retired clergyman on the premises may come in handy. Mr. Craig, I hope it won't inconvenience you and your guests, but I should like to attend midnight mass. I believe you have an Episcopal church in Alderwood. If I might borrow a car later tonight—"

"Nonsense, I'll have Felton or John drive you over," Craig said. "The only thing is, the road to the main highway may be impassable in a few hours. I haven't heard the plows go through."

"Please don't put yourselves out, Mr. Craig. If necessary I'll walk. I noticed it's only a mile or so. I haven't missed a Christmas Eve mass in fifty-some years, and I don't think at my age it would be wise to begin lapsing from grace."

"We'll get you there," John said. "Attention, everyone!" Marius Carlo awoke with a start. Ellery noted that the

38

blonde girl perched on his chair-arm had gripped Carlo's hair hard.

"Now that Mr. Gardiner's come, completing our party," John beamed, "I can announce the third colossal event of January sixth. Mr. Gardiner's staying through the entire holiday and beyond for more than social reasons. Immediately after midnight of January fifth the Reverend's going to perform a marriage ceremony. Yep! Rusty and me."

In the uproar that followed, Ellery managed to hang back so that he might observe Valentina and Marius. The actress was overvivacious, her throaty voice shrill with tension, as she embraced Rusty and John. She was so pale Ellery thought she was about to faint. Evidently Marius thought so, too, for he gripped her arm and squeezed hard. Valentina fell back after a moment, shaking the musician's hand off fiercely. Ellery heard Marius say to her, "You're a lousy actress after all," and her hissed, "Shut up, damn you!" Then they both smiled and held their glasses out as Felton, resuming his butler's role, came around to fill them for a toast.

Afterward, Rusty herself demanded of the groom-to-be, "But darling, you said four things were going to happen on January sixth. What's the fourth?"

"Ah, that's my big secret," John laughed. "That's one nobody knows—and nobody's going to know until *the* night. Not even my bride."

And no amount of wheedling on Rusty's part, or of good-natured quizzing by the others—including Arthur Craig, who kept smilingly insisting that he hadn't the faintest notion what John was referring to—would induce the young poet to reveal his secret.

It was in the oak-paneled dining room later, with the flames leaping in the fireplace and the party settling about the huge holly-decked oak table, that Ellery said to Ellen, beside whom he had been seated, "Here's an amusing coincidence."

"What, Ellery?"

"December twenty-fifth through the night of January fifth—Christmas through what's officially known as Twelfth Night—that makes a holiday party of twelve days, Ellen."

"What of it?"

"Look around. Twelve people in the party. Doesn't that strike you as interesting?"

"Not in the least," Ellen retorted. "What a peculiar mind you have."

At that moment Olivette Brown exclaimed, "Twelve of us. I must say I'm ever so relieved there isn't another guest!"

"You see?" Ellery murmured to Ellen Craig.

*In Which a Mystifying Santa Materializes from
Limbo, and an Ox, a Little House, and a Camel
Take the Center of the Stage*

ARTHUR BENJAMIN CRAIG'S guests awakened to a picture
postcard world of spotless snow and frosty evergreen. Even
the taller shrubs had only their crests showing. There was no
sign of driveway or road. The drifts dipped and swooped in
clean parabolas wherever the eye turned.

Most of the household were up early, exclaiming over the
beautiful view from the bay windows and enjoying the
Christmas day buffet breakfast prepared by Craig's brawny
cook-housekeeper, Mrs. Janssen, and served by the red-
cheeked Irish maid. The dining room was noisy.

The Reverend Mr. Gardiner was disconsolate. He had
missed celebrating his Christmas Eve mass in church after
all. It had proved impossible to take a car out the night
before, and even he had seen the folly of attempting to
struggle through the drifts on foot. Craig had soothed his
distress by switching the radio on at 11:30 P.M. and tuning
in WOR so that he might hear the Choir Invisible and St.
Thomas's carillon; and then at midnight they all joined the
old clergyman in listening to the midnight mass being broadcast over WEAF from the Shrine of the Sacred Heart. Rusty
and John sat hand in hand on the floor before the radio, and
Ellery was struck by the rigid white Benda mask of Valentina
Warren's face as she watched them, and the sardonic curl of
Carlo's lips. Ellen had noticed, too, and had seemed troubled.

Afterward, they sang carols and decorated the big tree in
the living room; and then most of them had gone to bed.

Breakfast over, John announced that he had a Christmas
morning surprise for everyone, and he herded them all into
the living room.

"Under the tree," John said, and stopped, looking silly.
There was nothing under the tree. He looked at Rusty, and
Rusty looked at her mother.

"I don't understand," Rusty said. "We set them down here
last night ourselves, after everyone went to bed."

"Funny," John muttered. "Mabel?" The maid stuck her
head in from the dining room. "Did you see any packages

40

under the tree when you laid **the fire in** here this morning?"

"No, Mr. John."

"If this is somebody's idea of a practical joke," John began rather coldly, and then he laughed. They all turned. In the archway from the hall stood Santa Claus, and his arms were laden with small Christmas packages.

"A Santa!"

"John, you should have been an actor."

"But *I* didn't—"

"Such a lovely idea!"

He was the classic Santa, with a great belly and a noble set of white whiskers and eyebrows. He set about distributing the gay little packages with wordless gusto.

"Why, John, what an exquisite brooch."

"A money clip in the shape of . . . What is this?"

"Mine seems to be a lamb."

"Don't you see?" Olivette Brown shrilled. "They're all your personal Signs. You're Aries, Ellen, so you get the lamb. Valentina, you're Sagittarius, so of course you get the archer. And so on. It was my inspiration, John, wasn't it?"

"It certainly was. Rusty designed them, and she had Moylan's, the Fifth Avenue jewelers, make them up."

"We had quite a time nosing out everyone's birth-date," Rusty laughed, "but we did it, and then it turned out that all twelve of us were born under different signs of the zodiac. Do you really like them?"

They were cunning little pieces in gold, with detail in semi-precious stones—brooches for the women, money clips for the men. Ellery's clip took the shape of an ingenious Castor and Pollux.

"We really ought to thank Felton," he said. "He did a noble job as Santa, John. Where is he?"

Santa Claus was gone.

"Felton?" John said. "Was that Felton?"

"You ought to know. Wasn't it?"

"But I don't know, Ellery. I didn't arrange for any Santa. Did you, Arthur?"

"I?" Craig shook his head. "I had nothing to do with it."

A little silence fluttered down.

"Well, it must have been Felton," Ellery said. "It couldn't have been one of us—all twelve of us were here when he handed out the gifts. It certainly wasn't little Mabel in that Santa costume, or Mrs. Janssen. It had to be Felton."

"I, sir?" They turned, startled. But it was only Felton, in the doorway from the dining room. He was wearing a green rubber apron and a pair of soapy rubber gloves. "I've been in the pantry doing the breakfast dishes. Mrs. Janssen can tell you."

The silence settled lower.

41

Arthur Craig said abruptly, "All right, Felton," and the houseman backed off and disappeared. "I wonder who on earth it could have been."

"Your orientation may be faulty, Arthur," Dan Z. Freeman murmured unexpectedly. "Maybe it was the ghost of Marley."

No one laughed.

"The thirteenth person," Mrs. Brown panted. *"Thirteen."*

John went over to the nearest bay and scowled out at the snow. Rusty joined him, saying something quietly. He shrugged.

"Mysteries are your specialty, Mr. Queen, aren't they?" Dr. Dark said in his cheerful squeak. "How about solving this one for us?"

It cleared the air. Everyone began to urge Ellery—as Valentina put it—to go into his act.

"It's probably depressingly simple," Ellery said. "Someone arranged for a Santa to come in from outside. How about the culprit's confessing here and now? I really don't feel sleuthlike this early in the day."

But all proclaimed their innocence.

"Wait a minute." And Ellery went out.

He came stamping back a few minutes later, slapping the snow from his trousers. "Not a print or mark of any kind in the snow anywhere near the house. So no one from outside stole in during the night, at least after it stopped snowing. Does anyone know just when the snow did stop?"

"About two-thirty this morning," Rusty said. "Just before John and I went upstairs."

"Then if someone did slip into the house, it was well before two-thirty A.M., or there'd be a trace in the snow. As I recall it, the rest of us went to bed about an hour before Rusty and John. I didn't hear a thing. Did any of you?"

But no one had.

"Hm," Ellery said. "Do you know, this is interesting."

Their host shook his head, smiling. "I suggest we forget the whole thing."

"It may not be so easy to do that, Mr. Craig."

"How do you mean?"

"The unbroken snow out there tells two stories. One, if Santa is an outsider, he entered your house well before half-past two this morning. Two, whenever he entered your house—whether last night or last year—*he's still here.* Even if, like old St. Nick, he attempted to get out via one of your chimneys, he'd need an airborne team of reindeer named Dancer, Prancer, Donner, Blitzen *et al.* to make his getaway without touching the surface of the snow."

"Maybe he's done it since you came back in, Ellery!" Ellen dashed out. But she came back shaking her head. "There's nothing out there except the tracks you just made."

"It's certainly odd, Arthur," Roland Payn remarked with a judicial frown. "Who could it have been?"

In the silence that followed, Marius Carlo asked, "How does the expert propose to proceed?"

"The prognosis doesn't seem too dark, Marius," Ellery said, smiling. "Whoever it was, he's still in the house, most likely hiding in one of the unused wings. If Mr. Craig has no objection, I'll make a search."

The bearded man waved in a troubled way. "Perhaps, Mr. Queen, that would be best."

"Ellen, you know the house inside out. Suppose you and I search together." Ellery added with a slight touch of dryness, "For tidiness, will everyone else please remain here?"

Ellen led the way upstairs, looking anxious.

"What do you suppose it means, Ellery?"

"Oh, someone's idea of a prank. Darned cleverly executed, too. Don't look so droopy, Ellen. Let's play it out in the same spirit of good clean fun."

An hour later Mr. Queen showed none of the signs of a man enjoying a game. They had gone through room after room in the unoccupied wings without finding a trace of anyone; they had even climbed to the attic, and searched the servants' quarters under the eaves and several storerooms. On returning downstairs Ellery insisted on searching the cellar. By this time the cook, the maid and Felton were infected by the general unease, and they huddled in the big kitchen whispering. At the end, even though the story in the snow was plain enough, Ellery waded over to the outbuildings. One was a two-story garage converted from an old carriage house, the other a stable. He searched them from floor to roof.

There was no sign of a thirteenth person.

"The trouble is," Ellery complained to Ellen, "there are so many rooms, cluttered with so much junk and so many closets, an intruder could hide out indefinitely just by dodging from one hiding place to another ahead of the search. I wonder what's behind this."

"Whatever it is, I don't like it."

"Twelve," Ellery mumbled.

"What?"

"Twelve people in the party, twelve days and nights of Christmas, and now a vanishing Santa Claus who distributes twelve signs of the zodiac."

"You're cuckoo."

"By the beard of Mrs. Brown's false prophets," Ellery muttered, "I don't know whether I am or not."

It was little Mabel, the maid, who made the discovery. She was preparing to set the table for lunch when she gave voice to a piercing screech. Ellery, who with Ellen, Mr. Gardiner and some of the others was in the living room listening to a special broadcast from WJZ—a Christmas Day greeting to the United States from Holland—ran into the dining room. The Irish girl was flat against the wall, staring down horrified into a big oak linen chest.

"I was—I was going for some place mats for the table," Mabel said, her teeth clacking, "I opened the chest, and"—she pointed a trembling finger—"*there it was!*"

In the chest, neatly laid out, was a complete Santa Claus costume—suit, hat, boots, stuffing, mittens, and false eyebrows, wig and beard.

While Ellen quieted the terrified girl, Ellery eagerly examined the costume. But it was new-looking, bore no labels, and showed only slight signs of wear.

"I must say whoever did this has a sense of humor," the fat doctor chuckled. "He must have known Mabel or somebody would be having to go to the chest sooner or later today."

Roland Payn uttered a dignified grunt. "I find him as funny as an off-color story at a Tammany clambake."

"Joke all you want," Olivette Brown said in a passionate vibrato, "but there's *something* in this house. *Danger.* I feel it. Yes . . . It's coming over me like a wave." She had her eyes fast shut, and for a horrid moment Ellery thought she was going to go into a trance. But Dr. Dark's amused comment galvanized her.

"You don't really believe that bosh, Mrs. Brown."

"Bosh!" She almost flew at him. "Don't blaspheme about things you don't understand, Doctor! There are more things in heaven and earth—"

"Than in my philosophy, for one," Ellery said, staring at the uncommunicative red suit. "I don't share the premonitions of your psyche, Mrs. Brown, but I have to admit I don't care for any of this, either. Didn't anyone catch even a glimpse of whoever put this costume in the chest this morning?"

But no one had.

The afternoon passed under a pall, not entirely identifiable with the gathering overcast. Gray clouds muffled the sun, the temperature rose, and Alderwood began to dig out of the drifts. Plows clanked by all day. A local garageman appeared with a small truck fitted out with a big wooden pusher, and cleared the Craig drive. John and Ellery seized shovels and helped Felton dig a narrow path around the house.

But the joy seemed squeezed from everything. Rusty, Valentina and Ellen tried a snowball fight and soon gave it up. There was some talk of hitching one of the horses from the stable to an old rusty-runnered sleigh standing in a corner of the garage, but that idea petered out, too.

In the music room Marius Carlo sat at the grand piano,

one eye closed against the smoking cigaret in his mouth, and played furious little arpeggios and wickedly warped snatches of opera, pausing frequently to freshen his highball; while, deaf to Carlo's musical sarcasms, Olivette Brown curled up in a corner with a book she had found in Arthur Craig's library of Americana first editions, Cotton Mather's *Wonders of the Invisible World*. They made a curiously harmonious picture.

Dan Freeman, Dr. Dark and Mr. Gardiner took a tramp in the woods beyond the house. They found themselves engaged in a heated discussion of two current best sellers, Axel Munthe's *The Story of San Michele* and Abbé Ernest Dimnet's *The Art of Thinking*, neither of which any of them would have ordinarily considered controversial.

Craig and Payn lolled in the library, arguing over the relative merits of the Hoover administration. It was a subject that usually struck sparks between them, but today the lawyer was doing a lackluster job of glossing over Black Thursday, and the best Craig could offer was a spiritless indictment of Senator Heflin and the Hoovercrats for having kept Al Smith—and presumably a sound economy—out of the White House.

The uneasy atmosphere was not cleared by Mrs. Janssen's elaborate Christmas dinner, which was served at five o'clock. Everyone seemed to be cocking at least one ear for a ghostly footstep overhead. Rusty and Ellen tried desperately to keep the table talk going, but it persisted in sputtering out into little silences.

"This is more like a wake," John exclaimed, throwing down his napkin. "Why don't we have our coffee and brandy in the living room? Maybe we can coax something cheerful out of the radio."

"Uncle Don is on at six-thirty," Marius said innocently. "Or would these giants of art and intellect prefer 'Amos and Andy' at seven, or the 'Happy Wonder Bakers' at eight-thirty? By all means let's listen to that great instrument of culture."

But there was no listening to the radio until much later Christmas night. For the first thing they encountered on entering the living room was a fresh mystery.

Under the tree lay a large package done up in red and green metallic paper, tied with gilt ribbon. To the ribbon was attached a Christmas card in the shape of a jolly Santa Claus, and on the card was neatly typewritten the name of "John Sebastian."

"Here's a pleasant change," John laughed. "Who's the modest sender?"

He turned the package this way and that, searching for a clue to its donor. But there was none.

Chill invaded the room.

"Oh, piffle," John said suddenly. "Someone's kind enough to give me a present, and we all stand around looking as if we expect it to blow up." He tore off the wrappings, revealing an unmarked white box. Removing the lid, he found a number of objects nested there, each swathed in red tissue paper. Upon them lay a plain white card with some typing on it.

John read it aloud, frowning.

```
On the first night of Christmas
Your true love sends to you,
A sandalwood   o x
In a holiday box,
An unfinished   h o u s e
For a soon-to-be spouse,
A gray and white   c a m e l
With skin of enamel.
```

"What the deuce," John said. "It doesn't make sense."

"Just gibble-gobble," Ellen said. "What's it supposed to mean?"

Ellery said abruptly, "May I see that, John?"

They clustered around, reading the queer doggerel over Ellery's shoulder.

"'Your true love,'" he mused. "I don't see whom that could mean except you, Rusty. Didn't you send this?"

"No," Rusty said. "I have a middleclass weakness for signing my name."

"You, Mr. Craig?"

"No, no."

Ellery said quietly, "See what they are, John."

John took the box over to the refectory table and lifted out the topmost object with extreme care. But then, violently, he tore off the tissue paper.

The object was a small hand-carving of lustrous brown sandalwood on a simple wooden base. It had been carved in the shape of an ox, with delicately sweeping horns.

"Looks Oriental," Ellery muttered.

Rusty shook her head. "East Indian, I'd say."

Ellery turned the little ox over and nodded. The words MADE IN INDIA were stamped into the base.

"Take that larger thing out next, John."

John removed it from the box, but this time it was Ellery who stripped away the tissue.

It was a house, as advertised—a sort of doll's house, rather crudely made. It was constructed with a certain ingenuity of miniature blocks painted red, to simulate brickwork, its roof, of tiny bits of black slate, lay on the upper story a trifle askew. Ellery removed it, exposing the upper story. There were little rooms and hallways and a flight of stairs leading up from the ground floor.

"'An unfinished house,'" Ellery pointed out. "This little doorway has a door missing up here on the upper floor, and see down here." On the ground floor, in one of the outer walls, a window was missing.

"But what does it mean?" Ellen demanded.

Ellery shrugged. There was no furniture in the toy house, and he turned the whole thing upside down, looking for a maker's mark, some clue to its origin. There was none.

"Home-made, undoubtedly. Well, let's have a look at that last thing, John—what did it say? a camel?"

It was a tiny camel, two-humped and heavy—Ellery guessed it was of some lead alloy, like the toy soldiers of an earlier generation—onto which a skin of gray and white enamel had been baked. As in the case of the little house, there was no clue to its make or origin.

"Mediterranean, I think," Rusty said.

"More likely Asiatic," Ellery said. "The two-humped camel is Bactrian, not Arabian. Well, I suppose it doesn't matter where these things came from, although someone's gone to the devil of a lot of trouble for the sake of whatever it is he has in mind. I wonder what the juxtaposition of these three objects is supposed to convey . . ."

"Lunacy," Dr. Dark said promptly.

"I don't think so, Doctor, tempting as the suggestion is. The verse seems a bit too lucid. By the way, has anyone seen any of these things before?"

There was a general shaking of heads.

"I don't get this at all," John said angrily.

"I do!" Olivette Brown cried. "There's a spirit-influence at work. I don't see it all yet, but the camel . . . in India, no ghost will cross the threshold of a house if camel bones are buried under it . . . and there's a house, isn't there—and, yes! isn't that little ox labeled 'Made in India'?"

"Doesn't that seem a bit on the complicated side, Mrs. Brown?" Ellery murmured. "Let's see, now . . . Two of the three objects represent animals, the third a house. That doesn't seem to tie in, unless this were a zoo house, which it clearly isn't. The materials vary—the ox is wood; the house is wood, simulated brick and slate; the camel is metal and

47

enamel. Their sizes are inconsistent—the ox is bigger than the camel, and the house is on a different scale from either. Colors? Brown, red and black and white, and gray and white."

"This is very much like reading *The Roman Hat Mystery* all over again," Publisher Freeman said. "Go on!"

"There's nowhere to go, Mr. Freeman. I can't see that these objects have anything in common except the irritating fact that they were given to John by an unknown donor for an undisclosed reason. John, does any explanation at all suggest itself to you?"

"Hell, no," John said. "Except that it has a nasty feel. Don't ask me why!"

"Oh, it's probably someone's idea of fun," Rusty said, taking John's arm. "Don't look so grim, darling."

"The ox," her mother exclaimed. "That's one of the signs of Taurus! Which one of us is Taurus again? Why, that's you, Mr. Craig."

The bearded host looked unhappy. "I suppose it is, Mrs. Brown. But let me assure you—"

Rusty said sharply, "Mother, don't be silly."

"Well, dear, he *is*."

"Ellery," Ellen said. "There may be a clue in the wording of the message."

"If there is, I'm blind to it. It's evident, of course, that the rhymester is taking off on that old English carol—what's it called ... ?" His mouth remained open. "I'll be double-jiggered," he said softly. "Of course. 'The Twelve Days of Christmas'!" At their blank looks he said, "I'd already remarked to Ellen the curious recurrence of the number twelve since these mysteries began. Twelve people in our party—for a holiday consisting of the so-called Twelve Days of Christmas—and among the twelve people, by coincidence (or is it?) we have represented the twelve different signs of the zodiac. Now these gifts come, and the verse that comes with them is a parody of the English carol actually known as 'The Twelve Days of Christmas'! Remember how the original goes? 'On the first day of Christmas/ My true love sent to me,/ A partridge in a pear tree./ On the second day of Christmas/ My true love sent to me,/ Two turtle doves and a partridge in a pear tree.' And so forth. The third day adds 'three French hens,' repeating two turtle doves and a partridge in a pear tree; the fourth day adds 'four calling birds'; and it keeps going that way, each additional item being followed by a repetition of all the preceding ones, until it winds up on the twelfth day with 'twelve drummers drumming.' "

"Charming," a voice said. "But so what?"

Ellery did not have to turn to recognize its owner. "I don't know, Marius. Except that we're plainly at the mere beginning of something. The carol would hardly be used as a model for these high jinks unless the user intended to follow it through."

"O happy day, O day of joy," John said. "Or is it?"

"I don't know that, either. I rather doubt, however, that the giving of joy is the motivating mood of whoever sent this. I'm afraid, John, for all its air of damfoolery, you'll have to take this seriously. People don't usually go to such elaborate lengths for the sake of a joke. Or, if it's a joke, its point is alarmingly obscure."

No one said anything. They were gripped in a sort of helplessness, not knowing whether to laugh or be nervous.

Ellery tapped the white card. "The only *modus operandi* I can suggest is to study this parody with an eye to its differences from the original. By the way, the spacing out of the words 'ox,' 'house,' 'camel' in the typing on the card I think we can construe as an effort at emphasis—to call particular attention to the nature of the gifts.

"Now as to the differences from the carol. They begin at once. In its first line the carol speaks of the first *day* of Christmas. In the card's first line *day* becomes *night*.

"The second line shows variation, too. The carol says, '*My* true love *sent* to *me*.' The message says, '*Your* true love *sends* to *you*'—particularizing John. In the third line the partridge in the pear tree becomes for some unfathomable reason a 'sandalwood ox,' and then the rhymester proceeds to throw in gratis two items that aren't in the original at all, even numerically—the 'unfinished house' and the 'gray and white camel.'" Ellery said suddenly, "I suppose all this sounds pretty silly, but nothing I can say about it is quite so silly-sounding as what it says in and of itself. Still, someone went to the trouble of gathering or making these things, packing them, writing out the verse, wrapping the whole production as a Christmas gift, and then skulking about in some hideaway in this convenient maze of a house until he found the chance to slip downstairs unobserved and deposit the box under the tree. With fifteen of us—we twelve and the three in help—moving unpredictably about down here, that safari to the tree was extremely risky if he wanted to remain unseen, or at least unseen in the cat-and-mouse role he's playing. No, the absurdities are on the surface only ... What's this?"

He had absently turned the white card over. Now he was frowning at some markings on the back.

They crowded about him, becoming a sort of panicky little mob. Even Mrs. Brown, for all her rapport with the spirit world, had developed a greenish pallor underneath her rouge.

The markings were in pencil:

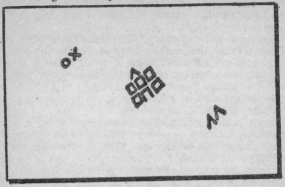

"There's the word 'ox,'" Freeman murmured, "clear as a publisher's conscience. But I'm damned if I can make sense out of the rest of it—I beg your pardon, Mr. Gardiner."

"It's quite all right, Mr. Freeman," the old clergyman said, waving his episcopal fingers. "I'm probably more familiar with damnation than anyone here. You know, this is most fascinating."

"Those two doodads at the bottom," Dr. Dark said intently. "Like two humps. The two humps of the camel!"

"And that central drawing," Mr. Gardiner muttered. "It strikes me, Mr. Queen, that may well represent the little house with the missing window downstairs and the peak of the roof."

Ellery nodded. "Yes, these markings undoubtedly refer to the three gifts in the box—the camel only begun, as if the pencil-user was either interrupted or for some other reason didn't get to complete the drawing." He shook his head. "I'm afraid I can't contribute anything more. Except the prediction that there will be further 'gifts' of this sort, perhaps a box of them for each of the twelve nights of Christmas. And that would add another twelve to the series of twelve-things taking shape. Twelve gifts, John, to you."

"And nuts to *him,* wherever he is," John said. "I'm fed up with this foolishness. Anyone feel like a hike into town?"

Apparently no one did except Rusty. The pair got into turtleneck sweaters, stocking caps and boots and left the house. A few minutes later Valentina and Marius decided that they might enjoy a tramp in the snow after all; and Ellery saw them slip out after Rusty and John. But he was too preoccupied with the esoterics of the number 12 to consider the human implications.

Ellery became conscious of a presence.

"Mind if I intrude on your thoughts?" Ellen said.

"You can hardly intrude on something that isn't there," Ellery grunted. "I'm afraid I'm not being very cavalier. Where is everybody?"

"Here and there. Some of the men are playing bridge, some are listening to the radio. Haven't you heard it?"

"I hear it now. Sit down by me, Ellen." He made room for her on the settle, facing the fire. "What do you make of all this?"

"Nothing. But it scares me."

"Who do you know has it in for John?"

"Has it in for him?" Ellen was genuinely surprised. "I can't imagine such a thing. John is charming and talented and lots of fun. I don't believe he's ever stepped on anyone's toes in his life."

Ellery nodded, although he did not entirely share Ellen's estimate of her uncle's ward. Ellery had seen John at Greenwich Village gatherings when the charm had worn thin, had sensed a hard layer under the poet's exterior, a streak of willfulness that Ellen either did not or would not recognize. John might well have stepped on someone's toes, Ellery thought; and if he had, he would have stepped ruthlessly.

"How about Marius?"

Ellen looked startled. "Marius is John's best friend."

"He has a curious way of showing it. Is Marius in love with Rusty?"

Ellen examined the fire. "Why don't you ask Marius?"

"Maybe I will."

"Well, while you're making up your mind, might a mere Fine Arts Major suggest something you, Mr. Queen, seem to have overlooked?"

It was Ellery's turn to be startled. "Overlooked?"

"The typing on the card. Typing means a typewriter. You said yourself whoever's behind all this is probably operating from a hideout in the house. Maybe he typed the card in the house, too. If you identified the machine—"

Ellery exclaimed, "I've been so bogged down in fantasy that the thought never occurred to me. How many typewriters are there in the house?"

"Two. One is in Uncle Arthur's library and the other is in John's old room."

"Let's mosey."

They got up and strolled toward Arthur Craig's library. The men at the card table did not look up. The Reverend Mr. Gardiner and Mrs. Brown were listening spellbound to the machine-gun delivery of the patch-eyed "Headline Hunter," Floyd Gibbons, crackling out of the big walnut, half-octagonal, six-legged Stromberg-Carlson.

Ellery glanced at his wristwatch. "Ten-forty. Gibbons will keep Mr. Gardiner and Mrs. Brown occupied, and those four at the bridge table wouldn't notice it if Voliva's end-of-the-world prediction came true under their feet. After you, Ellen."

They slipped into the library and Ellery gently shut the door. He had appropriated the card from John's mysterious gift-box, and he directed Ellen to type a copy of its message on the battered machine belonging to Arthur Craig. She did so with a light, swift touch. Ellery compared her copy with the original under the direct light of the desk lamp, and shook his head.

"No. This machine has a great many partly chipped or out-of-line letters that aren't duplicated on the card. The card was typed on a newer machine—and a machine of a different make. Let's examine John's."

They made their way casually to the hall, then ran up-stairs.

"Oh, dear," Ellen said outside John's door. "Is all detective work so sneaky?"

"No attacks of conscience, Miss Craig. This was your idea, remember."

They were in and out in three minutes.

The card had not been typed on John's machine, either.

"You're certain, Ellen, there's no other typewriter on the premises?"

"They're the only ones I know of."

"We'd better make sure. Or suppose I make sure, and you go back downstairs and kibitz the bridge game."

Ellen tossed her fair hair. "Don't try to scare me any worse than I'm scared already. Anyway, we're in this together, aren't we?"

So she knew he had decided to make another search for the vanished Santa. Ellery squeezed Ellen's hand, grinning, and led the way.

They found neither a third typewriter nor the elusive uninvited guest.

Before he got into bed Ellery dug from his suitcase one of his father's Christmas gifts to him—the only one of the Inspector's gifts he had brought along to Alderwood. It was a 1930 diary that began with some blank pages for the last week of December 1929. Diary-writing was an old vice of his; and it had occurred to him that it might prove useful now in keeping track of what promised to be a complex of events.

Ellery began at the first blank page, dating it: "Wed. Dec. 25, '29," and in a miniature hand wrote for half an hour.

Then he went to sleep to dream of oxen and camels and turtle doves and Ellen Craig's pert, wholesome face.

Chapter IV ✠ Second Night: Thursday
December 26, 1929

In Which the Mysterious Prankster Plays the
Deadliest Game of All, and Mine Host's Ward
Is Tendered Another Surprising Gift

THURSDAY DAWNED GRAY and warmish. By a curious inversion, everyone came down to breakfast in good spirits.

"Has anyone looked under the tree yet?" Valentina Warren asked dramatically. She was wearing a Bergdorf Goodman tweed, a bright plaid of blue, green and beige that deliberately accented her pallor and focused the fascinated eye on her heavily rouged lips.

"May I investigate with you, Miss Warren?" Roland Payn asked gallantly. The white-haired lawyer had been looking Valentina over with an auction-bidder's caution.

The blonde girl's long lashes drifted to her cheeks. "Why, Mr. Payn, I'd love it . . ."

"Val brings out the butter and eggs in every Republican," Marius said from a mouthful of ham. "Five will get anyone ten she's pumping him right now to see if he has a producer-client in Hollywood."

"Swine," Rusty said pleasantly. "John, do you suppose there *is?*"

"Something under the tree? I don't know, honey child, and I don't care," John said. "It's funny-paper stuff, and I'm not amused."

"Val and Payn won't find anything under the tree this early in the day," Ellery said. "The card last night said, 'On the first *night* of Christmas.' Consistency of time and place is one of the blessings of this kind of Barney Googleism."

"Then he's going to have to deposit his largess under my nose," Marius Carlo said. "WEAF is broadcasting excerpts from *Aïda* tonight with Rethberg in the title role and Lauri-Volpi singing Rhadames. I wouldn't miss that for a dozen Barney Googles."

Ellen cried, "Well?"

Valentina came in pouting. "Nothing."

"Except a few pine needles." The lawyer steered the blonde girl around and back toward privacy. "Why not tell me a little about yourself, Miss Warren? I do have a few influential connections on the Coast . . ."

"May I point out that to my alleged swinery," Marius

asked of no one in particular, "has been added the odor of goatishness?"

"At least Mr. Payn is a gentleman," Olivette Brown snapped.

"A gentleman-goat," Marius nodded, "even a poetic gentleman-goat, since he's exercising his goatishness under the Sign of Capricornus—isn't that right, Mrs. Brown?" She glared at him. "Well, Payn's itinerary for the day now being taken care of, what shall we folks do to improve each shining hour?"

"Mrs. Brown's annoyance turned to hope. "I have my Ouija board with me ..."

The exodus was hasty.

So it came about that until lunch was served people were everywhere but in the living quarters downstairs, where Mrs. Brown lurked like a lady-spider for a twitch on her web. And even she sallied forth occasionally in the hope of ensnaring a victim.

After lunch they all drifted into the living room to sit about torpidly. Somnolence enveloped them, induced by Mrs. Janssen's fare and the nodding flames in the fireplace. So when the discovery was made, it came like a lightning bolt at a picnic.

It was John Sebastian who made it. Craig had dispatched him to the library to fetch a certain Poe first edition for Dan Freeman's inspection. John was in the library not more than ten seconds. He reappeared, making futile little gestures behind him.

"Arthur." He paused to wet his lips. "There's a dead man in there."

In the vacuum created by this extraordinary announcement Craig said blankly, "What, John? What did you say?"

"A dead man. Somebody I never saw before in my life."

The skinny old man on the library floor lay on his potbelly with his head twisted to one side and his mouth partly open. He looked tired, as if he had died more in resignation than protest. The haft of a bronze knife protruded from the center of a dark and hardening stain between his shoulder blades, like the anther of a withered flower.

"My knife," Craig said with some difficulty. "It's from the desk there. An Etruscan artifact I use as a letter-opener."

"An Etruscan dagger," Dan Z. Freeman mumbled. "I'll bet it's tasted blood before."

"Please," Ellery said. "No one beyond the door. Except Dr. Dark. Would you come in, Doctor?"

The fat doctor pushed his way into the library. The others huddled in the doorway, too stunned to be horrified.

"Without moving him," Ellery said. "Can you give me a rough idea how long he's been dead?"

Dr. Dark knelt beside the body. Before he touched it he

felt for a handkerchief and blotted his forehead. Finally he got to his feet. "I'd say not more than a couple of hours."

Ellery nodded and stooped over the corpse. Dr. Dark rejoined the others.

The murdered old man had a shapeless, gone-to-seed look that was not entirely the work of death. His gray wool suit had seen many years of use. So had the shabby tweed overcoat, the tarnished Homburg, the cheap woolen muffler and mittens that lay tumbled on the floor nearby. The old-fashioned bluchers, unprotected by rubbers or galoshes, needed resoling.

The lividity of the naked scalp was underscored by a few tufts of colorless hair. There was a small pathetic cut in the skin below the exposed ear, as if his hand had trembled in shaving.

"Anyone know who he was?" When no one answered, Ellery looked up sharply. "Come now, someone here must recognize him. Mr. Craig?"

The bearded man shook his head. "He's an absolute stranger to me, Mr. Queen."

"Mr. Payn? Mr. Freeman? Marius?" Deliberately, Ellery named them one after the other, forcing each to speak. But he could make nothing of their denials. They all sounded honestly puzzled.

"Well, identifying him shouldn't be too hard. Then we'll see. Who admitted him to the house?" There was another silence. "Now that's obviously ridiculous," Ellery said. "He didn't materialize on Mr. Craig's library rug like a jinni, or one of Mrs. Brown's ectoplasmic friends. He's been in the house long enough for his shoes to have dried out. Felton, are you back there? Did you let him in?"

"Not me, sir!"

"Mrs. Janssen? Mabel?" After a moment Ellery said in a depersonalized tone, "Mr. Craig, you'd better phone the police."

Alderwood's police force consisted of five men, four patrolmen under the command of a chief named Brickell who had held his job for over twenty years. Brickell's prime function over that span was to haul out-of-town motorists before the local justice to pay the fines that relieved Alderwood's taxpayers of most of their police department's budget. His office was a shadowy cubicle in one corner of the town hall; his lockup consisted of two rusty cells in the basement, whose only visitors were occasional Saturday night drunks.

Chief Brickell's first words on entering the Craig house were, "My God, Mr. Craig, how did you happen to get a killed man dumped in your house?"

Craig growled back, "My God, Brick, how would I know?"

The man evidently had not the cloudiest notion of where to begin. He could only stare down at the corpse and mutter, "Stuck in the back, huh? Hell of a note," while his weathered face registered a deeper shade of green. When he was told that all present disclaimed knowledge of the dead man's identity, he actually looked relieved.

"Then I don't think we got much to worry about. He's likely some tramp. Maybe him and another 'bo sneaked in to steal something, got in a fight, and the other one stabbed this one and beat it. That would explain this."

"It certainly would," Ellery murmured. "But we don't know that evidentially, Chief, do we? Don't you think you'd better go into it a little more thoroughly? I'd be glad to help."

"You a police officer?"

"No, but I've had some experience in police work."

"This is Ellery Queen, Brick," John said. "His father is Inspector Queen of the New York police department. Ellery's the fellow who solved that big New York murder case last year, the killing of Monte Field in the Roman Theater."

"Oh!" Chief Brickell shook Ellery's hand heartily. "Glad to meet you, Mr. Queen! Got any suggestions?"

"I'd notify the county police, Chief."

"Give them the headache, hey? Mind if I use your phone, Mr. Craig?"

"Go right ahead," Craig said, not without humor.

"Oh, Brickell. While you're phoning. Is it all right with you if I look the dead man over?"

"Hell, yes."

"Wait till I tell my father," Ellery said *sotto voce* as the police chief tramped off. "Letting a suspect in a murder investigation be the first to examine the body!"

By the time Brickell returned, Ellery had the dead man's pockets turned inside out.

"I'm afraid the county police are being handed a pig in a poke, Chief."

"They'll be over right away. .... What say, Mr. Queen?"

"His pockets have been cleaned out. No wallet, papers, keys, jewelry, money, handkerchief—nothing. Just to make it more interesting, all the labels have been removed from his clothing, even the sweatband in his hat." Ellery studied the little corpse thoughtfully. "So his killer didn't want him recognized. Thus making the question of his identity crucial. Is there a coroner's physician in Alderwood, Chief?"

Dr. Dark answered. "Dr. Tennant."

"Might be a nice idea to notify *him*, too, Chief."

"Oh! Yeah, sure." Brickell hurried out, leaving a wake of silence.

"That Santa Claus yesterday morning," Rusty said suddenly. "Could this man be—?"

"No," Ellery said. "Our little visitor from outer space couldn't have stood more than five-four or five in life. Whereas friend Claus was taller than I, and I'm six feet. He was as tall as John, I'd say. You're about six-two, John, aren't you?"

"Six-one and a half."

And there was the silence again.

Valentina Warren said hysterically, "Two unknown men, one vanished and one murdered. *Two* ghosts! What's this all about, anyway?"

No one answered, not even Olivette Brown.

Lieutenant Luria of the county police brought an alarming note of sanity to the proceedings. A black-browed, quiet-mannered young man with heavily muscled calves, he slipped into the case without dramatics, disposing his detail of troopers and technicians from the county crime laboratory efficiently, and then sitting down to ask unaccented questions of unavoidable point.

It was evident from the first that he held everyone on the premises suspect, including Ellery—until that worthy produced certain credentials. Even then Luria was not satisfied. He telephoned Inspector Queen at police headquarters in New York for confirmation.

"The Inspector wants to talk to you." Luria handed Ellery the telephone."

"What have you got into now, son?" Inspector Queen's voice was ready for anything.

"I don't know, dad."

"Can't talk, hm? Just tell me this: Your nose clean?"

"Spotless."

"Want me to run out there?"

"What for?" Ellery hung up. "How can I help, Lieutenant?"

"Tell me everything you know about this."

Ellery told him—about the ephemeral Santa Claus, the queer gifts, his unsuccessful searches of the unused wings, and the discovery of the stranger's body.

Lieutenant Luria seemed unimpressed. "That Santa Claus business and the package—sounds to me like somebody's idea of a rib, Queen. Doesn't seem to go with the murder at all. The two may not be connected."

"I think they are."

"In what way?"

"I don't know."

Luria shrugged. "We'll give the place a roof-to-cellar runthrough and see if we can't come up with something on your Santa. Right now I'm more concerned with the dead man." He turned to the coroner's physician, a bald and fish-eyed country doctor wearing pince-nez glasses attached to his lapel

57

by a black silk ribbon. The physician was just rising from his examination of the corpse. "What's the bad word, Dr. Tennant?"

"I can't tell you much, Lieutenant. Dead about three hours. Doesn't seem to be any question that the knife in his back caused death. No other wounds, no contusions except a slight bruise on the forehead, probably made when he struck the floor. Age—oh, late sixties, say."

"Any scars or other identifying marks?"

"None on superficial examination."

Ellery said, "What about his teeth, Doctor?"

"As far as I can tell, they're his own. No bridgework. Some back teeth are missing, but I doubt if that's going to help. They look like pretty old extractions to me."

"Okay," Lieutenant Luria said. "Release him to us, Doctor, and we'll haul him over to the county morgue for a more thorough going over. You boys all finished with the photos?"

When Dr. Tennant and the corpse were gone, Luria turned suddenly to Ellery. "Here's an old party, shows up in the middle of a Christmas celebration, nobody knows who he is, what he wants, how he lands in the library, or who stuck a knife in his back after he gets here. And to give it more of a kick, all identifying papers and clothing labels have been removed. Any ideas, Queen?"

Ellery looked at his cigaret. "I'm in something of a spot, Lieutenant. As Mr. Craig's house guest . . ."

"You're not talking, either?"

"I was about to say: However, I was brought up to believe that murder most foul cancels Emily Post . . . It seems likely someone here is lying—knows this man, admitted him to the house, perhaps during the night. He could have been hidden out in that labyrinth upstairs for weeks. I can't help connecting the murdered man and Santa Claus, who I *know* has been hiding out here. They may even have come together."

Lieutenant Luria grunted.

"Unless we find Santa," Ellery said to his cigaret, "this whole case could hinge on identifying the corpse. The killer is probably afraid that if we knew who the dead man was, there'd be a clear trail to *him*."

"I understand you got a good squint at the corpse," Luria said. "That Brickell! What do you make of the little guy?"

"Not much. Unless the worn clothing was camouflage, he was down on his luck in a genteel sort of way. He hadn't given up—his clothes were neatly mended, fairly clean—but he'd reached a pretty desperate stage. A man who'd once been able to afford clothes of that quality doesn't wear a Homburg hat with a tweed overcoat unless he can't help himself. He wasn't a manual laborer, by the way. I mean unskilled work."

Luria grinned. "You spotted his hands, too."

"Certainly. No calluses, no broken or grimy fingernails, palms soft and well-scrubbed. Rather sensitive hands, in fact. The hands of a professional man, or an artist, perhaps a musician—"

Ellery stopped

They looked at each other.

Lieutenant Luria grinned again. "Two minds with but a single thought. How much do you know about this Marius Carlo?"

But nothing came of anything. Luria queried Carlo, and Val Warren, and Payn and the rest—not excluding Mr. Gardiner and Mrs. Brown, who was in a half-trance most of the afternoon—and in the end he had a notebook full of meaningless notes and a time schedule of people's movements during the morning that told him nothing at all.

"The Brown woman had the door to the library under observation practically all morning," the lieutenant said to Ellery, "and if I understand her right—which I'm not sure I do—the reason she didn't see the killer go in or come out is that she wasn't in tune with the spirits. What spirits? Bootleg?"

"I could bring up camel bones in this connection," Ellery said, "but I'll spare you. The fact is, Lieutenant, not only the killer but the corpse got by her—I mean while he still had motive-power—which means that she was either snoozing or out of the room at the strategic moments."

"What's this act she's been putting on, staring into space google-eyed, like she'd just lost her step-ins during a flagpole-sit?"

Ellery said gravely, "That's a demonstration of detection Olivette Brown-style."

"Detection?"

"By divination, Lieutenant. Mrs. Brown has a direct line to the Underworld."

Lieutenant Luria was astounded. "You mean this old jazzed-up tomato has a tie-in with the mobs?"

"Her Underworld has mobs, all right, but not the kind run by the Dutch Schultzes and Bugsy Morans of this world. Don't worry about it, Lieutenant. It's just that, mentally, she's a little crocked."

Search of the premises by Luria and several troopers was equally unproductive. They found no unknown person, nor any trace of one.

"You know, it just occurred to me," Ellery said suddenly. "Whoever's holing up here has to eat, doesn't he?"

"Say, that isn't a bad hunch."

The lieutenant questioned Craig's cook-housekeeper about her larder, but even this was inconclusive.

"With so many folks to feed three meals a day, and so many vittles having to be on hand at all hours," Mrs. Janssen told him, "I'd have to have eyes in the back of me head to keep track of it all. Sure food's missing, Lieutenant. Mostly it goes down the gullet of Mr. John, who's an icebox-raider from away back and never has been able to put an ounce on his bones, bless his heart."

Before Luria left, he assembled the entire company in the living room, including the three domestics.

"We'd better have an understanding," the lieutenant said calmly. "This is an unusual case, and I'm going to handle it—for a while, anyway—in an unusual way.

"A man was murdered on these premises this morning who, according to your statements, is a stranger to all of you. I'm not saying he wasn't. I've seen screwier things. For all I know, Chief Brickell may have hit the nail on the nub when he said the dead man might have been one of two tramps who broke in to steal something, had an argument with his buddy, got knifed, and the buddy lammed. There's no evidence to back that theory up—nothing stolen, according to Mr. Craig, who's checked the rare books in his library—no one seen running away, and so on. But it still may be true.

"And then again," Luria went on quite pleasantly, "the dead man may be directly connected with one or more of you. The removal of all identifying papers, labels, contents of pockets and so forth seems to back that likelihood up. So the first order of business is to identify the victim. That's going to take time."

He looked around at the tense faces. "Until we know better where we're at, I've got to have you all where and when I want you. I understand this house party's supposed to last at least through New Year's Day, maybe longer. That makes it easier for everybody. But a week may not be enough for us. In that case . . ."

Roland Payn's lush baritone enriched the air. "You realize, Lieutenant, that you have no evidence warranting the detention of anyone here. I personally have no intention of leaving until after New Year's, but if some unexpected matter should call me back to New York . . . I believe I speak for all of us when I say we'll cooperate to a reasonable extent, as we did with the fingerprints. But not beyond that."

"I understand, Mr. Payn," Lieutenant Luria said with a slight smile. "You'd like to make a deal."

"I beg your pardon?"

"I'm prepared to make one. I take it no one here, not even Miss Warren, particularly cottons to the idea of being splattered all over the newspapers in connection with a murder case?"

"Good God, no," Dan Z. Freeman said pallidly.

60

"I can see the Bishop's face now," old Mr. Gardiner said, not without a note of regret. "However, speaking as a good Christian, it would be my duty to spare him."

"Go on, Lieutenant!" Payn said.

"Well, if you all promise not to go legal on me about staying here, I'll do what I can to keep the newspaper boys off your backs. All I have to do is be vague about just where in Alderwood the man's body was found. I'll vouch for my men. I can't, of course, promise that Chief Brickell or Dr. Tennant will keep their mouths shut."

"I happen to know—if you'll forgive the unfortunate figure of speech—where a body or two is buried," Dr. Sam Dark said in a grim tone. "I'll shut Tennant up, all right. And Arthur, you ought to pack enough weight as a heavy taxpayer to do the same with Brickell."

The bearded man nodded. "This is decent of you, Lieutenant. You agree, Roland, don't you?"

"I always look a horse trade in the tushes." The New York lawyer shrugged. "However, I'll ride along."

Luria was amused. "Then that's settled. Oh, by the way. I'm leaving a trooper here, Sergeant Devoe. Sergeant?"

"Yes, sir."

A gigantic young man stepped into the room. He made a handsome picture in his trooper's uniform.

"Routine, Sergeant. Don't get into anybody's hair."

"No, sir."

"Golly!" Valentina breathed. "Sergeant, you can get into my hair any time you want."

To her disappointment, Sergeant Devoe followed Lieutenant Luria out, and for the rest of the day they caught only an occasional glimpse of him.

Dinner that night was a morose affair. The dead image of the old man hung heavily over the table; little was eaten, and the conversation flared and flickered dismally. After dinner they settled down in the living room. There was no box under the Christmas tree and no one seemed to have expected any.

"If this gift-and-carol business was a joke," Rusty said, "that poor little old dead man's put an end to it."

"I wonder who it was," Ellen said, frowning.

"Is," Marius corrected her.

"Is?"

"Well, my little chicken, he's probably still here, no?"

No one said anything after that about "Number Thirteen," as Ellen had christened him. The outrageous absurdity of someone's roaming about over their heads—of his very existence in the house—made any rationale about him impossible.

Marius wandered into the music room and played a tormented and percussive little thing on the piano, a composition of his own, that he called "Lullaby." Mrs. Brown drifted from group to group trying to interest people in astrological readings, with no success whatever. John and Rusty, curled up on the velvet-padded window seat in one of the bays, talked earnestly in undertones. Ellen and Valentina got Marius to play some orthodox carols and sang them in sweet, spiritless harmony. The older men sat around discussing books and plays and the ravages of Prohibition and, after a while, sports. Surprisingly, Mr. Gardiner disclosed that he was an ardent baseball fan, a discovery that enlivened Dr. Dark wonderfully. For a time the minister and the physician engaged in a spirited argument over the future of Babe Ruth, who had finished the 1929 season with a mere forty-six home runs.

"He's on his way out, I tell you, Reverend," the fat doctor squeaked. "Sixty homers in 'Twenty-seven, fifty-four in 'Twenty-eight, and now forty-six. You watch next year. 'Way down!"

"O ye of little faith," the clergyman muttered. "Sell not the Babe short, Doctor. I suppose you consider Lefty O'Doul the greater hitter?"

Ellery remained by himself, restlessly.

At ten o'clock Marius announced that anyone who did not care to listen to grand opera had his permission to go to bed. And he tuned in WEAF and shushed them with fierce little cries of pleasure as the powerful voice of Lauri-Volpi singing "Celeste Aïda" invaded the room. And for the better part of an hour Marius Carlo held them there, listening to Lauri-Volpi and Elisabeth Rethberg.

Poor Carlo was destined to have his Verdian pleasures foreshortened. He never heard the end of the program. For at 10:43 P.M. the great figure of Sergeant Devoe loomed in the archway from the hall, and his bass young voice drowned out the radio.

"Did you know about this, Mr. Sebastian?"

His big hand was holding up a Christmas package.

Ellery sprang to the radio, silenced it.

"Of course he couldn't leave it in this room tonight—no opportunity," Ellery said feverishly. "Where did you find that, Sergeant?"

"In the hall on that little table. I didn't notice it there before I went into the kitchen for my supper. Then I left by the back way and I've been patrolling outside." Sergeant Devoe looked at the silent company quite frankly. "Nobody's come near this house . . . from outside."

Ellen said a little shrilly, "Friend Santa again."

"May I have that, Sergeant?" Ellery said.

"I better get instructions first, Mr. Queen."

"All right, call Luria. But hurry, will you?"

62

Sergeant Devoe retreated, still clutching the package. No one said a word. When he reappeared, he handed the package to Ellery. "Lieutenant says it's okay, Mr. Queen. But he wants you to call him on it after you see what's inside."

There was the same kind of Santa Claus tag with the name "John Sebastian" typewritten on it, the same red and green metallic wrapping paper, the same gilt ribbon.

The box inside again was white and unmarked. Ellery raised the lid. Two small objects lay there, each wrapped in red tissue paper; and on them lay a plain white card displaying a typewritten verse.

Ellery read the verse aloud:

```
    On the second night of Christmas
    Your true love sends to you,
    A pine-paneled  d o o r
    For the upper floor,
    A stained-glass  w i n d o w
    For the floor below.
```

"For the love of Mike!" Dr. Dark said.

Ellery unwrapped the objects. One was a miniature pine-paneled door, the other a tiny stained-glass window.

"John."

"Yes, Ellery."

"After I showed last night's box to Lieutenant Luria today, what did you do with it?"

"Took it back to my room."

"Get the doll's house, will you?"

No one moved while they waited. But Val Warren laughed hollowly. "Joke's over, Rusty? It looks to me as if it's just starting its run."

Rusty did not reply.

John came hurrying downstairs carrying the toy gingerly. In silence he set it down on the refectory table, and in silence Ellery took the little pine-paneled door from the new box and fitted it into the doorless doorway in the upper story of the house. It fitted perfectly. And when he tucked the miniature stained-glass window into the frame on the ground floor where a window was missing, the window fitted perfectly also.

63

"Ellery." Ellen sounded frightened. "Are there any pencil marks on the back of this one?"

"No." It was the first thing Ellery had checked.

"It's insane!" John cried. "Who the devil's doing this? And why? Even a dirty joke has a point of some sort. What's the *point* of all this?"

Ellery said to the tall trooper, "What's Luria's number?"

When he came back he said abruptly, "All right, somebody's playing games. Like John, Luria's inclined to think it's the work of a psychopath. I don't agree. There's sanity behind this, and deadly purpose."

Ellery glanced over at the little house. "Last night John received an 'unfinished' house, tonight he receives two parts that seem to finish it. What that's supposed to mean I have no idea. But I don't believe the mysteries are going to deepen. For these events to have any rational motivation, they've got to become clearer as the game goes along. Let's see what we have so far."

Ellery began to walk about, addressing the floor, the fire, the timbered ceiling. "The number of the gifts has now become a variable factor. Last night's consisted of three items, tonight's of two. We may expect, then, further number-variations. Actually, these internal variations don't affect the external probability that there will be twelve groups of gifts—one for each night of Christmas. In the final count the total number of individual gifts may have some significant relationship to the number twelve. Beyond that we can't go at this time."

His publisher asked incredulously, "Are you being serious, Queen?" and looked about him with a timid smile, as if to include the others in his incredulity. But no one smiled with him.

All Ellery said was, "I'm simply playing the game, Mr. Freeman."

One by one they drifted off to bed, until only Ellery and John Sebastian were left in the living room.

The two young men sat before the dying fire in silence. But finally John said, "I can't see *any* light in this damned thing," and got up to mix of couple of whiskies. He handed one to Ellery and sat down with the other.

"Ellery. This sort of thing is up your alley, isn't it?"

"Not at the moment."

"You know what I mean. You have the involved type of mind that sees things average dumbbells miss. At least that's your reputation. Isn't there anything in all this that makes sense to you?"

Ellery shook his head. "I'm over my depth, John. So far, anyway. It's probably because there are still too many unknowns." He set his glass down. "Are you sure there isn't something *you* know that might help?"

The young poet was startled. "I? How do you mean?"

"I know of at least one item of information you've been holding back. You said that on January sixth four things were due to happen. You'll come into your father's estate, you'll have your book published, you'll marry Rusty ... and what? The fourth thing, you said, would be a surprise. What is it?"

John nibbled his lip.

"Conceivably, John, it could have something to do with these gifts."

"I don't see how. In fact, I know it hasn't." John got up and went to the whisky decanter again. "No, that has nothing to do with these Christmas boxes."

Ellery said quietly, "And with the murder of the old man?"

"Nothing!"

Ellery raised his brows. "You say that as if you aren't sure."

"Of course I'm sure! I'd stake my life on it."

Ellery picked up his glass and drained it. Then he rose and said gently, "That may be exactly what you're doing, John. Good night."

He went up the wide staircase slowly. He had remarked his friend's growing irritability of the past two days without attaching importance to it. Now it seemed to Ellery that it might have a secret connection with the mystery. What was John concealing? His bewilderment at the events of the last forty-eight hours had seemed genuine enough. Was it an act?

Something made Ellery look up.

He had paused on the landing. The upper hall ran across the landing, past bedroom doors in either direction. At each end the hall made a turn to a wing beyond his vision. Two nightlights, one in each branch of the hall, dimly illuminated them.

The dark figure of a man had appeared from around the corner of the hall to Ellery's left. As the figure passed under the nightlight, Ellery saw the face clearly.

It was John's.

The glimpse was brief. At once John opened the door of his bedroom and disappeared.

Ellery stood on the landing feeling stupid. He had left John downstairs in the living room a minute before; how had John managed to get up here ahead of him? It wasn't possible. Unless ... Of course. John must have taken the backstairs from the kitchen.

Ellery went to his room, dug out his diary, and sat down

to record the events of the day and evening. But all the time he was writing, a minute thought kept picking at the lock of a dark door in his brain. It annoyed him so much that he finally stopped writing to haul the thought out into the light.

Consciously examined, it annoyed him even more.

The thought was: How had John managed to reach the upper floor via the backstairs *so fast?* True, Ellery's direct-route pace from-living-room-to-hall-up-front-stairs-to-landing had been leisurely. But John had had to traverse the length of the living room, had had to cross the dining room and enter the butler's pantry, go through the pantry into the kitchen, climb the backstairs from the kitchen up to the landing at the end of the left wing of the upstairs hall, and then walk down the length of the wing and around the corner. Did he do it on the dead run? Even at a dead run . . .

But aside from that . . . why?

In fact, why use the backstairs route at all?

Ellery shook his head, impatient with himself. The general atmosphere of hocus-pocus surrounding the grimy fact of the old man's murder, he thought, must be getting me, too.

He locked the annoying thought back in its cubby and prepared to resume work on his diary. At that moment the big grandfather clock on the main landing upstairs began to strike the hour.

Automatically, Ellery counted the strokes.

His scalp prickled.

Twelve . . .

He began to write angrily.

Chapter V ✠ Third Night: Friday December 27, 1929

In Which a Summerhouse Sets the Scene for a Winter's Tale, and an Iron Gift Keeps the Roof of the Little House from Being Raised

AFTER TOSSING for hours trying to keep the annoying thought closeted, and failing, Ellery awoke to find that he had overslept. He went downstairs Friday morning not hopefully, and he was right. Mabel was clearing the table.

"Oh, Mr. Queen," the Irish girl exclaimed. "We'd given you up. I'll set a place for you."

"No, no, Mabel, the late bird doesn't deserve the worm, or

some such disgusting thought. Just coffee will be fine. No cream or sugar."

"And you so skinny!" Mabel giggled.

Ellery walked into the living room with his coffee to be greeted by jeers and a hurled copy of *The New York World*.

"Drink your coffee, read Broun and F.P.A., and shut up," John Sebastian growled. "You're interrupting the What's-Going-On-Outside-the-Bughouse Hour."

Everyone was reading a newspaper. Ellery wandered about, sipping his coffee and glancing over shoulders. Marius was absorbed in Lawrence Gilman's review of the Carnegie Hall début of a new young cellist, Gregor Piatigorsky. Roland Payn was studying a four-column halftone of curvaceous Helen Kane, the "Boop-Boopa-Doop Girl," who was making a Christmas week appearance at the Paramount Theater. Valentina and Ellen were reading the theatrical page, Freeman the book page, Craig the editorial page, and the Reverend Mr. Gardiner Dr. S. Parkes Cadman's counsel for the day. Dr. Dark was in the sports section, Rusty in women's fashions, and her mother—oddly—in the stock market quotations.

But it was John's choice of reading matter that interested Ellery most of all. Apparently he was being fascinated by an advertisement for a new type of electric toaster that toasted both sides of a slice of bread simultaneously.

Ellery dropped into a chair beside John and said, "You aren't reading at all. What's the matter, John? Didn't you sleep well? You look seedy this morning."

John mumbled, "What?"

"Skip it. I'm going to ask you what may sound like a fantastic question."

"Sorry. What did you say, Ellery?"

"Last night—"

John's fogginess cleared. He glanced at Ellery sharply. "What about last night?"

"When I said good night and left you alone down here, did you go directly upstairs?"

John blinked. "What kind of question is that?"

"What kind of answer is that?"

"Directly upstairs? To tell the truth, I don't—"

"When you did go upstairs, whenever it was, did you use the front stairway or the backstairs?"

"Backstairs?" Everything in John's face smoothed out. "I may have. What difference does it make?" And he buried himself in an advertisement for Rocky Ford Cigars, 5 Cents.

Ellery gave his friend a queer look.

"Forget it," he said pleasantly, and opened his *New York World*.

He wished he could take his own advice.

It was a tense day, with a curious waiting quality. It was not improved by Sergeant Devoe, who kept popping in at unexpected moments and popping out again.

In mid-afternoon Ellery looked up from his book to find Ellen Craig toe-tapping before him.

"What are *you* reading?"

"Anthony Berkeley's *The Poisoned Chocolates Case*."

"Poisoned pig's knuckles," Ellen said. "You're almost as dull as Uncle Arthur. How can everyone just sit all day? Come on out for a walk, Ellery."

"You have the energy of Jimmy Walker," Ellery complained. "Look, dear heart, the little I've read in this thing tells me Mr. Berkeley has some wows of surprises up his British sleeve. I've got to finish it in self-defense. Go be an outdoors girl with Sergeant Devoe."

"I could do worse! In fact, I just almost did." And Ellen strode off, head high.

Ellery looked apologetic, but he picked up his detective story.

Ellen went up to her room, changed into a French zipper ski suit, slipped on a pair of overshoes, jammed a white stocking cap over her curls, grabbed a pair of mittens, and ran downstairs and out onto the porch, slamming the door behind her hard enough to be heard—she hoped—in the living room.

The snow had settled grayishly under the higher temperatures of the past few days; it looked like shaved ice. Flinty clouds surrounded the sun; the slight wind had an edge. Ellen would have turned right around and gone back into the house but for her pique with Ellery.

She stepped off the porch, circled the house, and began to wade through the drifts toward the woods. The snow was crisscrossed with human tracks and had the mussed, untidy look Ellen detested. But then she caught sight of the summerhouse and her spirits rose.

The summerhouse lay a good distance from the mansion, at the edge of the woods, and it had been Ellen's favorite retreat from her uncle and Mrs. Sapphira when she was a child. Some of the most satisfactory memories of her childhood were associated with it. Here she had brought her dolls, played at being an actress or a nurse, and later dreamed of wonderful romances with the crushes of her adolescence. It had always been understood by John that the summerhouse was her private domain, not to be trespassed and sullied by a mere boy. He had occasionally dishonored their unspoken agreement, but not often.

Ellen approached her summerhouse eagerly; she had not been inside for a long time. But then she stopped in her tracks.

Someone was in it, talking. Two people, a man and a

68

woman, as Ellen could tell from their contrasting murmurs. She could not quite place the voices.

Disconsolate again, Ellen made a detour around the summerhouse toward the woods. And at that moment her right foot came down on a stone under the snow, her leg buckled, and she sank to her haunches with a muffled cry of pain.

"Miss Craig! You all right?"

Ellen looked up, annoyed. It was that big trooper, and he was hurrying to her from the bush behind which he had been skulking. Ellen had no doubt whatever about his purpose in skulking. He had been trying to eavesdrop on the people in the summerhouse. Even his exclamation of concern had been uttered in a cautious tone.

"I'm fine—" Ellen began in a loud, clear voice, when to her horror Sergeant Devoe's vast palm clamped over her mouth.

"Sorry, miss," the sergeant whispered, not relaxing his pressure for an instant, "but I've got to hear this."

"You big—you big Peeping Tom!" Ellen bumbled furiously. "Let go of me!"

He shook his massive head. "You'll warn 'em, miss. I don't like this any more than you do, but it's my duty. Shh!"

Very suddenly, Ellen stopped struggling. The voices in the summerhouse had risen. One was Rusty Brown's; the other belonged to Marius Carlo.

"Yes—love!" Marius was shouting. It was really more of a yell. "L-o-v-e! What's the matter, do you think I'm incapable of it? Or maybe John's a better man, Gunga Din?"

"You know perfectly well, Marius. Love has nothing to do with who's better and who's worse." Rusty was using a *grande dame* voice, by which Ellen knew she was trying to be reasonable and preserve her dignity at the same time. "Marius, let go of my arm. *Marius!*" The last was a shriek of pure outrage. Scuffling sounds came from the summerhouse.

"One kiss, just one," Marius was panting, "the kiss of a man, by God, not a puling adolescent who thinks because he doesn't rhyme 'love' with 'shove' he's a poet. Rusty, I'm crazy about you. Crazy in love . . ."

. . Swack!

Ellen flinched. Sergeant Devoe was beginning to look sheepish.

Rusty was shrill with rage. "You do that again, Marius Carlo, and I'll—I'll . . . Call yourself a man! Making passes at me behind John's back—your best friend! Why, if John had never existed, if you were the only thing in pants in the whole cosmos . . . *Love* you?" Rusty laughed scornfully. "I've never been able to stand the *sight* of you. You turn my stomach, Marius, do you know that? Anyway, it's John I love, and it's John I'm going to marry. Is that clear?"

Marius's voice was all but unrecognizable. "Very clear

69

indeed, Miss Brown. Marius the Crab revolts the fastidious Rusty Brown. Okay. So be it."

"And you can thank your lucky star I'm not the sort who'll go running to John about this. He'd break your neck."

"That's just what I'm going to do!"

"Uh, uh," Sergeant Devoe said.

"Oh, *dear.*" Ellen realized as she said it that the sergeant's mitt had long since unsealed her mouth.

John Sebastian appeared wildly from the opposite side of the summerhouse and plunged with a howl into the shadowy interior. He must have come up from the other side noiselessly, crouched in the snow, and listened as they had been listening.

From the flimsy structure came a drumfire of boots, a thudding of blows, a snorting of male nostrils, and little half horrified, half delighted yips from the maiden who was the cause of it all. The summerhouse trembled.

Sergeant Devoe listened judiciously.

"Don't just stand here, you lug," Ellen snapped. "What are you waiting for, a couple of corpses?"

"Those two?" The sergeant seemed surprised. "I guess it's time to break it up, though." And he stalked around to the entrance, stooped, and stuck his big head into the darkness. Ellen heard him say, "Okay, fellows, you've had your licks. Now lay off." When the sounds of carnage continued, Sergeant Devoe said regretfully, "I said lay off, didn't I, fellows?" and his monumental figure disappeared.

Immediately Marius and John appeared side by side in the summerhouse doorway, scratching at the frosty air, a great disembodied paw clamped about each of their necks. Then the rest of the sergeant came into sight, followed by a wild-eyed Rusty. The trooper marched the two friends out into the snow.

"Let go, you—Cardiff—troglodyte!" John panted, trying to get at Marius. "I'll kill the bugger!"

"Let—him—go, officer!" Marius screamed, flailing like a symphony conductor at the climax of a Wagner festival. "We'll see—what bugger—kills who!"

"No bugger's killing any bugger, and I'll remind you there's ladies present," the sergeant said sternly. "You two going to be good?"

With no discernible effort on the sergeant's part, the combatants buckled at the knees and sprawled prone in the snow, where they made various swimming gestures and gulpy sounds. Sergeant Devoe, on one knee holding them there, asked Rusty plaintively, "How do you turn these two off, miss?"

"You make them make up, Sergeant," Rusty said acidly.

70

"This is all a lot of hooey, anyway. Make them shake hands."

The sergeant looked flabbergasted. At this moment Marius's face emerged from the snow like a sounding whale's, and out of his dripping mouth came a spout of language that made Ellen, crouched behind the summerhouse, put her hands to her ears. So she missed the dénouement. The last she saw of the group, Sergeant Devoe was hustling the rivals along toward the main house, speaking to them reasonably, while Rusty trotted along behind, exhorting and advising.

Ellen sighed and straightened up. Immediately her ankle flopped over and she sank into the snow again.

"Oh, *dear!*" Ellen began to cry.

"Physical or emotional?" asked a male voice.

Ellen squeaked and slewed about in the snow. Ellery was coming out from behind the screening bushes.

"*You,*" Ellen said, and jumped up and fell back into the snow and began to cry again.

"A little of both, I observe." Ellery sprang to her side and raised her carefully. "Attagirl. Cry on Cousin Ellery's bosom. Horrible scene, wasn't it?"

"*You were there all the time.*"

"Every minute," Ellery said cheerily. "I circled around to get bêhind you and the sergeant, wondering what was up. I found out."

"Snoops. You *and* Sergeant Devoe. I'll never think a policeman or detective romantic again! Oh, Ellery," Ellen wept into his shoulder, "what are we going to do? It's gone from bad to worse. Poor Uncle Arthur . . ."

"We'll do the post-mortem later. Right now we're getting you back to the house and doing something about that ankle. Hand on my shoulder, Ellen . . . that's it."

It was as they were nearing the house that Ellen suddenly uttered a cry and halted.

"What's the matter?" Ellery asked anxiously. "Twist it again?"

"No." Ellen was star-eyed. "It just came to me . . . What were you doing out there in the first place?"

"What was I . . . ?"

"I thought that book was so enthralling."

"It was. It is."

"But you decided to come with me after all."

"Well—"

"You adorable man." Ellen squeezed his hand. "I forgive you. I really do."

Ellery mumbled something and they resumed their limping progress toward the house. He did not have the heart to tell the poor girl that he had deserted *The Poisoned Chocolates Case* and Mr. Berkeley's crafty divagations solely in order to trail John Sebastian across the snowy landscape.

Dinner was consumed with an attentiveness to the decorum of knife and fork and serviette that would have done credit to a delegation of Iowa schoolteachers invited to dine at the White House. Little was said beyond murmurs of "May I have the Yorkshire pudding, please?" and "Would you pass the chutney?"

Sergeant Devoe had apparently been successful in arranging a cease-fire, for the former friends addressed each other when the necessities of that table demanded, although not with any noticeable warmth. Rusty's attitude had in it something of the above-it-allness of a woman who knows that she has been fought over, and that everyone present is aware of the fact. That Valentina had heard the dismal details was evident from the way her handsome nostrils kept testing the wind throughout dinner.

The exodus to the living room had something in it of a disorderly retreat. Like any battle casualty, Ellen found herself bringing up the rear. Dr. Dark had pronounced her ankle sprained only superficially and he had taped it under her uncle's anxious eyes, but she was limping.

She came into the living room just in time to hear Sergeant Devoe say from the fireplace, "Nothing doing, Mr. Queen. Either he was too cute to come out from under cover, or I missed it."

"What's this, now?" Ellen asked.

"It's the 'third night of Christmas,'" Ellery said. He sounded glum.

All eyes turned at once to the Christmas tree. There was nothing beneath it.

"I'd forgotten about that business," Arthur Craig exclaimed. "What did you do, set a trap?"

"Of sorts. The sergeant staked himself out where he could spot everything going on in the hall and living room here, forgoing his dinner to do so. And you saw nobody, Sergeant?"

"Nobody and nothing."

Ellery muttered, "I don't understand that. There has to be a third gift. He's not going to stop at two ... Go get your dinner, Sergeant, and thanks."

Devoe left the room with a hungry stride.

"Doesn't he ever sleep or change his clothes?" Dr. Dark asked irritably.

"He has a relief who comes on at midnight and goes off before anyone's up," Ellery said. "It gives Devoe a chance to run over to the barracks for a few hours' sleep."

"Relief?" Roland Payn snarled. "Has anyone laid eyes on him?"

No one replied. Providentially, Felton appeared to serve brandy to the men and liqueurs to the ladies, and after a moment conversation became general.

It happened, almost as Ellery had come to expect, unexpectedly. On one of his serving tours about the room, Felton passed close to the Christmas tree. A projecting ornament at the tip of one of the branches brushed a cordial glass on his tray, and in trying to grab the glass before it fell Felton lost his balance and blundered into the tree. A shower of tinsel balls fell.

"Devoe!" Ellery roared.

The sergeant came running, a napkin tucked in his collar, jaws still grinding away at a mouthful of roast beef.

"What's the trouble?" He looked around frantically.

"Look."

The sergeant's eye sighted along Ellery's accusative arm. There, under the tree, nestling among the fallen ornaments, lay a tiny package of red and green metallic paper, bound with gilt ribbon.

Sergeant Devoe began to stutter, "But nobody—"

"Of course not," Ellery snapped. "Because it was done this afternoon, while you and I were out of the house, or at the latest early this evening before we arranged your watch. He simply tucked it deep among the branches. One of us would have found it eventually. Damn his playful soul, he's toying with us!"

Ellery snatched the little package from under the tree. The now familiar Santa Claus tag, with its typewritten "John Sebastian," he tossed aside. He stripped the wrappings from the plain white box. Inside lay something wrapped in red tissue paper, and on it a small white card with another typewritten verse:

> On the third night of Christmas
> Your true love sends to you,
> A hooked iron n a i l
> Your roof to dovetail.

And that, precisely, was what the tissue paper concealed: a plain iron nail that had been bent double in the crude shape of a hook.

Ellery went to the oak cabinet he had commandeered the night before as a storage place for the gifts, unlocked it with the key his host had given him, and took out the much-handled little house. He set it down on the refectory table and lifted the roof off.

"Here it is," he said through his teeth. "Two little metal eyes for the nail to slip into and hook the roof securely to the upper story. I remember wondering what they were for. Now we know."

"Know what, Mr. Queen?" Mr. Gardiner asked with unworldly innocence. "It fails to convey anything to me."

Olivette Brown's fanatical green eyes were on fire with triumph. "Iron!" she cried. "How could any of you know? Yes, including you, Mr. Gardiner—"

"Olivette," the old gentleman said.

"*Especially* you. But I've studied these things. Oh, I know that makes a bad Christian out of me, Mr. Gardiner, but some of this knowledge was old when our Lord walked the earth. Did you know that iron has the power to drive off evil spirits?"

"Then how is it, Olivette," Mr. Gardiner asked mildly, "that in all the literature of witches and sorcerers I've ever run across, evil spirits invariably use vessels and instruments of iron to prepare their brews?"

"Hear, hear," Dan Z. Freeman said.

"Mother, *please*," Rusty begged.

Mrs. Brown, constrained by some inner discipline from attacking her former pastor, turned on the unfortunate publisher. "I know your kind, Mr. Freeman! Tear down, tear down!"

"But my dear Mrs. Brown," Freeman protested, "*I* didn't—"

"Then why is iron *proof against ghosts?* Or didn't you know that?"

"Frankly, no." Freeman was plainly distressed at being the focus of a controversy. "But then I don't understand why all the ghosts of European castles I've ever heard of spend their nights dragging heavy chains around the premises."

"You can sneer at these things all you want, Mr. Freeman!" The woman's neck was stringy with rage. "But this I can assure you: from the dawn of time, when an epileptic goes into a fit they'll drive *an iron nail* into the ground to pin the demon! What do you think of *that?*"

"It ought to be called to the attention of the American Medical Association," Dr. Sam Dark said gravely.

"*Oh!*" Olivette Brown stamped out. Rusty ran after her.

"I'm sorry," the fat physician said. "But I can't believe she's serious about half the blither that comes out of her mouth."

Mr. Gardiner rose, shaking his head. He hurried after mother and daughter.

As if there had been no interruption whatever, Ellery said, "The other side of the card is blank . . . again."

That night, writing in his diary, Ellery added to his account of the day's events a short paragraph:

> Three gifts of the twelve now . . . subdividing into six different objects: an ox, a house, a camel, a door, a window, a nail. On the surface, idiocy or sheer malicious nonsense. Yet I can't get over the feeling that they have a connective meaning. The only thing is: *What?*

Chapter VI ✠ Fourth Night: Saturday
December 28, 1929

In Which Mr. Sebastian Develops a Puzzling Loss of Memory, Lieutenant Luria Tries Guile, and Mr. Queen Is Once Again Outwitted

AT BREAKFAST, Marius looked hung over. He ate silently, taking no part in the debate going on at the table.

Dr. Sam Dark had brought the subject up by announcing that he was putting in his bid for the use of the radio in the late afternoon—Army was playing Stanford in Palo Alto, and both CBS and NBC were broadcasting the game beginning at 4:45 Eastern time. This led naturally to a discussion of Chris "Red" Cagle, the Cadets' great All-American halfback, for whom the struggle with the Cardinals would be his last college game. Would Cagle tip the scales? Would the fact that it was his last football game spur him to feats of gridiron prowess extraordinary even for him? These were the burning questions of the argument, with Dr. Dark taking the anti-Cagle tack and Mr. Gardiner, Roland Payn, Arthur Craig and, in spite of himself, Ellery supporting the romantic view.

Chapter and verse were cited, including the crushing statistic of Army's defeat by Knute Rockne's undefeated Notre Dame team the month before—the good doctor delivering this blow; whereupon Mr. Gardiner sniffed that a 7—0 final score was hardly Armageddon, and the doctor retorted, "Yes, but what did Cagle do? Nothing but toss the pass that Jack Elder intercepted and ran ninety-eight yards for the only touchdown of the game!" This was deplored by Mr. Payn as an argument *ad hominem*, although he granted that Mr. Cagle had not had as good a year as in '28 . . .

And so it went, while Marius's jaws chomped and ground, and he never raised his eyes from his plate.

John Sebastian, on the other hand, seemed fully recovered this morning; he was cheerful, if on the absent-minded side, several allusions to the previous day's difficulties seeming to pass over his head; for the most part he heckled the disputants, taking one side and then the other where his partisanship might do the most mischief. Rusty kept looking at him queerly; but then Valentina was directing the same sort of look at Marius.

The young musician refused a second cup of coffee, hesitated, rose, excused himself and left the dining room. Immediately Val Warren followed. A minute later she returned, slipped into her chair and resumed her breakfast. And a moment after that Marius reappeared.

"John." He seemed to be having some trouble swallowing. "Could I see you for a moment? You and Rusty?"

John looked surprised. "Okie-doke. Excuse us?"

They followed Marius into the living room.

"Well, it's about time," Olivette Brown snapped. "Though I should think he wouldn't need *somebody else* to talk him into apologizing after the beastly way he acted yesterday."

"More coffee, Mrs. Brown?" Craig muttered.

Valentina said nothing.

Five minutes later Marius returned, alone. His dark features were eloquent with astonishment.

"Mr. Craig, I don't mean to worry you, but is anything wrong with John? Have you noticed any, well, absent-mindedness on his part lately?"

The bearded man was puzzled. "I don't know what you mean, Marius. Why?"

"I hoisted a few too many yesterday." The musician reddened. "I mean, that business with Rusty . . ."

"I understand. But I don't really see—"

"Apologizing isn't my forte, but . . . Anyway, I just apologized to Rusty and John. Rusty was very understanding—"

"And John wasn't?" Craig smiled in relief. "Well, young people in love, my boy . . . What does Dryden call jealousy? 'Thou tyrant of the mind.' "

"I don't mean that, Mr. Craig. What I mean is . . . it seems John doesn't remember what happened yesterday."

Craig looked blank.

"At first I thought he was pulling my leg. But he wasn't. He actually didn't recall our fight, Sergeant Devoe's stepping in—anything about it."

"But how could he possibly have forgotten?" Valentina exclaimed. "In less than twenty-four hours!"

The bearded man glanced in bewilderment at Dr. Dark.

The fat doctor was thoughtful. "It sounds to me like an amnesic episode of some sort, Arthur. Maybe a result of a head blow during the fist fight. I'd better have a look at the boy."

"May I look first?" Ellery asked quickly. "If you don't mind?"

Before anyone could answer, he jumped up and went into the living room.

John was seated stiffly in a chair. Rusty sat at his feet, talking to him carefully. She flashed a grateful glance at Ellery as he came in.

"Imagine, Ellery," Rusty said in a bright tone. "John doesn't recall a thing about that summerhouse business yesterday. He doesn't even remember being there. Isn't that amusing?"

"I don't know why everyone's making such a fuss," John said irritably. "All right, I forgot. Is that a crime?"

"We've all been under a strain the past few days," Ellery said, "and the old bean can play us queer tricks sometimes, John. Like that backstairs episode Thursday night."

"Backstairs?" Rusty repeated apprehensively.

"I don't care to discuss it!" John sprang from the chair, almost upsetting her.

"But darling, you know you've been having headaches—"

"Hangovers!"

"Look, John," Ellery said, "as long as Dr. Dark's a house guest, anyway—"

"I'm all right, I tell you!" And John rushed out of the living room and vaulted up the stairs.

The others immediately trooped in through the swinging door from the dining room. Rusty seemed about to burst into tears. Craig patted her helplessly.

"I don't understand it," he kept saying. "Sam, I'd better go up to him alone—"

"Nonsense, Arthur," Dr. Dark said. "I've explored him inside and out since he was a twerp in kneepants. We'll go up together."

"I don't think," Ellery said softly, "that will be necessary."

For John was running back down the stairs. The lines of worry and peevishness had smoothed away. He was smiling as he strode back into the room.

"I must have given you people a scare," he said. "Rusty baby, I'm terribly sorry. Of course I remember now. It just came back to me. Did I sound awfully obtuse? And Marius, you don't have to apologize. It's no disgrace being in love with Rusty—I am myself! Forget it."

For once Marius was at a loss for words.

"John Sebastian," Rusty said firmly. "You tell me this one thing: When Sergeant Devoe went into the summerhouse to stop you and Marius from fighting, how did he go about it? What exactly did he do to you?"

John grinned. "He clamped those meathooks of his on the backs of our necks and hauled us out into the snow as if we were a couple of squabbling kittens." He rubbed his nape ruefully. "I'm still sore."

"You do remember!" Rusty flung herself at him. "Oh, darling, you had me so frightened . . ."

Everyone began to talk at once.

Ellery slipped out of the room. He shut the door of his host's library, sat down at the extension phone, and put in a person-to-person call to Inspector Richard Queen at New York City police headquarters.

"Dad. Ellery. Look, do me a favor?"

"Hold it," the Inspector said. "What goes on up there?"

A bit impatiently, Ellery told him.

"Sounds mad," his father said. "I'm glad I'm out of this one. Or am I?"

"All I want you to do is get some information for me. Rusty Brown, John Sebastian's fiancée, designed a number of Christmas gifts for everybody here and John distributed them Christmas morning. Each one was in the design of a different sign of the zodiac—"

"Sign of the what?"

"Zodiac."

"Oh," the Inspector said.

"—and they were all made up by Moylan's, the Fifth Avenue jewelers, on special order. Eight of the pieces were money clips, four brooches. Will you question Moylan's about them?"

"In person, I suppose."

"That won't be necessary. Send Velie down, or Hesse or Piggott or somebody."

"Do you know, my son, you have no sense of humor?"

"What?"

"It's not important," the Inspector said. "What sort of questions are to be asked? Or do we make them up as we go along?"

"I don't really know. I'm playing a hunch, dad. A really wild one out of left field. Just get Moylan's to tell you all about the transaction. Especially if there was anything unusual about it. Understand?"

"Nope," his father said, "but who am I to grasp the finagling of genius? I suppose this is to be a confidential inquiry? No leaks?"

"That's right."

The Inspector sighed and hung up.

Lieutenant Luria dropped in during the early afternoon.

"No," he said to their questions, "no luck yet in identifying the dead man. We're beginning to send his photo out of state. How have you all been getting on? I hear, Mr. Sebastian, you're still getting your nightly gifts."

"Do you understand Greek, Lieutenant?" John asked.

"You mean like 'Timeo Danaos et dona ferentes'?" Luria grinned.

"That's Latin, but I guess you get the idea."

78

"I don't blame you. See here, folks," the lieutenant raised his voice, "you've been awfully cooperative about staying put, it's a nice day—how would you all like a couple of hours' skating? I don't imagine anyone's going to run out on me." He laughed. "I noticed some people whizzing around the ice on Alderwood Pond coming up here, and they told me the skating's good today."

The girls were delighted. Even Dr. Dark allowed himself to be persuaded, although only on condition that they get him back to the house in time to tune in the Army-Stanford game. The younger people had brought skates, and Arthur Craig thought that between John's old storeroom of discarded athletic equipment and the resources of a neighbor with a large family, he could manage to supply those who had none. They all hurried upstairs to change into warm clothing.

"Aren't you going, Queen?" Lieutenant Luria asked.

"I've had a bellyful of skating since the days when I read *Hans Brinker*." Ellery lit his pipe and sat back. "Nothing from the lab, Lieutenant?"

"Not a thing." Luria stared at him. Ellery stared back. "All right, I suppose I can't force you. But don't tip my hand, will you?"

"You are gazing upon what the Bard called a veritable 'pigeon-egg of discretion.' How about fingerprints?"

"No strange prints in the library but the dead man's."

"The dagger?"

"Some prints of Mr. Craig's, but they're old and smudged. The killer wore gloves."

" 'Twas ever thus, *nicht wahr?*"

Before the party left, Ellen said to Ellery, "I might have known you'd be different. You staying home to make sure the police don't steal anything?"

"Something like that," Ellery smiled. "Well, toodle-oo. And let's hope everyone stays off the thin ice."

Ellen sniffed. "Really, Mr. Q., you're not half as clever as you think you are." And off she went, linking arms with Marius Carlo and Dr. Sam Dark as if they were the two most desirable males in the universe.

As soon as the party had driven off in the Craig and Freeman cars, Lieutenant Luria went into the kitchen. "All right, ladies, put on some warm duds. You're going for a ride."

"Are we, now," Mabel said, dimpling.

"You are. You're entitled to some fresh air, too. That includes you, Felton. Sergeant Devoe will take you for a spin."

"That's awful nice of you and the Sergeant," Mrs. Janssen beamed. "But what about me dinner?"

"You'll have plenty of time. The football broadcast doesn't even start till nearly five o'clock."

Luria waited until the police car drove from the grounds. Then he went into the living room.

Ellery took the pipe from his mouth and said, "Santa?"

"The hell with Santa," Luria said. "Now shut up and let me earn my pay."

He took the cushions off the chairs. He probed furniture, opened drawers, rifled cabinets. He poked up the chimney. He removed the back of the Stromberg-Carlson. He explored the Christmas tree, not neglecting to peer under the red crepe paper apron draping the stand. He went over the walls inch by inch, looked under pictures, tapped, rapped, thumped. He tested the floor, shifted rugs. He took the living room apart and put it together again.

He repeated the process in the library, music room, dining room, butler's pantry, kitchen and hall.

Ellery tagged after him, smoking peaceably. When Luria had completed his inspection, Ellery said, "Mind if I ask what you're looking for?"

Luria said cryptically, "Nothing—I hope," and added, "Nothing personal, Queen, but I'd like to search you."

"Search me?" Ellery grinned. "A pleasure."

He raised his arms high while the lieutenant made rapid passes over his body.

"Now would you stick to me like a brother?"

It was almost 4:30. Luria went back to the living room, Ellery at his heels, and took a comfortable chair.

"Let 'em come," the lieutenant said, and he lit a cigaret and blew an enigmatic puff.

The ice-skating party returned first, at a few minutes past the half hour, chattering in good spirits. Luria met them at the front door, blocking it.

Craig was surprised. "You still here, Lieutenant?"

"I'm afraid you're going to have to put up with me for quite a while yet, sir."

The bearded man's soft rumble took on an edge. "What is it this time?"

"I'll explain later. For now, would you all be good enough to do exactly as I say? I assume you'll want to get out of these clothes, freshen up or whatnot. Please go directly to your rooms. Whenever you're ready, come downstairs. Use these front stairs." He stepped back. "All right."

Baffled, the entire party trooped in. Luria stood alertly at one side of the hall as Arthur Craig and John Sebastian and their guests filed by and went upstairs. Luria remained in the hall.

A few minutes later Sergeant Devoe returned with the three domestics. The lieutenant repeated his instructions, adding, "You go on up with these folks, Sergeant, and bring them back down."

80

Even Felton's imperturbability was shaken. The three preceded the sergeant up the stairs nervously.

Ellery's silver eyes glittered. "I get it now."

"Whatever you think you've got, hang onto it."

Dr. Dark was the first to come hurrying down. "I don't know what's going on here," he panted, "but I'm listening to that football game. One side, gentlemen."

"Hold it a minute," the lieutenant said. The bulk of the Alderwood doctor quivered to a halt at the foot of the staircase. "Mind if I slap you around a little? It won't hurt." He was smiling.

"A body search?" Dr. Dark asked curtly. "What for?"

"You don't really mind, do you, sir?" Luria was still smiling.

The doctor's sandy mane bristled. But then his little eyes twinkled. "Why should I mind? You go ahead, son."

When he was finished, Luria said politely, "Thanks, Doc. Now please go into the living room and stay there. Turn on the radio, do what you want, only don't step out of that room."

Dr. Dark made directly for the Stromberg-Carlson. He turned the dial to the CBS wave-length, adjusted the volume control, lit a long cigar, and leaned back in an armchair beaming at the voice of Ted Husing.

John was the next to appear, and after him, one by one, the others descended the stairs. One by one Luria stopped them. The men all submitted to a body search; the ladies Luria was content to scrutinize closely, merely asking permission to open their handbags. Each was sent straight to the living room with a repetition of the request not to leave it.

When Sergeant Devoe reappeared with Mrs. Janssen, Mabel and Felton, the lieutenant said reassuringly, "Don't be jittery, girls, nobody's going to snatch you baldheaded. Go ahead into your kitchen, Mrs. Janssen, and get going with your dinner. You work right along with Mrs. Janssen, Mabel, don't you?"

"And how," the Irish girl said. "I have to peel the potatoes, set the table—"

"In the dining room? Not tonight, Mabel." Luria pursed his leathery lips. "Mrs. Janssen, what's on your menu for tonight?"

"Ham and cold cuts, potato salad—"

"Perfect. You'll prepare it buffet—to be eaten in the living room."

"Mr. Craig will want me to serve cocktails and canapés before dinner," Felton said.

"That's okay. You three can have the run of the kitchen, butler's pantry and dining room. You, Felton, will also serve in the living room. But make sure to come in by way of the dining room and go back the same way. Sergeant, you're

81

accountable for every movement of these three people."

Sergeant Devoe said with amusement, "Yes, sir." He escorted the trio up the hall, held the door to the butler's pantry open for them, and followed them in. Luria hesitated. Then he hooked the door shut from the hall side and went quickly into the living room.

They were standing about whispering. All except Dr. Dark, who was concentrating on Ted Husing.

Arthur Craig said stiffishly, "Lieutenant, I'd appreciate an explanation now, if you please."

"Yes, sir, if the doctor will turn the radio off. The game won't start for a few minutes yet, Doc." The fat man glared, but he reached out and shut the machine off.

Lieutenant Luria drew the brown velvet ceiling-to-floor drapes securely across the living room archway. Then he turned around, a chunky figure against the brown backdrop.

"It's simple," the lieutenant said. "I've got a murder to crack, a toughie I can't get to first base on till the murderee is identified. Meantime, there's this tricky business of the anonymous Christmas present to Mr. Sebastian nightly.

"I don't know what's behind that monkey business, or how it ties in to the murder, or even if it has a connection with the murder at all. So here's what I've done today.

"I got you all away from the house early this afternoon, even the servants. All but Mr. Queen, but he didn't get preferred treatment. I'm not leaving him out of my calculations just because his old man is a high police officer."

You certainly are not, Ellery thought with a grin.

"While you were all away from the house, Mr. Craig," Lieutenant Luria continued, "I took the liberty of searching the main living quarters downstairs here. By the way, I came prepared with a search warrant in case you felt like getting technical. If you'd like to see it, sir . . ."

Craig waved him on testily.

"Each of the presents addressed to Mr. Sebastian the past three nights has been left somewhere on this main floor." Luria said with a smile, "My purpose today was to satisfy myself that the fourth box—tonight's gift—*hadn't already been planted to be found.*"

"Damned clever of you, Lieutenant," John said rather coldly.

"Common sense. When you all got back to the house I sent you directly upstairs, and kept an eye on you till you'd got up there. In that way I made sure no one planted the box down here *on the way up.* And when you came back down, I searched the men and looked the ladies over before sending you into this room. So I'm satisfied that nobody brought a box *downstairs with him.* In other words, as of this moment, I'm ready to testify under oath that this downstairs floor is clean. There's no box here. And since we're all going to stay

82

right here in this living room till midnight"—there was a corporate groan—"why, this now-you-see-him-now-you-don't Santa Claus you've been telling me about has the run of the house. We ought to find out all sorts of interesting things from what does or doesn't happen. Right, Queen?"

Seven hours turned out to be a long time for over a dozen people to be shut up in a room without hope of escape, even a room as spacious as Arthur Craig's manorial hall. The siege began in an atmosphere of strain that thickened detectably as the evening ground on. It quite spoiled Dr. Dark's football game. He kept alternating between silencing the ladies and gluing his large ear to the loudspeaker. When Stanford repeated its 1928 triumph over Army, defeating the Cadets by a score of 34—13, the good doctor scarcely savored his victory. He was too put out with the talkers. He could not even summon a just retort when Roland Payn pointed out that— Army defeat or no—the fabulous Mr. "Red" Cagle had acquitted himself with valedictory brilliance, having made both Army touchdowns and thus accounted for all his team's scoring.

Emotions were not soothed when a pale Felton was passed through the dining room doorway by Sergeant Devoe, bearing the unmistakable paraphernalia for a buffet dinner. Craig half rose, then sank back mute. There was a high-pitched comment (from Olivette Brown) that "This has gone quite far enough, Mr. Craig, wouldn't you say?", and scattered mumblings (notably from Dr. Dark, who said that he had never chosen to learn the vaudeville knack of balancing a plateful of food on his knee and he did not intend at his age to begin). But for the most part there was little protest, only a tightening of the tension. They ate their dinner with no conversation at all. Luria was courteous and watchful throughout. His own chair stood squarely before the velvet drapes masking the archway, and he did not leave it for a moment.

After dinner there was a general quiet toping. Marius Carlo got drunk in a businesslike way and fell asleep, his spasmodic snores not improving morale. Some desultory bridge was played; Rusty located a jazz band on the radio and persuaded John to dance with her, and then with Valentina and Ellen (Ellery remaining in his corner, blind to Ellen's signals); and late in the evening, out of desperation, the company agreed at Valentina's urging to play charades. This enabled the leggy blonde girl to display both her legs and her unchallenged histrionic abilities, but it did little for anyone but Roland Payn, whose distinguished glance did not lift once above Valentina's fashionably high hemline. Finally, at eleven o'clock, they abandoned the game to tune in the news. This evoked hollow laughter. President Hoover's Commission on Law Enforcement and Observance was ready to report to

Congress, the newscaster announced in sincere tones, looking "with confidence" toward a more adequate enforcement of the Prohibition law; one of Dutch Schultz's bonded trucks had been hijacked on New York's East Side, and on Chicago's North Side two well-stapled corpses, who had been worked overy by a "typewriter" in a carbon copy of the St. Valentine's Day massacre, were scraped up from an alley and filed away as memoranda of the Bugsy Moran-Scarface Al Capone "alky" feud; and Police Commissioner Whalen of New York City had come out with a positive solution of Manhattan's traffic problem by advocating an end to all parking in the business districts.

After the news they sat around soddenly, waiting for midnight.

When it came, with the muffled bonging of the grandfather clock on the upstairs landing, heads were scarcely lifted.

"I'm very tired, Lieutenant," Mr. Gardiner said with a sigh. "May I retire now?"

"Just a minute, Reverend!" Luria had jumped to his feet. He strode over to the dining room door. "Devoe!"

The sergeant stuck his head into the living room.

"Get those three in here." When Mrs. Janssen, Mabel and Felton had dragged themselves in, Luria snapped, "You stay in here with all these folks, Devoe. Nobody's to move!" and, running back to the archway, he plunged through the velvet drapes and disappeared.

The house was still.

"The witching hour," Freeman said suddenly, and laughed. The laugh almost raised an echo.

They stood and sat there for a long ten minutes in total silence. Then the drapes parted, revealing Lieutenant Luria. He took a pack of Melachrinos from his pocket slowly, slowly extracted one, slowly lit it.

"End of experiment," he said.

"What's that supposed to mean?" John croaked.

Luria said deliberately, "There's no Christmas box tonight. Anywhere downstairs—or, for that matter, on the porch. And do you know why, ladies and gentlemen? Because whoever's been leaving them nightly to be found *couldn't* leave a fourth box tonight. And who couldn't leave a fourth box tonight? Why, any of you people in this room.

"May I say that I never did believe in your Santa Claus? Now I know there's no Santa Claus. Or if there is, or was, he didn't have a thing to do with these gifts. The one who's been dropping presents all over the place is one of you. Now how about letting us all in on the joke? What do you say?"

But no one said anything.

Oddly, Lieutenant Luria lost his temper. "All right, play your kid games!" he snarled, waving his arms. "From now on I'm concentrating on the murder in this case. I'll leave the fancy stuff, Queen, to you."

"But Lieutenant," Ellery began, wondering how he was going to point out with sufficient delicacy the large holes visible in Luria's experimental fabric.

But the lieutenant barked, "Good night!" and stalked out of the house.

"I hear my relief. Night," Sergeant Devoe said with a discreet cough, and he followed Luria out.

No one moved until the sounds of the two police cars racing down the drive became soft with distance.

Then they all went wearily up to bed. At least, they thought they were bound for bed. But with doors opening and closing along the upper halls, John—who had been one of the first upstairs—came running out of his bedroom laughing like a demon.

"No box tonight," he said. *"I just found this on my bed!"*

He was holding aloft a little Christmas package in red and green metallic paper, bound by gilt ribbon. On the familiar Santa Claus tag was typewritten the familiar "John Sebastian."

John had to be sedated. Dr. Dark remained with him until he fell asleep.

When he went downstairs the doctor found the company assembled around the new box, which Ellery had opened.

"How's John, Doctor?" Rusty asked in a subdued way.

"It's just nerves, my dear. He's always been highstrung, and this mystery stuff is beginning to get him." Dr. Dark reached frankly for the Scotch decanter. "Well, what's the leprechaun handed out tonight, Queen?"

Ellery held up a miniature wooden picket fence, painted white. "It's a perfect fit around the house, Doctor."

"And the message?"

Ellery handed him a white card. It contained four neatly typed lines:

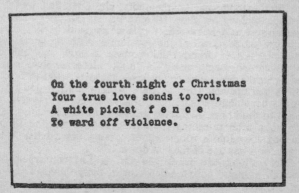

```
On the fourth night of Christmas
Your true love sends to you,
A white picket  f e n c e
To ward off violence.
```

85

"Not even decent doggerel," the doctor muttered, and he held out the card.

"No, this time there are markings on the reverse side again. Make anything of them, Doctor?"

The fat man turned the card over quickly, staring.

"Looks like a child's drawing of a picket fence. What does it mean?"

"I wish I knew."

"Violence," Arthur Craig said heavily. "It uses the word violence. This is the first time there's been a suggestion of ... of anything like that."

"Except the corpse in your library, Mr. Craig," Ellery said, not without irony.

"Yes, but this is directed against *John*."

Rusty giggled, "I think I'm going to upchuck," and she ran out of the room and up the stairs. Dr. Dark followed hurriedly, clutching his glass. Olivette Brown ran after him. Val Warren rose, too, but at Ellery's glance she sank back.

Ellery stared down at the toy house, with its latest addition. "Luria's experiment didn't prove a thing, and this development only emphasizes its futility. If some unknown is hiding in the house, he could have placed this fourth box on John's bed upstairs after we were all immobilized down here by the lieutenant. Or, if the gift-giver is one of us, as Luria seems to think, he could have suspected Luria's intentions this afternoon after returning from Alderwood Pond and slipped the box into John's room before coming downstairs. You'll recall John was one of the first down."

Ellery shook his head. "As far as I'm concerned, I'm through trying to balk the deliverer of these things. The odds on his being able to leave a small box somewhere about the house are too one-sided. From now on, all I'm interested in is the contents. To date we've had seven objects in four units. There's a pattern here somewhere. So far I don't see it. With more objects to go on, maybe I will."

Craig asked in a rumble, "You're convinced this isn't a practical joke, Mr. Queen?"

"Yes."

"Then I can't tell you how glad I am that you're here." The bearded man sank into a chair. "If you can possibly see what it all means . . . before it's too late . . ."

"Go to bed, Arthur," Dan Freeman said gently.

Ellery said, "I suggest we all do."

They left Marius, still snoring, in the living room.

Chapter VII ✣ Fifth Night: Sunday
December 29, 1929

In Which Capricornus Sprouts Four Horns, X Marks the Spot, and Divers Explorations into the Applicability of Twelves Comes to Nought

LURIA WALKED IN while they were at breakfast, spoiling it. One glance at his overcrowding brows, and Ellery knew that the lieutenant was in no mood for Christmas boxes this morning.

"I'll be wanting you one at a time in the library," Luria announced without preliminary. "Where's Gardiner?"

Craig said, "In town, at church."

"He's included when he gets back."

He went at them from behind the library desk all morning in a one-man Star Chamber proceeding, making notes in a fat notebook. Ellery hung back until last, then discovered that nothing new had been added—Luria was merely exercising the Hobson's choice of all policemen and going over the same old ground . . . they had never seen the dead man before?—and where and when exactly were you on Thursday morning last? *et cetera ad nauseam.*

When Lieutenant Luria slapped his notebook shut and rose, Ellery said, "And by the bye, just after you left last night, John Sebastian found the fourth gift box in his bedroom."

Luria sat down again. And rose again. "Never mind!" Then he said, "What was in it?"

"A little white picket fence—cutest thing you ever saw—and an implied promise of violence to come."

"It's the bunk. You know you're all nuttier than fruitcakes? I've got to be going."

"Wait a minute, Lieutenant. What about the dead man?"

"A big nothing. We haven't had a nibble from B.I.s anywhere on his mug, his description, his prints; and my hunch is he had no record. He certainly doesn't come from anywhere in this vicinity, as much as we've been able to check so far. So how do I like it? I'm crazy about it!"

Shortly after lunch there was a phone call from New York for Ellery. He took it in the library behind a closed door.

"Inspector Queen reporting," Inspector Queen reported. "How do you want your astrology, Mr. Queen—straight or around the bush?"

"Straight always," Mr. Queen said grittily.

"You said this Rusty Brown number designed eight men's money clips and four ladies' brooches, each with a different sign of the zodiac?"

"That's what I said."

"Your arithmetic is wrong. Eight and four make twelve, or did when I went to school. The only thing is, Moylan's say they made up *thirteen* pieces." When there was silence at the other end of the wire, the Inspector said, "Ellery? You drop dead or something?"

"I'm recovering from a heart attack," Ellery said in a faint voice. "Made up thirteen, you say? On order, of course. Not by mistake."

"Sure on order. Moylan's don't make mistakes."

"And tell me this," Ellery said, his voice growing steadily stronger. "The thirteenth piece was not an unrelated design? It was also a sign of the zodiac—a duplicate of one of the twelve, in fact?"

"Yes. It was—"

"Hold, sire. Let me guess. The duplicate pieces were in the form of goats? Capricornus, that would be. Two money clips for Capricorn. How am I doing?"

"Colossal," his father said, genuinely astonished. "How did you know, son?"

"You know my methods," Ellery said modestly. "Oh, well, I have no secrets from you. John Sebastian's birthday is January sixth. January sixth comes under the Sign of the Goat."

"Oh? But how did you know it was a duplicate of Sebastian's?"

"That's a fascinating yarn I won't go into over the phone. Dad, I have another job for you. Dad? You there?"

"I'm here," Inspector Queen said glumly "I sometimes wonder why I don't send you a monthly bill. What is it this time?"

"Have you a good man you can spare for a couple of days' confidential legwork? Like Sergeant Velie, for instance?"

"Ask for my right arm! All *right*. What do you want Velie to do?"

"I want him to dig into the circumstances surrounding John Sebastian's birth."

"His *birth*?"

"You hear me. All I know about it is this: John's parents were Mr. and Mrs. John Sebastian of Rye, New York. Mrs. Sebastian's Christian name was Claire. On the evening of January fifth, Nineteen-O-Five—are you taking this down, Dad?"

"Yes, sir," the Inspector sighed. "Nineteen-O-Five."

"The Sebastians were driving back from New York City in a snowstorm. Near Mount Kidron they had a smashup. That's Mount Kidron. As a result of the accident Mrs. Sebastian went into premature labor and gave birth. She died in childbirth, John's father dying about a week later because of his injuries. That's all I know. I want to know more about that accident and *accouchement*—lots more."

Ellery found Rusty behind the house. John was watching Valentina, Marius and Ellen compete in a snowman-building contest. Rusty was watching John, who did not look as if he was enjoying himself.

Ellen yelled to Ellery. He merely smiled and waved and said to John, "May I borrow your fiancée for a couple of minutes?"

"If you don't try to talk her out of marrying me. By the way, are you in love with her, too?"

"Madly," Ellery said, and walked Rusty aside. Ellen's pink cheeks turned carmine, and when Marius said something to her she grabbed two handfuls of snow and leaped on him.

"I don't know why you want me," Rusty said, "when I'm not available and Ellen is."

"Because Ellen can't answer the question I want to ask," Ellery smiled, "and you can."

"What question?"

"How come you didn't mention the thirteenth zodiac gift, Rusty?"

"Oh, that," Rusty said. "Didn't I?"

Ellery said gently, "No, you didn't."

"Well, I ordered it all right. The thirteenth was a duplicate of John's."

"And why did you order a duplicate of John's?"

"Because John asked me to. Any further questions, Mr. Queen?"

"One. Why did John want two Capricorn money clips?"

"I could say that it's probably because he's coming into so

89

much money January sixth he'll need two, but that would be a guess." Rusty was very cool about the whole thing. "The fact is, Ellery, I don't really know why."

"And you didn't ask?"

"Of course I asked."

"And what was John's explanation?"

"He laughed and kissed me and said we weren't married *yet*. Why don't you ask him yourself?"

"At risk of being kissed," Ellery said, "I believe I will."

His mock gravity concealed a real grimness. But Ellery did not let it show when he took John aside.

"What about it, Johnnykins?" he asked. "Why the duplicate goat design?"

"How did you find out?" John asked sharply. "Has Rusty been talking?"

"No. She merely confirmed what I already knew."

John said in an unhappy way, "You've been checking up on me."

"Only in idle pursuit of a notion. Why, John? Do you mind being checked up on?"

"I think I do," John said slowly.

"Look, friend. A murder's been committed in this house—"

"Good God," the young poet cried, "are you suggesting that I had anything to do with that? Ellery, I'm as much at sea about that old man and how he got himself killed on these premises as you are!"

"Then why don't you tell me about the duplicate clip?"

John said coolly, "Because I don't choose to just yet. Any other questions?"

"I think not."

Ellery lingered for a moment. John rejoined the group, said something to Rusty, got a delighted kiss in response and, at once, with her enthusiastic assistance, he began to build a snowman.

Ellery strolled back to the house. The instant he was out of their view his stride briskened. He entered the house quietly, ran into old Mr. Gardiner and Olivette Brown, murmured something about lying down for a nap, trudged upstairs ... and swiftly let himself into John's bedroom.

It was an immense room with a sweep of bay windows, its own fireplace, an oversize bed, and two enormous walk-in closets. The walls were busy with old college banners and a miscellany of teen-age accumulations—signs saying STOP, NO PARKING and KEEP OFF THE GRASS, crossed fencing foils speckled with rust, a motheaten raccoon tail, some French travel posters and a great many other tidbits of John's salad days.

Ellery went directly to the nearest closet and opened the door.

He stood there for some time, staring.

Then he opened the other closet.

He was still standing transfixed when an icy voice said behind him, "I've always equated snoops with Peeping Toms, cockroaches and other vermin. Just what do you think you're doing?"

"Similar insensitive remarks have been made about John S. Sumner, Bishop Cannon and Canon Chase," Ellery said without stirring. "One man's snoop is another man's crusader. I'm on the trail of truth as I see it, with no appreciable help from you." He turned around. "Still, I owe you an apology, John, which I hereby tender. Now will you tell me why every suit, coat, sports outfit, hat, sweater, pair of shoes and so forth in these closets has an exact duplicate hanging or standing immediately next to it?"

Surprisingly, John's handsome mouth lifted in a grin. "You mean to say you guessed that simply because I had two matching money clips made up by Moylan's?"

Ellery looked pained. "Guess is a dirty word in my dictionary. No, I had a bit more than that to go on, John. But you haven't answered my question."

The grin widened. "It probably won't make sense to you. I've always been hipped on clothes, and since I'm hard on them I've got into the habit of buying everything *en double*. I know, it's mad. But what's the advantage of being a poet if you can't indulge a whimsy or two?"

"As simple as that, eh?" Ellery murmured.

"As simple as that. Here, I'll show you." John began to yank bureau drawers open. "Duplicate shirts, handkerchiefs, tie clasps, belts, suspenders, socks—"

"Even monograms." Ellery fingered two identical neckties monogrammed *JS*.

"The madness extends to identical wallets, signet rings, cigaret cases . . . Are you going to call for an alienist?"

"For such a methodical madness?" Ellery shook his head, smiling.

John seemed amused, too. "You don't believe me."

"Well, you remember what Oscar Wilde said: Man can believe the impossible, but never the improbable."

"I agree. For instance, I'd never have believed the improbability that you'd come pussyfooting into my room like the celebrated thief in the night."

"I said that's what Oscar Wilde said. Personally, I not only can but frequently do believe the improbable. All I require is that the facts point to no other conclusion."

"And the facts in this case point to some other conclusion?"

"Those that I have at the moment," Ellery said, "—yes."

Their smiles crossed, and then Ellery left.

It was Ellery who found the night's gift.

It was during Major Bowes's "Capitol Family" broadcast after dinner. Ellery found that he had run out of pipe tobacco. He went up to his room to refill his pouch, and there on his bed lay a Christmas box, gay with its telltale green and red metallic paper and gilt ribbon and typed Santa Claus tag.

It was a rather larger box than the last two had been. He took it downstairs carefully.

"Number five," he said.

Craig hastily turned the radio off.

Ellery took the box to the refectory table. In silence they ranged themselves about the table. He stripped the wrappings away, revealing the usual plain white box. Inside lay some object swathed in red tissue, and on the red tissue a white card:

On the fifth night of Christmas
Your true love sends to you,
A plaster h a n d
(You still don't understand?)
A black spot in the p a l m
(Does that give you a qualm?)

And when he removed the tissue, a hand it was—a man's hand in plaster, bony, almost emaciated, with the fingers curling slightly and the thumb stuck out in supplication or surrender. On the white plaster of the exposed palm the sardonic sender had used a black pencil with a soft lead. Etched into the palm was an X.

"There's no misunderstanding what he means this time, is there?" John said with a short laugh. He turned to the liquor cabinet automatically.

"Rusty," Ellery said. "Would you say this is a life cast?"

"No." Rusty's disturbed glance was on John. "It looks more to me like an art class model for anatomy study. You can buy things like this in any art supply store."

"X marks the spot," Arthur Craig mumbled. "But why a hand?"

"Palmistry," Mrs. Brown said suddenly. "The palm—the lifeline—X cutting the lifeline . . ."

"Shall I slit my throat and end the suspense?" John asked with the same odd laugh.

"I think we can do without the bad jokes, John," his bearded guardian said snappishly. "Mr. Queen, does this make any more sense to you than any of the other things?"

"Not a particle." Ellery turned the card over. "And here's another pencil jotting."

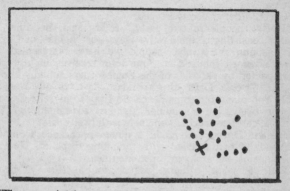

"The essential hand," Ellery murmured. "Form stripped to its skeletal function. Complete with X—in case John can't read, I presume. It's so inane it's frightening."

He tossed the card on the table and turned away. One by one they drifted back to their chairs. No one, not even Dr. Dark, seemed disposed to turn the radio on.

"John darling," Rusty said.

"What?"

"Darling, you're not really taking this seriously, are you?"

"Oh, no," John said. "I've been weaned on death threats. They don't mean a thing to me, sweet Rusty Brown. I eat 'em for breakfast, belch 'em for lunch and digest them for dinner. They roll right off my backside, girlie. Serious!" he exploded. "What am I supposed to do, Rusty, die laughing?"

"John, John," his guardian said.

"Come on, Ellery," John cried. "This is your stuff. The screwball-de-luxe type. Don't hold out on us. Expatiate."

"Hear, hear," Marius said, banging his glass on the arm of his chair. "Speech."

"In English," Roland Payn said darkly.

"In spades," Dr. Dark said, watching John.

"In God's mercy," Mr. Gardiner said in low tones.

"In any damn way at all!" John shouted; and he sat down and drained his glass.

"All right, I'll take as the subject of my discourse this

evening the Curious Coincidence of the Twelves," Ellery said on exactly the right note of amiability. Rusty looked her thanks.

"I'll listen to anything," Ellen said disagreeably, "but are we back to that again?"

"We've never left it, Miss Craig," Ellery said, bowing to her. John looked up rather vacantly. Then he settled back in his chair.

"Go on, Ellery," Rusty begged.

"Twelve people in our party," Ellery said, nodding. "A holiday consisting of the Twelve Days—or Nights—of Christmas. Among the twelve people we have represented the twelve signs of the zodiac. And John receives nightly gifts accompanied by parodies of the English carol actually known as 'The Twelve Days of Christmas.' Twelves all over the place. Too many for coincidence. So I say to myself: Can the number twelve be a planned signpost to something? For example, can I connect anyone here with twelveness?"

Sergeant Devoe had made a quiet appearance from the hall, and he had listened with mounting disbelief. Now he leaned against the archway, open-mouthed.

"Well, let's see." Ellery looked around. His eye lit on Roland Payn. "Suppose we start with Mr. Payn."

"Me?" The lawyer was taken by surprise. "I'd appreciate it if you left me out of this nonsense, Queen."

"No, no, you can't be left out of it. That's the whole point of the inquiry. Think, Mr. Payn, hard. Does the number twelve—in any context—strike fire anywhere in your personal experience?"

"Of course not!" Payn replied, not with grace.

"Your professional life? You're a lawyer. Lawyer ... Of course!" Ellery said, beaming. "What could be clearer? Lawyer—jury. Twelve good men and true. You see?"

"I hardly ever try a case in court," the white-haired estate attorney snapped. "Anyway, I'm in the civil law, not the criminal."

"Oh, come, Payn," Freeman said unexpectedly. "This could be fun. Surely—?"

"Well, I really don't know of any twelve."

"Roland, how can you have forgotten your postgraduate thesis?" Craig asked solemnly. "You were so proud of it that years later you had me design and print a private edition of it for distribution among your legal friends. Don't you remember? It was about that fifth century B.C. code of Roman law."

"My God," the lawyer groaned. "Arthur, never mind!"

"The title of it, of course," Craig chuckled, with a side glance at John, "was *Lex XII. Tabularum*—I have a copy of it around somewhere. *The Law of the Twelve Tables*, by Roland Payn."

"Yes, yes, that's right, Arthur," Payn said with a feeble smile. "I'd forgotten. And I don't thank you for reminding me."

"So there we are," Ellery said cheerfully. "Mr. Payn, you at least have now been connected with twelveness. In fact, come to think of it, you're also a douzeper."

"I'm a what?" Payn gasped.

"Douzeper," Ellery assured him. "The douzepers were the twelve paladins of Charlemagne. Surely you can't have forgotten the most famous paladin of them all? Doesn't *Chanson de Roland* ring a bell for you, Mr. Payn? 'A Roland for an Oliver'? *Childe Rowland?* My dear sir, you're up to your quiddities in twelves. Now, who's next? Dr. Dark?"

John was smiling. Rusty moved over to him and curled up in his lap. Her hand slipped into his and squeezed. He kissed the tip of her nose.

"Doctor, we're waiting," Ellery said in a chiding tone. "What does twelve mean to you?"

"The hour when I'm usually wakened from a sound sleep by a patient who's positive she has the Australian pip," the fat man said. "However, I could refer you to the twelve cranial nerves, an inescapable part of the anatomy, which terminate in the twelfth, or hypoglossal, nerve—"

"Remote, remote," Ellery said with a frown.

"Think, Samson," Craig chuckled.

"Samson! Did you say Samson, Mr. Craig?" Ellery cried.

"Certainly I said Samson. That's his name."

"And I thought it was Samuel! Well, that makes all the difference," Ellery said with satisfaction. "You see that, of course."

"Frankly," Ellen said, *"no."*

"What do they teach you at Wellesley? Samson is the Biblical equivalent of the Greek Hercules. And what does Hercules suggest?"

"The Twelve Labors!" Freeman said, smiling broadly.

"You see the advantages of an ivory tower."

"Ivory tower my foot. It reminds me of Mrs. Jabotinsky," Dr. Dark said. "Or at least it seemed like twelve labors to me before I got her on the delivery table."

"And he said the hypoglossal nerve was *remote!*" Ellen shrieked.

John laughed a big booming laugh.

After that it was easy. Marius Carlo qualified as a musical disciple of Schönberg's, with his twelve-tone system; Mr. Gardiner was linked with the Twelve Apostles, one of whose names—Andrew—he actually bore; Mrs. Brown and the twelveness of the zodiac were natural affinities; Arthur Craig was accepted through one of the annual staples of his press, the famous Craig Calendars; Valentina, denying that she had ever played Shakespeare's *Twelfth Night,* nevertheless insisted on inclusion because she was Sagittarius, the archer, and her birthdate was December twelfth—the twelfth day of the twelfth month! Rusty was a problem until Ellery ferreted from her the information that her baptismal name was not Rusty at all, but Yolanda; which, having seven letters, combined with the five letters of her surname to add up to the magic twelve; and Dan Z. Freeman, who was of the Jewish faith, was unanimously voted—by John's nomination—Grand Twelveness, since his Jewishness not only suggested the Twelve Tribes of Israel and their chiefs, the Twelve Sons of Jacob, but his first name, Dan, was the name of one of the twelve and his middle name, Zebulon— "after my maternal grandfather, *olav hasholem,*" Freeman assured them gravely— was the name of another.

By this time Sergeant Devoe's lower jaw was perilously close to his chest.

The effect was rather spoiled when it was discovered that neither John nor Ellen could join the club. In spite of the best efforts of Ellen, she could think of no twelve in her life, nor could her uncle. As for John, if anyone thought of bringing up the twelve nightly gifts he was being threatened with, the thinker thought better of it.

"What about you, Mr. Queen?" Craig smiled. "You mustn't leave yourself out."

"Me? I'm in John's and Ellen's boat, Mr. Craig. I can't think of a twelve that applies to me."

"Your name," Freeman suggested. "It has eleven letters. If you had a middle initial—"

"Unfortunately, I don't."

"Books!" Craig slapped his thigh. "You're in this club on the basis of your association with books! One of the technical book sizes is duodecimo, what we call 12mo. You see?"

Ellery said reverently, "Mr. Craig, I believe you've struck it."

"That gets me in, too," John said, grinning. "I've written a book, haven't I? Poor old Sis. You're the only one left out."

"Come around twenty years from now," Ellen said through her little white teeth, "and I'll show you. A dozen kids!"

On this happy note the Impromptu Sebastian Nonsense Therapy came to a close. The patient, with every appearance of complete recovery, suggested a raid on the refrigerator and persuaded the confused Sergeant Devoe to head the raiding party; Marius scuttled to the piano and began banging out *Marche Militaire;* Dr. Dark seized Olivette Brown's ropy arm and insisted on escorting her in the grand manner; Roland Payn slipped his arm about Val Warren's waist and gave it a paternal little squeeze; and the whole party trooped gaily kitchenward.

But later, in his bedroom, writing in his diary, Ellery paused to wonder just how much of it was nonsense and how much was not . . . or if it was nonsense at all.

He concluded his diary entry for the day:

> The absurdity of tonight's exhibition is like laughing in the dark. Through the nonsense-fabric of this thing runs an invisible thread full of menace. But what, what? Where is the sense in the nonsense? What do the gifts mean? Who's dropping them all over the place? . . . *And who is the dead man?*

Chapter VIII ✠ Sixth Night: Monday
December 30, 1929

In Which the Reverend Mr. Gardiner Has an Unclerical Adventure, The House of Freeman Totters, and Young John Goes to Bed with a Whip

MR. GARDINER came downstairs Monday morning with a heart as heavy as his tread. The old clergyman had been sleeping poorly since Christmas night, but the fatigue he felt was largely of the spirit. He had viewed with increasing misgiving the events in the Craig household; each night, in his bed, he prayed earnestly that the explanation might turn out, by some miracle, full of laughter and grace. The dead man in the library he had firmly put out of his thoughts. That was an event that only his Lord could set to rights, and Mr. Gardiner knew in his heart that the Second Coming was not for the world of his existence.

Because he was bewildered, and because in his bewilderment he saw some vague sin of his making, or at the least a wavering of faith, Mr. Gardiner chose this morning to deny the flesh. He would eat no breakfast. Avoiding the dining room, from which he heard the murmurs of various of his fellow-guests, the old gentleman crossed the living room and went quietly into his host's library. He would, he thought, write a long letter to his Bishop. That was a regimen the Bishop himself recommended to his retired rectors for their times of trial and self-doubt, for did it not say in John 10:11, "The good shepherd giveth his life for the sheep"?

So Mr. Gardiner sat down at the desk, opened the writing case he had brought downstairs with him, unscrewed the cap of his fountain pen—how many sermons had flowed from that blunted nib!—prayed momentarily for guidance, and then began to write.

How long he wrote he could not have said. He was dimly aware of the passage of people through the living room—voices, laughter, footsteps—but some time afterward he became conscious that these sounds had long since ceased. They must all have gone outdoors or back to their rooms, he thought; and he began to read what he had written, his lips moving soundlessly.

At this moment he heard two voices in the living room. They were not loud voices; indeed, Mr. Gardiner would scarcely have heard them if not for the profound quiet. One voice belonged to the little man with the large, half-bald head and the beautiful sad brown eyes, Mr. Freeman, the publisher; the other was John's. It seemed a business conversation, and since the voices were pitched low Mr. Gardiner gathered that it was confidential. He wondered uncomfortably if he should not go to the doorway and make his presence known. But that might prove embarrassing, he decided on reconsideration, especially to shy Mr. Freeman. Mr. Gardiner resolved to remain where he was, neither attempting to subdue his natural movements nor calling attention to himself unduly. Perhaps one of them, in moving about, would catch sight of him through the doorway.

And then, suddenly, Mr. Gardiner hoped with fervor that that would not happen. For what he had thought a business conversation had begun to take on a sinister sound.

John was being nasty, very nasty. He had begun by recalling that Mr. Freeman's publishing house, The House of Freeman, had been founded by his, John Sebastian's, father and Arthur Craig; and that while Arthur Craig had voluntarily sold Sebastian & Craig after John Senior's youthful death he, John the son, had long regarded that sale as a blight on his father's memory and for years had brooded upon how he might "right the wrong." And then he had seen how it could be done. On January 6, 1930, he, John, was coming into the principal of his father's estate; he would be worth millions. He would simply buy the publishing house back.

All this was said in a smily, mocking sort of voice that Mr. Gardiner found very nasty indeed.

Mr. Freeman sounded uncertain, as if he hoped but was not quite sure that the young man was being facetious. The publisher, too, had interpreted that tone as, at the least, unpleasant.

There was a pause, as if Mr. Freeman were cogitating and John were waiting; then Mr. Gardiner heard the older man say with a nervous laugh, "For a moment, John, I thought you were serious."

"And you were dead right."

Another interlude, during which Mr. Gardiner tried to

forget both the words and the way they had been uttered. But he could not.

Mr. Freeman's voice said, "I ... I don't quite know what to say, John. If this is actually a serious offer for The House of Freeman, I'm touched, really I am, especially because of the sentiment involved. But The House of Freeman is not for sale."

"You're quite sure of that."

"Certainly I'm sure," the publisher said, nettled. "What sort of question is that?"

"Mr. Freeman, I want that publishing house, and you're going to sell it to me—or your controlling stock, which amounts to the same thing. I won't hold you up. I can pay what the business is worth, and I will. But you've got to understand, the choice isn't yours. It's mine."

Mr. Gardiner almost sprang to his feet.

The poor man was saying helplessly, "John, you're either pulling my leg or—or you're very ill. But if you insist on playing this out, I'll be as serious as you say you are. I had nothing to do with the original sale. That was strictly a result of your father's tragic death and, as I understand it, Craig's feeling that, alone, he wasn't equipped to carry on. Since that time the firm has gone through a number of hands. I'm merely the current owner. When I took over, it was close to bankruptcy. I've put a lot of hard work into it, John. I've built it up to perhaps the best of the smaller publishing houses in New York. Now you say you want to take it away from me. I could ask, Why? By what right? but I'm not going to. I'm simply going to ask—and I'd like a straightforward answer, without any of this childish byplay: Exactly how is the choice yours? How do you propose to make me sell?"

Mr. Freeman's voice had grown stronger as he spoke, and Mr. Gardiner was tempted to utter a resounding "Bravo!" But he continued to sit at the desk and strain his ears.

"Through your father," John Sebastian said.

"Through my father." Mr. Gardiner could feel the publisher's stupefaction all the way in the library. "My *father?*"

"I wish you'd be reasonable," the hateful young voice said plaintively. "I don't care for this any more than you do. Don't force my hand, Mr. Freeman."

There was a spluttering from the living room and the *thwack!* of a fist hitting a chair. "What—what cheek! See here! What has my father to do with this? What do you mean by dragging an ailing old man you don't even know into this nightmare?"

"He is old, isn't he? In his seventies ... All right, Mr. Freeman, you're asking for it. When I decided to buy the publishing house back, I knew I had to have a sales argument a little stronger than cash. Frankly, I did a bit of rooting around. When I couldn't dig up anything on you, I went after your family. Your father was an immigrant to this country, wasn't he?"

"Yes?" Freeman said. Mr. Gardiner's heart bled for him.

"An orthodox Jew from Germany who skipped the country under an assumed name. He was in a lot of political trouble with the Imperial German government."

"Whom have you been talking to?" the publisher whispered. "What Judas?"

"I suppose he was afraid of not being accepted here. Anyway, he made certain false statements to the American immigration people. After that, he was scared to apply for citizenship papers. In fact, he never has become an American citizen. He's still a German national, and if those misstatements to which he falsely swore were brought to the attention of the immigration authorities, he might very well—even at his age—be deported back to Germany."

"Impossible!" Freeman said in horror. "They'd never do it. He's seventy-four. It would kill him. It would be a sentence of death. They'd never do it, I tell you!"

John Sebastian asked politely, "Are you willing to take the chance, or do you sell me The House of Freeman?"

There was a long silence.

Then Mr. Gardiner heard the publisher say in a terrible voice. "A partnership. I'll give you a partnership, and to hell with your money."

"But I don't want a partnership, Mr. Freeman. I want my father's publishing house. Do I get it?"

"This is intolerable. You're insane—paranoid! No! I won't do it!"

With great charm John said, "Think it over, Mr. Freeman. You have time. You'll be here at least another week."

"Another week?" Freeman laughed wildly. "Do you suppose that after this I could stay here another hour? I'm leaving—at once!"

"I'm afraid Lieutenant Luria would have something to say about that. Have you forgotten that a murder's been committed here—and that you've been confined to this house as, technically, one of Luria's suspects?"

Mr. Gardiner heard John stroll from the living room.

He could imagine the poor publisher sitting there, staring after the monstrous ward of his host, his delicate hands clenched impotently, grief and confusion in his heart. Mr. Gardiner could have wept.

After a time, he heard the unfortunate man's low step leave the room.

Mr. Gardiner found Rusty in the old carriage house. She was cuddled against John on the dusty front seat of the ancient sleigh, listening raptly to the young monster read poetry. Their backs were to him, so that for a few moments the old gentleman could observe them unnoticed. The poetry was love poetry of a particularly brittle, clever sort, and from the immense self-satisfaction with which the young man read it Mr. Gardiner gathered that it was his own. Rusty, whom the clergyman could see in profile, was drinking in the verse with parted lips.

Mr. Gardiner composed himself and coughed. He had to repeat the cough before they heard him.

"Oh, Mr. Gardiner," Rusty cried, her red bob flying. "You should hear John's poems. They're magnificent!"

"Hi, Reverend," John said shortly.

"Then I'm interrupting. I'm sorry." Nevertheless, Mr. Gardiner did not stir.

"I take it I'm not wanted," John said.

"Well, I've been lax," Mr. Gardiner said, unmoved. "With the wedding date so near, I really should have a talk with Rusty. Of course, if you'd rather I deferred it—"

"Oh, hell," John said. "Get it over with." He jumped from the sleigh and strode out.

"Don't pay any attention to John," Rusty said with an embarrassed laugh. "You know what a strain he's been under the past few days. Do you want to sit up here beside me?"

Mr. Gardiner climbed spryly into the sleigh. He took Rusty's hand and smiled down at her. "Well, my dear—alone at last, as the spider said to the fly." It was Mr. Gardiner's standard witticism for such occasions. Then his big Yankee nose tightened at the nostrils as he set himself for what he had to say.

At that instant Rusty gave a little shiver of pure happiness. "Oh, Mr. Gardiner, I'm so full of everything wonderful and ecstatic I could burst. Not even what's been happening can spoil it."

Mr. Gardiner's mouth closed. It was written in I Samuel 2, *If one man sin against another, the judge shall judge him.* Still . . . Matthew 7:1, *Judge not, that ye be not judged.*

"You love John dearly," Mr. Gardiner said in a troubled voice.

"Oh, yes."

"And John loves you?"

Rusty laughed. "He'd better!"

Mr. Gardiner did not smile. "You have no doubts, my dear? Either for yourself, or for him?"

Rusty hesitated, and Mr. Gardiner took hope. But then she said thoughtfully, "I don't think so. I have been kind of worried the past few days, I admit, John's acted so—well, not himself at times. But it's just all this mixup. You can't really blame him. He feels the responsibility of getting every-

101

one together, and then murder ... and those dreadful Christmas boxes ..."

"Rusty." The old clergyman cleared his throat. "Suppose you discovered that John isn't what you think he is. Would you still marry him?"

"You're a darling." Rusty squeezed his hand. "But I can't answer a question like that, Mr. Gardiner. It has no reality for me. John couldn't be otherwise than I know he is. He wouldn't be my John. I can't imagine not marrying him."

Mr. Gardiner kissed her on the forehead and began to climb out of the sleigh. "In that case," he said, "we'll say no more about it."

To you, poor child, Mr. Gardiner thought as he tramped back to the house. But I cannot leave it there.

He sought out Olivette Brown, not in hope but out of duty. He knew Rusty's mother thoroughly—a stony, almost sterile, vineyard in which he had labored without success for many years. Her obsession with the claptrap of psychic manifestations, divorced from any communion with true spirit, he had long since stopped trying to exorcise. Indeed, he had often felt that Olivette Brown did not believe half the drivel she dispensed. This, to Mr. Gardiner, was an even greater sin than her devotion to magic. It made her a vessel not only devoid of grace but full of hypocrisy.

He found her in the kitchen, reading Mrs. Janssen's fortune in some tea leaves.

"Olivette," Mr. Gardiner said abruptly, "I should very much like to talk to you in private."

"I was just going up to help Mabel with the beds," Mrs. Janssen said hurriedly. She fled.

Mr. Gardiner seated himself on the other side of the porcelain-topped table.

"You're going to scold me again," Mrs. Brown said coyly.

"No, I'm going to ask you what you think of your future son-in-law."

"John?" Mrs. Brown became incandescent. "Such a dear, fine boy! I'm so happy for my Rusty."

"Olivette," Mr. Gardiner said, "suppose you discovered that John isn't all he seems to be. Would you still be happy for your Rusty?"

"Well, of course! You don't think I'm fool enough to believe the lovey-dovey period lasts very long, do you? I remember Mr. Brown." Rusty's mother sniffed at the memory. "Certainly John isn't all he seems to be. What man is when he's courting a girl?"

"Suppose," Mr. Gardiner persisted, "you discovered he was dishonest."

"Fudge," Mrs. Brown said. "What would John have to be

dishonest about? Certainly not material things, and if it's anything else I'm sure *I'm* not wise enough to set myself up as his judge."

Judge not, Mr. Gardiner thought unhappily. Then he remembered the Devil's gift for crooking Scripture, and he drew himself straighter.

"I wasn't born yesterday," Mrs. Brown was saying, "and, dear soul that you are, neither were you. Nothing would surprise me about a man. But John is young, handsome, charming and talented and he's going to be *very* rich, and whatever you're talking about, Mr. Gardiner, I'd much rather not hear it. If anything should happen to call this marriage off, I think I'd *die.*"

"And would you fear no evil, Olivette?" Mr. Gardiner asked; and he excused himself and went looking for Arthur Craig, who had been his only real hope from the first.

"Are you sure, Mr. Gardiner, are you sure you didn't misunderstand?" Craig kept repeating.

"I did not misunderstand, Mr. Craig."

"But that isn't like John. I mean—he's talked about his father a good deal, and the publishing house, but as for getting it back, I never heard him express . . ."

"I can only tell you what I overheard."

"Blackmailing Dan Freeman." He pulled at his beard. "I can't believe it, Mr. Gardiner. I can't!"

Mr. Gardiner rose. "I understand. Indeed I do. And I'm truly sorry. But I felt it my duty . . ."

"No, no, please sit down." Craig's big fingers clutched the minister's arm. "A boy you brought up—thought you knew inside out—whose integrity you'd have sworn by . . . how do you approach him with a thing like this, Mr. Gardiner? What does one say?"

"Out of the abundance of the heart the mouth speaketh," Mr. Gardiner quoted gently. "Say what you feel. The boy loves and respects you. He'll listen. He must."

"Will he? Do I know him at all? At times during the past few days . . ." Craig got up suddenly and addressed the fire. "I've been trying to maintain an equilibrium · of sorts, Mr. Gardiner, in the midst of . . . I don't know what. Something terrible." He swung about, and Mr. Gardiner's heart contracted in compassion. "What is happening in my house?" the bearded man cried. "What can I do? How do I cope with it?"

Mr. Gardiner touched the rigid shoulder of his host. "On the last night of His earthly life, Mr. Craig, Jesus 'went out into the Mount of Olives,' as Mark tells us, unto 'a place which was named Gethsemane,' and there He underwent His agony of mortal fear and sorrow. *Gethsemane* is an Aramaic word meaning 'oil press,' and there, while Jesus's heart—like the olives that gave the place its name—was being pressed and tormented, He still found it possible to say, 'Not what I will, but what Thou wilt.' "

The old clergyman smiled. "I know it will sound old-fashioned, Mr. Craig, but have faith and you will see the way."

But as he left Arthur Craig, Mr. Gardiner's smile expired. He had been preaching faith for half a century, he thought, with sadly small result. True faith worked miracles, he knew, but it was so rare, so rare. And this was a problem in which time might be of the essence.

Mr. Gardiner sighed. It was sometimes necessary to render unto Caesar the things which were Caesar's. He sought out Ellery and told him all about John's ultimatum to Mr. Freeman.

Ellery listened tensely. "Thank you, Mr. Gardiner. I'm glad you came to me with this. It begins to add up, add up. One fragment of it, anyway."

"Add up to what, Mr. Queen?" The clergyman was puzzled by the joy, almost the predacity, of the young man's expression.

"I can't be positive yet. I'd rather not say any more now."

Mr. Gardiner retreated to his room, utterly bewildered.

Mrs. Janssen served an early dinner. "Monday's one of Mr. Craig's favorite nights for the radio," she confided, "what with Roxy and all—and, to tell the truth, I like to listen meself." She had an old crystal set in her bedroom which she was forever taking apart and putting together again.

So 7:30 found them ensconced in the living room, listening dutifully to "Roxy and His Gang" on WJZ. At 8:30 Craig switched over to WEAF for the "A & P Gypsies." "I hope you don't mind, Marius. I know the music is conventional, but I like it."

"What's wrong with conventionality, Uncle Arthur?" Ellen demanded. "They play standard works familiar to everybody, and they play them beautifully. I don't see why people have to apologize for liking what a lot of other people like, just because a handful of nose-looker-downers sneer." And her scornful glance sped arrow-like to Ellery.

"Who, me, coach?" Ellery murmured.

"After that," Marius chimed in, "who could be so vain as to refuse to listen to this *schmaltz?*"

It was not a good night. There was a snappy undertone to everything. Marius seemed to have regained his bad form, John was abstracted, Valentina querulous, Payn abrupt, Dr. Dark sulky, Mrs. Brown shrill, Mr. Gardiner troubled, Craig despondent, Ellen touchy, Rusty restless, and Freeman a disembodied spirit floating in some bitter ether on another plane.

The evening dragged by. At eleven o'clock someone turned on the news. In the middle of it Freeman rose and said, "Trouble, nothing but trouble. Would you excuse me? I believe I'll go to bed." He went out with a tired step.

They were sluggishly discussing the news—U.S. Coast Guard liquor patrols had killed three smugglers and captured three boats carrying illicit cargoes worth half a million dollars; in India, Mahatma Gandhi was calling for "civil disobedience" to British rule—when the publisher reappeared and said stridently, "I just found this in my room."

He was holding up a small Christmas package in green and red metallic paper, with gilt ribbon and a Santa Claus tag.

Ellery took it from Freeman quietly. "Addressed to you, John, of course. Shall I do the honors?"

John laughed with great bitterness. Mr. Gardiner, listening closely, could hear little in that laugh of the nastiness and mockery he had heard come out of the same mouth that very morning. A strange boy, he thought, so many-sided . . .

The pale publisher did not look at John at all. He seated himself outside the immediate circle of the party and watched, blinking.

Arthur Craig was chewing on a wisp of his beard and eyeing his ward furtively, as if he were seeing John truly for the first time. Then he caught hold of himself and sat up straight, watching Ellery open the package.

Inside, on the red tissue-wrapped object, lay the white typewritten card. Ellery plucked it from the box and read it aloud in a perfectly flat voice:

```
     On the sixth night of Christmas
   — Your true love sends to you,
     A leather-plaited  w h i p
     Of clever workmanship.
```

It was a wicked-looking little whip of some tough leather, heavily plaited at the handle, with a relatively long lash. A whip for Lilliputians.

"It's a reproduction in miniature of some authentic whip," Rusty said, examining it, "but I don't know of what. It may represent a bull-whip, although it's not of the South African *sjambok* type. It might be of South American origin."

"A bull-whip," Dan Z. Freeman said clearly, "or a man-whip?"

Rusty looked baffled. "What, Mr. Freeman?"

"I was just thinking" the publisher said. "My birthday is March the third—and that, if I'm to judge by your little zodiacal gift to me the other morning, comes under the sign of Pisces. You're our astrologer, Mrs. Brown—refresh my recollection. What is the common interpretation of Pisces?"

Rusty's mother looked suspicious. "A symbol of bondage."

"Slavery," Freeman nodded, and he smiled. "I never took any stock in constellational influences until today." And he looked directly at John Sebastian. But John was worrying his thumb and staring at the floor.

"Another one?"

They turned with relief. It was Sergeant Devoe, from the hall.

In silence, Ellery took the little whip from Rusty and handed it to the trooper along with the white card. The sergeant took them, scratched his chin, and turned away. A moment later they heard him telephoning. When he hung up, he reappeared and thrust the whip and the card back at Ellery.

"Lieutenant says you hang on to 'em, Mr. Queen."

"No, I think this gift is one John might like to keep." Ellery paused. "John?"

John took the whip with a start. He turned it over and over.

"Yes," Dan Z. Freeman said from the background, "yes, it looks quite natural."

"Natural?" For the first time the young poet looked at his publisher. "What do you mean, Mr. Freeman?"

"Now don't tell me you're in the throes of another amnesia attack," Freeman said.

"I don't know what you're talking about." John's eyes flashed. "I'm going to bed."

"John," Rusty began.

But he kissed her hastily and ran out.

Only then did Ellery realize that he had not examined the back of the card. He turned it over quickly.

But the other side was blank.

*In Which Two Triangles Become a Quadrangle, the
Misses Brown and Warren Go Back to the Cave,
and a New Year Is Ushered in Unhappily*

THE LAST DAY of the year came in fair and fresh, with
southwest winds.

"I feel like getting on a horse," Ellen announced at breakfast. "Anyone for a ride?"

"I'm your man," Ellery said.

"Are you?" But Ellen looked pleased.

"I want to ride, too," Rusty said. "John?"

"Sure, sure," John said. "What do we do, ride double?
There are only two horses."

"Double would be *fun*," Rusty said.

"Not for me it wouldn't," Ellen said coldly. "Suppose we
break it down into two shifts, Rusty. We'll meet you and
John back at the stable in an hour, and you can take the
horses from us."

Felton had the Morgan gelding and the pinto mare ready
for them, and they rode out into the woods in a dignified
silence. It took Ellery some time to thaw Ellen, but he was
contrite for having neglected her, and he kept at it with a
single-mindedness he usually reserved for his intellectual pur-
suits. Finally he earned a smile, and after that the woods
trail, the gold-speckled snow, the smoothly working horses
were a joy.

They rode back out of the woods at a walk, to spare their
mounts for Rusty and John. Ellen's cheeks were pink, her
eyes danced, her slender jodhpured leg bumping his was soft
and dangerous; and Ellery realized suddenly that not once in
the past hour had he thought of a dead old man or mysterious gifts or cryptic messages. So he spoke a great deal of
nonsense rapidly, hardly aware of what he was saying, and
Ellen listened with mounting color; and so it came about that
they rode into the stable and almost trampled Valentina
Warren and John Sebastian before they realized what they
had blundered into.

"Val, for God's sake," John was saying. She had him
backed against a stall. "We've got company."

"I don't care!" Valentina said with passion, not bothering

to turn around. "I never thought you were so shallow as to fall for a dimple and some coarse red hair."

"Hi, Sis, Ellery," John said feebly. "Look, Val, Rusty will be here any minute—"

"I tell you I don't *care!*"

They sat their horses like idiots, immobilized.

"John, I'm human. I've played my part like a trouper—the best friend—the good joe—'I hope you'll both be very happy'—like hell I do! Darling, I have to say it before it's too late. I love you, John, love you, love you, love you! Are you blind as well as stupid? I loved you long before you met Rusty. We used to have the swellest times together—"

"I know, Val, I know. Don't think I've forgotten. Have a nice ride, you two? How's the woods trail?"

"F-fine," Ellen said. She looked as if she were trying to get off her horse and remain in the saddle at the same time.

"John, never mind *them*—"

"Can't we talk this over some other time?" John asked, trying to duck under Valentina's well-planted arms.

"When? After you're hitched to that poor man's Clara Bow?" Val stifled a sob. "Oh, Johnny, Johnny . . ."

"Val, let go. Let go of me! In front of Ellen and Ellery. Val, are you out of your ever-loving mind? *Val . . . !*" John's exclamation ended in a strangled mumble. Fascinated, Ellen and Ellery watched the blonde girl wrestle him helpless and kiss his mouth wildly. He managed to wrench his lips away long enough to say, "Oh, ye gods and little fishes," and laugh in sheer exasperation. "Hello, Rusty."

Guiltily, Ellen and Ellery twisted in their saddles. There, behind them, on foot in the snow, stood Rusty. She slapped Ellery's horse on the rump and strode into the stable.

"Well," Rusty said. Her voice might have come from a crevasse at the South Pole. "What are you doing, Val, the grappling scene from *Sink or Swim?*"

Ellen said from stiff lips, "Why, Rusty, that's just what Val *was* doing. Illustrating a scene—"

"Oh, shut up," Valentina said sulkily. "All right, Rusty. So now you know."

"Now I know what, Val?" Rusty's ice-encrusted voice said. "That you're a snake-in-the-grass, a man embezzler, a two-legged, two-faced bitch?"

"This damn *stirrup*," Ellen said fiercely.

John cleared his throat. "Look, Rusty—"

"You keep out of this, John Sebastian!" Rusty shrieked. "You've probably encouraged her! It's a good thing I found out in time!"

"Oh, boy," John said wearily. "Look, baby, believe it or not, I was waiting for a street car when I got boarded and bussed. I've got witnesses to prove it. Wasn't I attacked, Sis? Ellery? For God's sake, speak up!"

"Yes," Ellen said. "Yes, Rusty."

"Yes, indeed," Ellery said. "That's how it was, Rusty."

"In front of an *audience*," Rusty said. "How low can you get?"

"Bitch am I?" Valentina was muttering. *"Bitch?"* she repeated, the word apparently exciting her. "Who stole who from whom, I'd like to know, you red-headed buccaneer!"

"Want to fight?" said Rusty in tinkling tones. And to their horror—and John's—the two girls sprang at each other with outstretched claws, and immediately the stable became noisy with scuffling boots, unladylike panting, little teeth-locked cries, and the prancing of alarmed saddle horses.

"Down!" Ellen shrieked, fighting her mount.

"More complications!" Ellery roared, fighting his.

So they had to fight for life and limb through the whole incredible thing—John's forcible intervention, the hysterical battle-chatter of the two enraged females, and finally the cessation of hostilities. Then Rusty ran, weeping and heedless of the rearing horses, and Valentina ran, also weeping and heedless, and John ran after them with one loud, explicit word of Elizabethan origin.

"As if," Ellery finished his thought a long time afterward, when they were creeping out of the stable, "as if there weren't too many already."

So Ellen began to weep, too, and Ellery found himself with his hands—literally—too full for further thought of Rusty-John, Rusty-Marius, John-Valentina and, for all he knew, Valentina-Marius.

As her uncle's hostess, Ellen had planned a traditional New Year's Eve party, "dress-up," with champagne, balloons, noise-makers, comical hats, festoons of crepe paper, and quarts of confetti.

Ellen called it off.

"We can't go through anything as gay and *normal* as that, Uncle Arthur," she said fiercely. "Not with the way this horrible party has turned out. It would be a farce."

"Worse," Ellery said. "It would fall flatter than one of Texas Guinan's suckers at six o'clock tomorrow morning."

"I agree, I agree," Craig said heavily. Ellen had insisted on telling him about their unedifying experience in the stable. He had listened with the dazed resignation of one who can no longer be surprised at anything. "Whatever you say, dear. Good lord, what's going to happen next?"

"Why won't that—that *policeman* let us all go?" Ellen cried.

That had been another unpleasantness of the year's last day. Lieutenant Luria had made an unheralded appearance just before lunch, for no other purpose apparently than to re-emphasize their house detention. The lieutenant had worn a harried look, from which Ellery gathered that there were still no developments in the hunt for the dead man's identity. Luria had had a tense conversation with Payn, who was becoming increasingly restive, and a hysterical scene with Val Warren, for whom the party had suddenly developed an abysmal tedium. In the end, with Luria's grim departure, all things remained as they had been, only worse.

As if in revolt at authority, Valentina appeared for dinner in full battle array. Her evening gown was of apple-green chiffon in the long lines of high fashion, with tier after tier of ruffles; and over it she wore a matching coat of transparent velvet, which she promptly insisted on John's taking from her. He did so sullenly. She wore a 16-button white glacé glove on her left hand and carried the other and a French evening bag of green faille silk embroidered with coral and pearl beads. Her iridescent green evening pumps had three-inch "needle" heels, and she towered over Rusty like a queen in a fairy tale.

Rusty was furious. She, too, had ignored Ellen's change of agenda; she, too, swept downstairs in full panoply. She had put on an evening ensemble of flat crepe with a jacket, furred in white lynx at the elbows, falling halfway to her knees. The dress was majestic with pennons and had a long irregular hemline full of drama. The only trouble was, by some fiendish coincidence, Rusty's outfit was also apple green.

They sat opposite each other throughout dinner glaring. Ellen, who was wearing a simple Poiret dress in red and yellow wool of Paisley design, was thoroughly miserable.

The postprandial recess proved even grimmer. For one thing, Lieutenant Luria had given Sergeant Devoe the evening off for whatever New Year's Eve celebration a trooper sergeant indulged in, and his substitute—a blue-skinned, beetle-eyed, flat-nosed hardcase—catfooted in on them every ten to fifteen minutes as if he expected to surprise them in the act of manufacturing a bomb. Mrs. Brown *eeked* every time she laid eyes on him.

The older men maintained a desperate conversation—about Hemingway's *A Farewell to Arms,* Julia Peterkin's Pulitzer Prize novel, *Scarlet Sister Mary,* Chic Sale's *The Specialist;* about Primo de Rivera's difficulties in Spain; about Professor Babson's market reports and Professor Leon Theremin's theremin; about the Senate committee's investigation of the sugar lobby and the rumors of sensational revelations; about the modernist movement in art, led by Picasso, Modigliani, Archipenko, Utrillo, Soutine—Soutine, who took a landscape "and threw it upon the canvas as if it were a dishrag, but one which suddenly caught fire!" as Dan Freeman quoted; about the recently developed ethyl gasoline being advertised; about Pan-American's overseas flights to the West Indies, Sir James Jeans's contention in *The Universe*

110

Around Us that "God is a mathematician; the universe was not created for human beings," the growing power of the Dutchman, the new IBM calculators, the exploits of Bobby Jones and Helen Wills, King George V's illness. But each subject sputtered out for lack of inspiration, and another was introduced only to thwart the deadly little silences that spaced them.

Once Ellery said, "I wonder who's going to find it tonight," but no one answered.

At midnight, mechanically, they drank a toast to the new year, exchanged the traditional pecks and handshakes—Rusty and Valentina touched cheeks in icy truce—and with deep gratitude sat down to listen to WJZ's newly instituted original program, "Pursuing Time Across the Continent," in which for five minutes before and after each hour, the announcer said, listeners would hear the new year ushered in musically in New York, Chicago, Denver and San Francisco successively. Even this alluring prospect was marred, however. In refilling her glass, Valentina upset it over her gown.

"Oh, *shaving* soap," Valentina said slurpily. "I may as well hit the hay," and she swept regally out of the room.

She was back two minutes later, looking over her shoulder wild-eyed.

"On *my* bed tonight!"

And Valentina sat down on the floor with the seventh Christmas box in her lap and quietly had hysterics. When no one paid any attention, she stopped.

The card bore four lines of typing:

```
On the seventh night of Christmas
Your true love sends to you,
W a t e r  and a golden  f i s h
(No, this isn't gibberish).
```

The red tissue in the box was damp; some of the color came off on Ellery's fingers. Under the paper was a little toy fish-bowl—scarcely larger than a plum—with an incredibly tiny tropical fish of some sort, of a golden translucency, swimming vigorously about in a thimbleful of water. Although the bowl had been tightly wedged in the box with wads of tissue, most of the water had slopped out.

"Not too far out of scale with the house," Ellery said. "This is a consistent maniac, at any rate."

"I thought the damn house was finished," John said, as if it mattered to him. Mercifully, no one was looking at him.

"Marks on the back of this card, too," Ellery muttered.

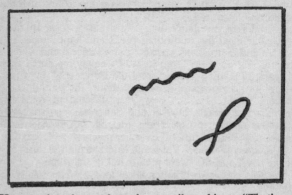

He stared and stared at the pencil-markings. "That's certainly a water symbol."

"That thing under it looks like a pair of pliers," Dr. Dark protested. "What do pliers have to do with anything?"

"Not pliers, Doctor. Don't you see? An extremely simplified drawing of a fish with a flowing tail. Water and fish, as announced. Water and fish . . ."

Most of them sat up late, seeking the dubious cheer of their host's champagne copiously while WJZ pursued the New Year to the Golden Gate. Then Ellen volunteered to cook up a mess of scrambled eggs and chicken livers, after which—somehow—Ellery found himself in a Stygian niche somewhere with two soft arms around his neck and a pair of perfumed lips on his and a voice, which was certainly Ellen's, murmuring "Happy New Year," which was undeniably pleasant, even exciting, but—Ellery recalled thinking—advanced nothing.

It was almost 5 A.M. before he fell into the chair in his bedroom and fumbled for his diary. In spite of the enveloping haze, Ellery managed to complete the entry for December 31st. His last paragraph had a desperate tone:

The pictures when they occur are crude, crude . . . *Crude.* Could they be meant to appear primitive? Cave drawings? American Indian? . . . Hieroglyphics! Could that be the key? If so, they're ideographic. They do resemble Egyptian ideographs, especially this last pair of symbols . . . But so what, so what? What do the damned things *mean?* I mean, I know what they stand for—water, fish—but what does *that* mean?

Chapter X ✠ Eighth Night: Wednesday January 1, 1930

In Which John Receives the Gift of a Head, Ellery Pursues a Phantom, and Inspector Queen Comes New Year Calling at an Odd Hour

IT COULD NOT be said that Mr. Queen greeted the dawn of 1930 with hope. For one thing, when he opened his eyes it was five minutes of one on Wednesday afternoon. For another, when he tottered to the window to gaze upon the bright new world he found it universally gray, with clouds as thick as the inside of his head, the air with a sludgy quality, and rain the obvious fate of the day. "Ring out the false, ring in the true," Lord Tennyson had written, but Ellery doubted that the bells clanging in his skull foretokened any such millennium.

The shrinking snow looked like a pall.

When he slunk downstairs, he found further cause for depression. Ellen was waiting for him armed with aspirin, a tomato juice and Worcestershire sauce concoction, and a pot of coffee, and that was good; but the glow in her cheeks and the light in her eyes were not good, not good at all. He tried very hard to remember what had happened after the kiss in the dark niche, but a fog overlay the night. She *clung* to him this afternoon. As if . . .

Ellery shuddered and gulped another cup of coffee.

Ellen crooned, "Poor dear," and the way she held on to him when they went into the living room had him fighting panic.

The room was strewn with the bodies of the survivors, trying apathetically to read their newspapers. Ellery reached pointedly for an unused one, hoping that the lovely parasite for whom he had become a host would sense his wish to suffer alone. Not so. She clung intimately as she steered him to a piece of furniture he recognized with a start as a love seat. They sank into it, inseparable.

"Read your paper, darling," the parasite said softly in his ear. "I'll just sit here and . . . look at you."

He read with desperation. New York police had made 19 liquor raids during the New Year's Eve gaieties. Mayor Jim-

113

my Walker was being sworn in today for his second hilarious term. General Smuts of South Africa had arrived on his first United States visit and told reporters that the horrors of modern war would undoubtedly outlaw it ... He read on, blindly.

The arrival of Rusty and John from a tramp outdoors rescued him. Ellery jumped up, said rapidly, "Excuse me, Ellen, I've been wanting to talk to John, be seeing you—" and made his escape.

"Ave, Caesar," Rusty hailed him. "You could do lots worse."

"What?" Ellery asked stupidly.

"Ellen's a lovely girl."

"Yes. Well. Good morning, you two. How are the heads?"

"Which one?" Rusty said.

"Mine is still with me," John grinned, "though for an anxious moment this morning I didn't think it would make it."

"At least you had an excuse."

"A what?" John said.

"I refer to the Embarrassing Incident of the Mews," Ellery said hollowly.

"Of the *what?*"

"That business in the stable yesterday, John. The big smooch scene."

John grinned. "Who was the lucky man?"

"Oh?" Ellery glanced at Rusty.

She was pale today. "It doesn't matter, Ellery. Anyway, it was silly. The best thing to do is forget it."

"Forget what, for heaven's sake?" John demanded.

Ellery looked at him. He was about to say something when Valentina drifted into the room like Lady Macbeth. Rusty murmured, " 'Scuse us, Ellery, we need coffee like *mad*," and virtually ran John into the dining room.

Ellery would have smiled grimly, except that the mere thought made him wince.

Happily, the Rose Bowl game was being broadcast by WEAF. Listening to Graham McNamee's running account of the Southern California 47—14 victory over Pitt—arguing afterward that it did not compare for thrills with last year's Rose Bowl game, when Roy Riegels, California's center and captain-elect, retrieved a Georgia Tech fumble and incredibly took off for his own goal line, to give the Southerners an 8—7 victory—got them through what was left of the day, and by the time they had consumed Mrs. Janssen's dinner the evening was well along.

Ellen was still clinging to Ellery. "I wonder who's going to find the box tonight," she said as they made for the living room.

Behind them Marius said, "Who cares?" and pushed by. They saw the light come on in the music room and heard Marius lift the lid of the grand piano. The lid immediately crashed. Marius ran in brandishing a small Christmas package done up in red and green metallic paper, with gilt ribbon and a Santa Claus tag.

"In the piano, by God!" Marius yelled.

Ellery took the package from him. The familiar "John Sebastian" inscription had been typed on the tag.

"Don't open it," John snarled. "I don't want to see it."

"John."

Rusty went to him quickly. She pulled him down into a chair and stroked his forehead as if he were a child.

"Same typewriter," Ellery said. Then he shrugged and tore the wrappings from the package.

The white card in the box said:

> On the eighth night of Christmas
> Your true love sends to you,
> A head with one closed e y e --
> A warning you will die --
> A head with m o u t h shut tight --
> For omen this eighth night.

John was rigid on the edge of the chair.

Ellery removed the red tissue paper from the object in the box. It was the head of a rag doll, apparently severed from the body with a scissors. The original face had been obliterated by white paint, and on the white paint had been painted in black two features: a single closed eye at the upper left and, centered toward the bottom, a slash of hard straight line, evidently intended to represent a closed mouth.

Ellery looked from the doll's head to the back of the white card, but it was blank.

Then John said, "A warning I will die," and sprang from the chair. Rusty put her fingers to her mouth. "All *right*," John said. "I can't treat this any longer as if it's a rotten gag, or the vaporings of a sick mind, or whatever the hell it is. I can't go on with the rest of you pretending this is a holiday get-together of congenial people—going through the social motions, eating, chatting, playing games, listening to the radio, sleeping . . . as if nothing out of the way was happen-

115

ing. I'm fed up. Who's after me? What do you want? *What have I done?*"

And that brought Ellery up against the massive wall that had thwarted him from the beginning. Knowing now what he knew about John, it was still beyond the bounds of credence that this should be a performance, a demonstration feigned for the occasion. John was *afraid*. He was almost out of his mind with fear. He could not possibly be behind the gift boxes. He knew nothing about them.

John ran out. They heard the pound of his shoes on the stairs. They heard him snatch open a door, slam it . . . lock it.

One by one they got out of their chairs and muttered or mumbled something and crept upstairs to seek safety in their rooms. The sound of keys turning over in locks became the sinister rattle of musketry.

When Ellery finished writing in his diary he looked at his watch and saw that it was still only a little past 10:30. The house was as still as if the hour were four in the morning.

Perversely, New Year's Eve head notwithstanding, he did not feel sleepy. He began to pace his floor.

He had never in his life wanted so much to solve a problem. It had nothing to do with the murder. The little old man on the library rug seemed far away. That was a sane aberration, anyway. Sooner or later the mysterious victim would be identified, sooner or later his identification would unlock the puzzle of who had driven the Etruscan dagger into his back.

But these boxes, with their fantastic contents. That was a puzzle for fools . . . or madmen . . . or someone like himself who had been born with the tapeworm of curiosity, driving him in perpetual hunger toward answers. That was what had steered him across the orchestra floor of the Roman Theater through the labyrinth of the Monte Field case. Or had that been a fluke . . . a "Roman" candle, he thought with irony, bursting for one brilliant moment and then dying forever?

He refused to believe it.

There's an answer here, he thought, something ties these objects together, something no doubt enormously simple. All he had to do was see it.

Ellery sat down and seized his head.

So far, eight nightly boxes. Making four to go, if there was any logic in this at all. No point in trying to anticipate the nature of *those* . . . Eight boxes, containing all told 13 objects. 14, if you counted the palm on which the "spot" had been drawn—the palm as differentiated from the hand of which it was really a part. But "palm" had been emphasized by the typist with the spacing-out device . . . Say 14, then. Eight—14. Was there a mathematical relationship? If so, it was obscurer than Eygptian hieroglyphics before Champollion deciphered the Rosetta stone ... Hieroglyphics! Ellery actually bolted up. But then he lay back and closed his eyes.

Assume the number so far as 14 ... An ox. A house. A camel. A door. A window. A nail. A fence. A hand. A palm. A whip. Water. A fish. An eye—a *closed* eye. A mouth—a *closed* mouth ... See no evil, speak no evil? That left out the ear. Or was the ear coming?

Three are animals, if you lump the fish with the ox and the camel. Five relate to a house. Four are parts of a body— specifically, of a human body. Leaving whip and water, which fit nowhere. Animals, house, parts of body, water and whip ...

He tried various combinations. Ox and whip went together. Yes, but where did they lead? Nowhere . . . Camel. Camel and eye. *It is easier for a camel to go through the eye of a needle than for a rich man to enter into the kingdom of God.* That might be John, who would soon be rich enough. A warning? "Don't take your patrimony, or you'll find yourself sizzling in Hell"? Then why not say so! ... House, window. "People who live in glass houses ..." That was interesting; that had possibilities. The secret in John's past? "Don't black-mail me and I won't blackmail you"? ... Nail. "For want of a nail the battle was lost . . ."

After a while Ellery gave up. It was a problem for Einstein, he thought—Albert *or* Izzy; both specialized in cracking cases with dreadful contents.

He looked at the bed; it did not invite him.

I'll read awhile, he thought. I'll get a book from the library and read myself to sleep.

He had not yet undressed. He let himself out into the dim corridor and crept downstairs. The living room was dark except for the glow of the fireplace embers, and he snapped on his pencil flashlight. But he snapped it off at once. There was a light in the library. Had Felton forgotten to turn it off? Or—?

Ellery's skin tightened. He crossed the room softly.

Someone was in the library, a motionless figure with slack legs under a dressing gown and one chillingly limp hand draped over the arm of the leather wingchair.

Ellery peered.

It was John.

John, sitting there under the reading lamp as if ... *A warning you will die.*

Ellery leaped into the library and stopped short. He almost cried out in relief. There was a book in John's lap; he was breathing, slowly and quietly. Restless, he had probably had the same impulse as Ellery. He had come downstairs for something to read and had fallen asleep over the book.

Ellery stooped to shake John awake. But then, stopped by

a diffidence he did not attempt to analyze, he straightened without touching the sleeping man and tiptoed to the nearest shelf. It displayed some new and recent books, among them one entitled *How Like a God* by someone named Rex Stout, published by Vanguard. It was a first novel, Ellery recalled, and the *New York Herald Tribune* review of it had said something about its plowing "straight, deep furrows through the black soil in which Gabriele D'Annunzio and D. H. Lawrence staked out claims." Ellery decided to investigate this literary nova; he took the Stout book from the shelf and quietly went out.

After the light in the library the darkness in the living room was profound, and it took him some time to make his way to the hall. Here the glow from the upper hall helped him, and he ran upstairs lightly, book under his arm. Reaching the landing, he turned into the corridor—and froze.

John was walking up the hall toward his bedroom.

There was no mistaking him, even with his back turned and in the feeble light. It was John, and he had *not* passed Ellery on the stairs, and yet—again—he had reached the upper hall first!

Ellery called out sharply, "John?"

John did not turn around. John did not stop. The instant he heard Ellery's voice, John ran.

Ellery said grimly, "Okay, Brother Jonathan," and he ran, too.

John ran past his bedroom door. He dashed to the end of the corridor, turned right, and vanished.

Ellery put his head down and ran faster.

The chase that followed was a bruising experience in all ways. It took place in hellish darkness through the unused wings of the house, in and out of unoccupied but cluttered rooms, and in silence except for the pad of toes and the occasional assaults of furniture on various parts of the Queen anatomy. By the time he remembered to use his pencil flashlight he was one all-inclusive ache, he had lost his quarry, and he was thoroughly disgusted with himself.

He hurried back downstairs, using his flash recklessly. The library was dark. He switched the light on. The wingchair was empty.

Ellery ran back upstairs and without hesitation threw open the door of John's bedroom and walked in.

John was standing there naked, in the act of putting a leg into his pajama trousers.

They stared at each other.

"Well, if it isn't Second-Story Pete," John said, completing the thrust of the leg. "I should have locked my door again. What's the pitch now?"

"I thought you'd gone to bed."

"I'll confess all. I did, but I couldn't sleep. So I went down to the library and read a while. Dozed off and just came to. What are you panting about?"

"Who's panting?" Ellery grinned; and he went back to his room, leaving John one leg in, one leg out, scowling.

The truth was, Ellery was panting like a puma. And the truth also was—he thought, still grinning—that John's breathing was as unlabored as an infant's with a bellyful of his mother's milk.

At the stealthy knock on his door, Ellery slipped his arm back into his coat sleeve and said, "Yes?"

"It's me. Open up, Mr. Queen."

Ellery opened the door. "I thought you'd gone long ago, Sergeant."

"My relief just came." Sergeant Devoe lowered his voice. "It's a break you haven't undressed yet. Come on."

"Come on where?"

"Outside. You've got visitors."

"Visitors?"

"They think it's better if they don't come in. They're waiting in the car."

"Who's waiting in what car, Sergeant?"

The sergeant, however, was already striding down the hall. Ellery shut his door and, baffled, followed.

Devoe and his relief, a young trooper named Cooksey, were conferring on the porch in low tones and paying no attention to the driveway.

Ellery stepped off the porch, peering. The car was standing there in the darkness without lights and with its motor off, a powerful sedan.

He said, "Yes? Who is that?"

A crackling voice said, "Happy New Year," and a bass one beside it said, "Ditto."

"Dad—Velie!" Ellery ran over and yanked the rear door of the squad car open and slid in. "What are you two doing up here at this time of night?"

"Rubbernecking is all," Inspector Queen said. "And Velie came along because he doesn't think I can be trusted at a wheel."

"You can't," Sergeant Velie said briefly.

"At midnight," Ellery said. "In the open."

"I didn't want to embarrass you in front of your ritzy friends," his father said.

"This is one snazz of a dump, the little I can make out," the sergeant said. "How's the other half live, Maestro?"

"Cut the comedy," Ellery said. "Oh, and Happy New Year to *you*. Now what did you two find out about John's birth?"

"Okay, Thomas," the Inspector said. "That'll be one buck. Fork over."

"Wait a minute, will you?" Sergeant Velie grumbled. "I knew it was a sucker bet the minute I let you con me into it."

There was the chink of coins, some rustling, and then the Inspector said, "Seeing that you legged it, Velie, you tell him."

"Well, I scouted around Mount Kidron and Rye," Sergeant Velie began, "and what with this and that, and putting a couple twos together hither and yon, I pieced the story out. The auto accident occurred during a blizzard, on the Boston Post Road, outskirts of Mount Kidron, on the night of January the five, Nineteen-O-Five, right outside the house of a local medic name of Hall, Cornelius F. Hall. There was a Mrs. Hall, too, the doc's wife."

"Time," Ellery said. "This Dr. and Mrs. Hall. How long had they been in Mount Kidron? Where did they hail from?"

"No info," the sergeant said. "All I got on Hall was that he had a kind of poor practice and he and his wife just about made out. Anyway, Sebastian, who didn't seem to be hurt much at the time, though he died less than a week later of a head injury from the accident, somehow got Mrs. Sebastian into the Hall's house and Dr. Hall went to work on her. She was in the eighth month or something and the accident brought on labor. She gave birth right there that night—well, January sixth. It was after midnight."

"And now," Inspector Queen said, "get set for a surprise."

"I'd be surprised if you surprised me," Ellery said. "I know your surprise. It's what made me ask you to dig into this in the first place. John wasn't the only Sebastian child born that night, was he? Mrs. Sebastian gave birth to twins, didn't she? Identical twin boys?"

"Listen to him," Sergeant Velie said with disgust. "If you already knew, Maestro, how come you had me chasing my tail all over Westchester County?"

"I didn't know, Velie, I hypothesized. Having observed certain curiosa of incident and behavior, I applied Queen's Law of the Displacement of Material Bodies, which states that not even a poet can be in two places at the same time. Then there's Queen's Law of Questionable Amnesias, which concludes that when a young man loses his memory about a specific incident that occurred only the day before, while recalling the other events of that day—and this occurs on two separate occasions—why, Sergeant, the amnesia just ain't, and the incident must be considered to have happened to someone else. All this, incidentally, was corroborated by Queen's Law of the Rising Eyebrow. Under this valuable law, when a man has hanging in his closets and lying in his bureau drawers exact duplicates of everything he wears, from a back-bow Burgundy hat to a pair of pearl-button spats, and he ascribes this odd state of affairs to the fact that he's 'hard on clothes' and thus buys two of everything—under this law, as I say, the eyebrow rises and stays there."

"What's he talking about, Inspector?" the sergeant demanded.

"Search me," Inspector Queen said. "Though if I get a vague kind of drift from this dribble, son, you're in for a surprise just the same."

"What?" Ellery said.

"Let's string the genius along for a while, Velie. Give him the buildup first."

"Yes, *sir*," Sergeant Velie said with a smack of his whale-like lips. "You see, Maestro, when I find out there's a second kid born that same night I says to myself, What happened to this other kid? That's a logical question, ain't it?"

"It certainly is," Ellery snapped, "the logical answer to which is as follows: Since the second son's birth was never made public, and John Sebastian Senior apparently never acknowledged his existence, said second son must have been brought up by strangers, probably under a different name, and most likely unaware of his origin, at least for many years. There's a good deal about this second son we may never find out—especially the reason why his father refused to acknowledge him—but you've confirmed what I deduced, and that's all I care about at the moment. There's an identical twin of John's in existence, and has been for twenty-five years less some five days."

"Through, Mr. Queen?" his father asked.

"Of course. What more is there?"

"Oh, a mere detail," the Inspector murmured. "Give it to him, Velie."

Sergeant Velie chuckled. "The twin son died on January the twenty, Nineteen-O-Five, at the age of fourteen days."

"*No!*" Ellery cried.

"Yes," Sergeant Velie said.

"*Impossible!*"

"Maestro, I can prove it to you both ways from the ace."

"*You made a mistake!*"

"Is that nice?" the sergeant growled. "Guys get their teeth shoved down their throat for cracks like that. When I say this kid—the twin—died at the age of two weeks, brother, *he died*. Get me?"

"You can't possibly be sure," Ellery said wildly. "Why, that would be—that wouldn't be tolerable! It would upset the universe! Produce this so-called proof of yours, Velie, and I guarantee, sound unheard, to punch forty-two holes in it!"

"Oh, yeah? It's true that about nine years ago the Mount Kidron town hall burned to the ground with all its files, so that I couldn't find any official records of the kid's birth, but—"

"Aha!" Ellery said. "And oho!"

"But," Sergeant Velie continued, unperturbed, "I've got living testimony. And my informants say that the folks who had custody of John Sebastian Senior's twin son after the first kid, your John, was taken up to Rye were the Halls—that's right, the delivering doctor and his wife. The thing is, they could only hang on to him two weeks. He got pneumonia and kicked off. Hall called in another Mount Kidron doctor, who's still in practice there, a Dr. Harold G. Martin. Dr. Martin remembers making out the death certificate. I've got his affidavit. Martin also remembers Hall telling him the whole story, seeing that the twin had died. About the kid's having been born right after the first one in his house two weeks before to a Mr. and Mrs. John Sebastian of Rye, and that Sebastian had *given* him the baby because during the second delivery the guy's wife died and he blamed this second kid for it, or something as screwy as that, and didn't want any part of him. That head injury must have made him wacky."

"So even that's explained," Inspector Queen said.

"That's Number One," the sergeant continued with satisfaction. "Number Two: I located the undertaker who buried this kid for the Halls. Hall told him the same story. Number Three: the minister who read the funeral service over the coffin is still living in Mount Kidron, retired. He took me over to the church and had the church records hauled out for me, and there it was in white and black: 'Second Sebastian Son, aged two weeks, died January 20, 1905.' I took a photostat of it, knowing my customer. Want to see it?"

"I don't understand any of this," Ellery said weakly.

"And fourthly," his father said, "Velie located the child's grave in Mount Kidron Cemetery. There's a cheap little headstone that just says: 'Sebastian-Hall. Born Jan. 6, 1905—Died Jan. 20, 1905. Rest in Peace.' We could probably get an exhumation order, but beyond establishing that the bones are those of a two-week-old child I don't see what it would accomplish. We have plenty of affidavits to prove the twin was born and that two weeks later he was dead. You sound sick, son. Is this very bad news?"

"The worst," Ellery groaned. "It's gibberish. It can't be. The Halls, Sergeant—what became of them?"

"They pulled freight around the middle of Nineteen-O-Six and nobody in Mount Kidron's seen or heard from them since. I couldn't find anybody who knows where they moved to. There's no record of such a move on the books of any local moving company, so they probably used an out-of-town van."

Ellery was silent. Then he said, "Thanks a lot, Velie."

"Want to talk about it?" his father asked gently.

"I wouldn't know what to say. This was one phase of this cross-eyed case I was sure I had the answer to. Now ..." Ellery was silent again. Then he said, "Well, it's my headache. Thanks, Dad. Take it easy going back, Velie. Good night."

He got out of the squad car and groped his way to the porch like an old man.

Chapter XI ✠ Ninth Night: Thursday January 2, 1930

*In Which the Mystery of John Sebastian Darkens,
Mr. Queen Despairs, and to the Growing
Menagerie Is Added Another Denizen*

THERE ARE tides in the affairs of young men which, taken at the ebb, lead on to folly. It is no exaggeration to say that as Ellery thrashed in his bed through the interminable night and the rain-gray daylight hours of the following morning, his thoughts were not full of wisdom. He was to encounter and surmount many difficulties in the course of his career; but he was young then, the Case of the Curious Christmas Packages was only his second investigation—really his first independent one—and it seemed to him the end of his world had come. There should be two John Sebastians; every fact in logic cried out for two John Sebastians; he had settled in his mind that there were two John Sebastians; and now it appeared that there was only one John Sebastian after all. If John II existed, it was as a cherub in heaven and a two-week-old skeleton on earth, interred for almost twenty-five years. These were facts, too. When fact met fact head on, what happened? Chaos.

Thus young Mr. Queen's despair. In his despair he thought many foolish thoughts, which twenty-seven years later he was to recall with burning blush.

He crawled out of bed at noon, wishing woefully that he had never heard of crime, John Sebastian or, for that matter, Christmas.

When he got downstairs, he found Lieutenant Luria on a quarterdeck quelling a mutiny. It was the second of January, Mr. Payn, the attorney, was saying with a ferment in his mellifluous voice, he had many large affairs to attend to, and he wished to return to the city post-haste. Lieutenant Luria said he was sorry, but that could not be. Dr. Sam Dark

123

protested that he must return to his practice of medicine, that he had promised to release his covering fellow-practitioners on January 2nd, this was January 2nd, and you must be reasonable, Lieutenant Luria. Lieutenant Luria said he was doing his job as he saw it, and please don't make it any tougher on me or yourselves. Mr. Freeman, the book publisher; Marius Carlo, the refugee from Professor Damrosch's orchestra; Miss Valentina Warren of the theater; Miss Ellen Craig of Wellesley—all pleaded their causes with varying degrees of heat and emotion, and all met Lieutenant Luria's tight-lipped rebuff. The dead man was still unidentified, he said; the area of investigation was now being widened to embrace the continental United States, and he would be loath to slap on a blanket warrant holding them all as material witnesses to a homicide, but he would do that very thing, ladies and gentlemen, if you force me to. This elicited from Mr. Payn, the lawyer, a tirade of legalisms which tried the lieutenant's temper; and the whole conference broke up into fragments of excited talk which, when the débris settled, found Lieutenant Luria gone and all parties still there.

Lunch was a stony affair. There was no longer even a pretense of sociability. Rusty and John had apparently fallen out again, and from the green glances Rusty shot at Valentina and the red glares John directed toward Marius, Ellery gathered that the delicate problems of the quadrangle were still very much with them. After lunch Dan Z. Freeman retired to a corner like a squirrel with a nut and frankly read a manuscript which had been delivered to him from the city by messenger. Olivette Brown, muttering, pored like a witch over an astrological chart. Roland Payn paced tigerishly up and down. Dr. Dark and Arthur Craig, engaged in two-handed pinochle, kept slapping cards down with vicious little splats. The Reverend Mr. Gardiner, after touring the premises with a distressed expression, murmured something about a headache and retreated mendaciously to his room. Ellen asked Ellery to go walking with her in the rain, received a blank stare, and stamped off in deep dudgeon.

In the end Ellery followed the clergyman's example, went upstairs, locked his door, and sat down in a reclining chair. But not to doze. Instead, he clutched his temples and thought and thought and thought.

Ellery came to himself with a start. The room was almost dark. He felt stiff and chilled. He had thought himself into a coma. He supposed he should be grateful to the voices . . .

Voices! He shook himself alert. It was the voices that had brought him back to the dismal world of reality. They were apparently coming from the next room.

That's the trouble with these old houses, Ellery thought,

with their time-riddled walls. Sneeze—or worse—and the whole place knows it.

Men's voices. Who had the adjoining bedroom?

Payn.

Payn!

Ellery scrambled to his feet, reached for a straight chair, set it noiselessly down at the communicating door, stepped onto the seat, breathed a prayer that the hinges would not creak, and with swift fingers let down the transom. The creak was outrageous. But apparently the owners of the voices were too preoccupied with their conversation to notice.

Payn's voice.

And John Sebastian's.

Ellery eavesdropped without shame.

"You loathsome little pup," Roland Payn was saying. "You haven't the scruple of a ward-heeler. Trying to blackmail me!"

"Calling me names won't get you anywhere, Payn," John's voice said. "The fact is—if you'll pardon the expression—I've got you with your pants down. I know the address. I know the name of the babe. She's nothing but a prostitute, and you're one of her preferred customers."

"Prove it," Payn said curtly.

"That's what I like. The legal mind. Cuts right to the belly of the matter. You want proof? Here."

"What's this?" The lawyer's voice sounded choked.

"Photostats of a little red book. It's Dolly's blue-chip list, the cream of her clientele. Dates, names, fees per session. Even some amusing comments. Like this one: 'This Rollie Payn is sure one athlete. What does he think I am, a one-gal harem?'"

"Enough," Payn's voice said hoarsely. "Where did you get this?"

"From Dolly," John's voice said. "I bought it. That is, the original. Don't worry, Rollie, I've got it locked away in a safe place. I wouldn't want to see photos of this splashed all over the New York papers. Imagine what the *Graphic* would do with it! Probably paste up one of their famous composographs, showing you and Dolly in a tender moment. I'm afraid it would just about ruin that stuffed-shirt practice of yours."

Payn was silent. Then his voice said, "All right. How much?"

"Money? Not a dime."

"I don't understand."

John laughed. "Man does not live by bread alone. Anyway, I have a whole bakeryful." He said abruptly, "You have a son, Payn. His name is Wendell Payn, he's one of the shining lights of the Princeton English faculty, and he's considered the coming man in the field of poetry criticism. A word from young Professor Payn—"

125

"You," Roland Payn said in a wondering way, "are a maniac, I'm absolutely convinced. You seriously suggest that I influence my son to write a favorable review of your piddling little book of verse?"

"Not merely favorable, Mr. Payn. Enthusiastic."

"It's evident that your prying into my private life didn't include an investigation of my son's character. Wendell would no more consider writing a dishonest criticism than he would consider breaking into the Princeton bursar's safe. He just wouldn't do it."

"Not even to save his saintly father from disgrace? You know, Mr. Payn, publication of that little red book might even result in your disbarment."

"It's out of the question! I can't ask him!"

"That's your problem, isn't it?" Ellery heard the rattle of a doorknob. "There's plenty of time. At my suggestion Dan Freeman sent a copy of my book to your son, with a personal note, for review. You have until the next poetry issue of the *Saturday Review* goes to press. I'll be looking forward to it. Yes, Mr. Payn? You were about to say?"

The attorney's voice came through the transom all breath and distortion. "Nothing," he said. "Nothing."

Ellery heard Payn's door open and close, both softly, and the stealthy sound of John Sebastian's steps down the hall.

He also heard a violent metallic clash, as if a man had hurled himself onto a bed.

Ellery found himself shaking.

This was not John. This could not be John, even the worst of him. The John Ellery knew was not like this. The John Rusty Brown had fallen in love with was another man entirely.

And yet he was John. He could be no one else.

He was. And he wasn't.

It was not to be borne.

And that evening it was Roland Payn who found the ninth Christmas box. He had gone upstairs directly after dinner, saying that he had some letters to write. Down he came two minutes later, his handsome face exercised, his white hair indignant, carrying the gay little package as if he had picked it up in a Chinese rice field. He dropped it on the refectory table, took out a handkerchief, wiped his hands pointedly, and then went back upstairs without a word.

Without a word Ellery reached for it.

"John Sebastian," the Santa Claus card said.

In the same typewriting.

The white card in the box had four typewritten lines tonight:

On the ninth night of Christmas
Your true love sends to you,
A m o n k e y for your zoo:
Your fifteenth clue.

The object in the red tissue paper was a stuffed animal, a raffish little monkey made of felt-like cloth. He was quite fetching. Under other circumstances he might have evoked squeals from the women and grins from the men. As it was, they all stared at him as if he were about to sprout horns and recite the Lord's Prayer backwards.

Ellery turned the card over. It was blank.

"Any suggestions?"

"Yes!" John shouted. "Burn the whole unmentionable mess!"

From his corner Dan Freeman chuckled. "There's an old Yiddish saying, John, that I commend to you. Literally translated, it goes: Somebody else's backside is good to spank." He rose, smiling. "I don't know but that I'm beginning to enjoy this."

Ellery paced his room that night with the iron desperation of Edmond Dantès in the dungeon of the Château d'If.

The animal motif again. An ox. A camel. A fish. And now a monkey. And the message for the first time introduced the concept "zoo," as if to call attention to the animals of the collection.

So he concentrated on the four animal gifts.

Ox. Camel. Fish. Monkey.

Bovine. Ruminant. Aquatic. Primate.

Horns. Humps. Fins. Hands.

He shook his head impatiently.

The materials from which they were made?

Ox—wood. Camel—metal and enamel. Fish—living tissue. Monkey—cloth. When he found himself adding, Queen—marblehead, he snatched his diary and tried to lose himself in recording history.

But the word "clue" in the evening's verse kept beating in

127

his head. It was the first time the word had been used in the messages. As if the writer were growing impatient with his dullness, making things plainer. . . . *My* dullness? Ellery thought. Why do I assume it's I he's baiting? The gifts are addressed to John.

Still, he had the queerest conviction that Queen, not Sebastian, was the target of the sender's taunts.

Fifteen individual gifts in nine nights.

"Clues."

Clues to what? To what?

Chapter XII ✠ Tenth Night: Friday
January 3, 1930

*In Which the Pale Rider Comes a Cropper, the
One-Eyed Doll Grows a New Tooth, and a
Baffled Sleuth Touches Bottom*

FRIDAY MORNING a hostile spirit was abroad in the house. Scarcely anyone was on terms of civility with anyone else. Befuddlement and lethargy had undergone a chemical change. Now everyone flashed anger, toyed with Mrs. Janssen's food, prowled the premises either singly or in resentful pairs, and made it nakedly evident that he wished for nothing so much as escape. Sergeant Devoe had his hands full.

The coldness between John and Rusty was colder. It was not thawed by the actions of Valentina and Marius. They kept up a barrage of malicious remarks, ostensibly addressed to each other but hitting their true mark each time. The sniping finally drove John out of the house.

Furious, Rusty followed him.

"Don't you see what those two are up to? Darling, what's happened to us? We can't let them spoil everything. John, what's come over you!"

But John was saddling the pinto mare, deaf.

"Don't go riding this morning. With all this slush the trail will be dangerous."

"I'll be fine. I just want to get away."

"From me."

"*Not* from you, Rusty. It's just that I feel like being alone. What's wrong with this damn girth!"

"I thought the idea of being engaged to be married was *not* to feel alone," Rusty said, knowing this was madness yet unable to stop. "Or is that what you're trying to convey to me?"

"Oh, for God's sake." John leaped into the saddle, yanked the mare's head around, bent double, and kicked. The mare shot out of the stable like a rocket.

With her hand to her mouth, blinking back the frustrated tears, Rusty watched him gallop across the mushy snow and disappear in the woods.

Panic seized her.

Fumbling, she saddled the gelding and rode out after him.

The woods trail was even worse than she had feared. Patches of snow and soft mud alternated with icy spots where the sun did not penetrate. The gelding picked his way primly, snorting his displeasure. Rusty's heart hammered. If John tried to run the mare at full gallop on this treacherous trail . . . She prodded the Morgan into a trot, straining to see ahead. Once he slipped and almost threw her. She hung on, trying to tell herself that the mare was surer-footed than the gelding, that John was an expert horseman . . .

She found him around a bend in the trail. He had been tossed clear and was lying in deep snow under a fir tree, face down. The mare had slipped and fallen—Rusty saw the telltale wallow in the snow—but apparently she was all right, for there was no sign of her.

"John?"

He lay still and pale. Rusty scrambled off her horse and flung herself at him. He can't be dead, she told herself. He *mustn't* be.

"John!" She shook him fiercely. "Oh, thank God . . ."

He was alive, but unconscious.

"Darling, wake up." She kissed him, patted his cheek.

John's eyes remained shut.

Rusty's relief drained out. He's hurt, she thought. He's hurt badly. I mustn't move him. I might . . .

Dr. Dark!

Rusty breathed a prayer, jumped into the saddle, sawed the gelding about on the narrow trail, and raced back to the house.

John's accident cleared the air. Ellery returned from the stable to find him holding court on the divan, with everyone chattering cheerfully. Rusty was caressing his head and smiling, and Dr. Dark was just shutting his medical bag. The only sign of injury was the bandage on John's right wrist and hand.

"The patient will live, I see," Ellery said.

"The damn fool, you mean," John grumbled. "It was my own fault. I don't know what all the fuss is about."

"It certainly was," Dr. Dark snapped. "You're lucky to have got away with a mere sprained wrist."

129

"You're sure no bones are broken, Sam?" Craig asked anxiously. "No concussion?"

"I could run him over to the hospital if it would make you feel better, Arthur, but it really isn't necessary."

"Of course not," John said. "Relax, Arthur. Where've you been, Ellery? Not that I deserve your sympathy, but you might have hung around to see if I'd broken my neck."

"I'd have been tempted to break it myself." Ellery filled his pipe. "Why, Sergeant Devoe and I went looking for the mare."

"She's hurt?" John exclaimed.

"Fit as Blue Larkspur and full of beans. We found her in her stall, devouring hay." Ellery blew out the match and dropped it gently into an ashtray. "Tell me, John. How did the accident happen?"

"I was running her hard, she slipped, and I took a header. That's all I remember until Dr. Sam brought me to."

"Nothing happened on the trail to pull her up suddenly, make her shy?"

"No." John looked puzzled. "Not that I remember. Why?"

"Mr. Queen." John's guardian was disturbed. "You aren't suggesting—?"

"I'm suggesting, Mr. Craig," Ellery said dryly, "that this is no time to take an accident to John at its face value. That's why Devoe and I looked the mare over. She might just possibly have had a shoe tampered with. I'm happy to report that she hadn't. It wasn't likely, since no one could have known that John was going horseback-riding this morning, or that he'd take the mare instead of the gelding, his usual mount. Still, in view of what's been going on, I'm not ruling out anything simply because it's unlikely."

Shadows crawled back over the party.

At Dr. Dark's insistence, John spent the rest of the day on his back. Since he balked at being put to bed, he occupied the divan in the living room all afternoon, becoming the vortex of small eddies of activity.

Today the subject uppermost in all minds insisted on surfacing. They discussed endlessly the meanings of the gifts. Ellery listened in silence, on the alert more for nuances of tone than for content. But he could detect nothing significant.

Throughout the day the question kept running through his head: What will the gift be tonight?

The answer to the corollary question: Who's going to find it? Ellery dismissed as foregone. If the pattern persisted— and, meaningless as the pattern was, it seemed consistent— the finder would be Rusty. Whoever was centrally involved with John on any given day turned out to be the finder of the

130

gift that night. This had been true at least since Sunday, the fifth night. On that day he, Ellery, had been surprised by John in John's room; that night he, Ellery, found the gift. On Monday John had had his blackmailing talk with Dan Z. Freeman; on Monday night Freeman found the sixth gift. On Tuesday Val Warren declared her passion to John in the stable; on Tuesday night it was she who found the seventh gift. Wednesday had been an exception: it was Marius who had found the eighth gift in the grand piano, although nothing special had happened during the day between him and John. But yesterday, after the literary blackmail in Roland Payn's bedroom, it was Payn who had found the ninth gift.

Ellery shrugged. He was not disposed to place too much importance on these juxtapositions. They were obviously not coincidences, but on the other hand the individual episodes of each day could not have been foreseen by the gift-giver. Whoever he was, he was simply taking advantage of events as they occurred. With so many people in the party, wandering upstairs and down and out of doors at all hours, it was no feat to snoop and keep informed as to what was going on. This phase of the mysterious donor's activities was apparently byplay, a derisive part of whatever deadlier game he was playing. And that he was playing it with Ellery rather than with John or anyone else, Ellery was becoming more and more positive.

Far more pressing, Ellery felt, were the questions: Who is the dead man and how does he fit in with the other pieces of the puzzle? How explain the brain-numbing fact that John must have an identical twin secreted in the house—when according to Sergeant Velie's information the twin had beyond question died at the age of two weeks? And finally, and always: What did the nightly gifts signify?

As Ellery had foreseen, Rusty found the tenth gift. She ran up to her room after dinner to fetch an extra blanket to tuck around John on the divan, and she came running back pale as the blanket, clutching the latest of the dread boxes.

"On my bed. Will somebody p-please take it?"

It was of a different shape from its nine predecessors—a flat square box of the kind used by linen shops for packing handkerchiefs.

It was unique in another way, also. For when Ellery took off the box top, he found nothing inside but a white card.

"No gift," Ellen said, staring.

"That's a switch." John actually looked relieved. "Maybe even the lackbrain behind this nonsense is beginning to realize his joke's laid an egg."

"I'm not so sure, John." Ellery read the typewritten message aloud:

John managed a grin. "Lovely sentiment. Don't look so tragic, Rusty. I'm through letting this get me down, I really am. I could never stand lame verse, anyway."

No one was fooled.

"No gift," Olivette Brown shrilled. "I must say that's weird. What can it mean?"

"Maybe he's run out of ideas," Dr. Dark suggested.

"Or couldn't get hold of a head?" Marius said.

"I don't find that remark particularly amusing, Carlo," Payn said coldly. "In fact, there's damned little about you that amuses me."

"Oh, be quiet, both of you," Valentina said. "What do you make of it, Ellery? Why no gift tonight?"

"There is a gift tonight." Ellery tapped the card. " 'The head predicting you'd be dead.' There was such a head, remember? 'A warning you will die'? The head with 'one closed eye' and 'mouth shut tight'?"

"The rag doll on New Year's night!" Ellen cried.

Ellery nodded. He went to the cabinet in which he had been storing the gifts. He examined the lock, nodded again, and then without attempting to use the key he pulled on the knob. The cabinet door opened.

"Lock forced, probably during the small hours last night. Full of surprises, isn't he? ... Yes, it's here," Ellery said grimly, "though in amended condition."

To the closed eye and slash of mouth on the white paint covering the doll's face had been added a third feature. It was a single short vertical line a bit to the right of the "mouth's" center, projecting upward from the mouth line. Crude as it was, its meaning was unmistakable. It represented a tooth—a grinning sort of tooth snaggling out of a mean sort of mouth under a leering sort of eye.

132

They had to help John to bed.

That night in his bedroom young Mr. Queen drained the bitter cup to its lees. It was no mere matter of the piling of obscurity upon confusion, or the fact that the current tally of 17 items over ten nights made another meaningless sum.

It was the taste of derision.

There could no longer be any question of who was being derided. John Sebastian might be the target of the threats, but "Mr. Sleuth" was the target of the taunts.

He's leading me around by the nose, Ellery thought savagely, and each night he gives it a tweak. And all I can do is submit to being led around and tweaked. He knows me, damn him! He knows I won't give up, that I'll stick it out to the end. And he isn't the least concerned about what I may come up with. He's leading me to a conclusion . . .

For an instant the odd thought flashed in Ellery's head: *a conclusion he wants me to reach.*

But then it was lost in the vaster questions: And when I've reached it, what then? What happens then?

He saw only one gain in the debits of the night. To have forced the lock of the cabinet the forcer must have been one of the people in the house. With Sergeant Devoe on duty all day, and his relief on duty all night, no outsider could have managed it.

But that was small consolation. He had known that all along.

Ellery stared into the darkness of the bedroom until it began to turn gray. Then, exhausted, he fell asleep.

Chapter XIII ✠ **Eleventh Night: Saturday January 4, 1930**

In Which Dr. Dark Gives John Some Unmedical Advice, and with the Sign of the Cross the Little House Is Finished—or Is It?

OVERNIGHT THE weather turned cold. It proved tonic. Even John managed a smile or two over Rusty's mother-clucking at breakfast; with his right hand *hors de combat* he had to have help, and Rusty swarmed over him like a hen. No one mentioned last night's sinister gift of the "tooth," or what fresh devilment might be expected tonight. At least part of the improved atmosphere, Ellery thought, was ascribable to the feeling that the gifts had almost run their course. This was the morning of the eleventh day of the holiday; and with the end only thirty-six hours away, everyone seemed to feel that even Lieutenant Luria would prove reasonable.

"If he doesn't," Roland Payn said grimly, "I'm going to start handing out legal advice—gratis."

"Oh, it isn't so bad," Marius Carlo said. "Because of it, I get to miss another Damrosch broadcast tonight." And he gave the lethal warning that anyone tuning in WEAF at nine o'clock would have the choice of weapons at dawn Sunday morning.

The humor was heavy, but as Mr. Gardiner murmured to Dan Z. Freeman, at least it had the merit of clarity.

So the day began well, and since Valetina and Marius had apparently agreed to pull in their horns the spirit of bonhomie promised to continue. Ellen was so encouraged that she got together with Mrs. Janssen and Felton and organized a wiener roast. They picnic-lunched in a clearing deep in the woods around a beautiful fire, carbonizing frankfurters, turning hamburgers into leather, frizzing onions, picking exploded potatoes out of the ashes, consuming quarts of bitter coffee and having a wonderful time.

Not even Lieutenant Luria's visit in the afternoon spoiled the day. He brought himself up to date on the messages and gifts, but not as if they mattered; he went through the motions of another round of interrogations; and in the end he announced that, barring unexpected developments, the party would be permitted to disperse Monday or Tuesday. A cheer went up.

Ellery remarked to Luria aside: "You've struck something."

The trooper hesitated a fraction of a second in applying flame to his cigaret. "What makes you say that, Queen?"

"I was weaned on gun oil and cut my first molars on a nightstick. What have you found out?"

"Well—something."

"About the dead man?"

"We're not sure yet."

"Who was he?" Ellery asked eagerly.

"When we're sure I'll let you know."

"Anything else?"

Luria shook his head. "I don't know that the identification is going to get us anywhere after all. There are certain possibilities if the little guy is who we think he is, but . . ." He shrugged. "Hell, you can't make an arrest on possibilities. There's no evidence of any kind to connect anyone here directly with the murder."

"Then you're serious about letting them go?"

"What else can I do?" Luria regarded Ellery through the cigaret smoke. "Make any sense yet out of those messages and boxes?"

"No," Ellery said briefly.

"Still think they're connected with the murder?"

"Yes. I mean—I don't really know, but I think so."

"If you ever find out give me a buzz." Lieutenant Luria uttered a soft, rich curse. "It would be my luck to hit a screwball case."

"And mine," Ellery muttered. "And mine!"

Dr. Dark knocked on the bedroom door. "John?"

"Who is it?"

"Sam Dark. May I come in?"

"Sure."

The fat man opened the door and walked in. John was lying on his bed and Rusty was seated beside it, an open book in her lap.

"Cheers," the doctor said. "How's my patient behaving?"

"Not too badly for such a nasty character," Rusty said. "Beefed, but took his nap, and he's been lying here listening to *Dodsworth*, although not without snide comments."

"Lewis couldn't write his way out of a paper bag," John snorted. "He and Dreiser!"

"*Dodsworth?* Oh, his new one," Dr. Dark said. "I haven't got to it yet. I don't know, John, I thought his *Arrowsmith* was pretty good. How's the carpus?"

"Painful, thank you. What are you practicing these days, Dr. Sam, bootleg medicine? Clapping me into bed for a sprained wrist!"

"I let you go to the picnic, didn't I? Anyway, you're not in bed for the wrist. Concussion can be tricky." The fat doctor glanced at Rusty. "My dear, I wonder if you'd mind—?"

Rusty rose. "I'll be back, darling."

"For crying out loud," John complained. "I don't blush when my wrist is exposed."

"The doctor-patient relationship is sacred." Dr. Dark winked at Rusty. "This won't take long."

"I hope he's sweeter-tempered with you than he's been with me." Rusty kissed John lightly under the Byronic curl and left.

"Okay, Dr. Sam, make it snappy. Hey!" John sat up in bed. "What are you locking the door for? What kind of examination are you going to give me, anyway?"

Dr. Dark set his vast back against the door. The twinkle was gone. "John, I want to talk to you."

John stared. Then he lay back on the pillow and looked resignedly at the ceiling. "Man to man stuff, hm?"

"Anything wrong with that?" The fat man came over to the bed. He stood there looking down at the young poet.

"I guess it's better than man to boy." John rolled his head idly. "You and Arthur have a tendency to forget that I'm not a Katzenjammer Kid any more. 'Thus the whirligig of time brings in his revenges.' That's from *Twelfth Night*, Sir Leech—speaking of twelves, which God forbid. It's later than you think."

"Yes," Dr. Dark said. "Exactly. You might remember that."

John looked at him. "What's that supposed to mean?"

"John." The fat man hesitated. "I've known you from infancy. I've helped you grow up, in a way. I suppose I've always thought of myself as a sort of uncle to you. Are you sure you know what you're doing?"

"You mean about marrying Rusty?" John grinned. "I told you back in the early part of November, the night I told Arthur, that's a consummation I can be devout about."

"I don't mean that and you know it. John, look at me. No, in the eye."

"The eye test for virtue?" John grinned. "I thought that went out with the chastity belt. You mean like this?"

Dr. Dark said heavily, "John, I know what you've been up to with Mr. Freeman and Mr. Payn."

"Do you, now." There was no perturbation in John's voice, only surprise and annoyance. "And just what is it I'm supposed to be up to with Freeman and Payn?"

"I don't believe it's necessary for me to spell it out, John. I tell you I know."

John examined the ceiling again. "So they're talking. I've misjudged them."

"They've told me nothing."

"Then where did you hear this *conte drôlatique?*"

"Does that matter?"

"It may," John said calmly. "How fast has this canard spread? How many others know about it?"

"I don't know," Dr. Dark said. "Only a few, I think. That's not the point. The point is, John, you're riding for a fall just as surely as you rode to one yesterday."

"Dr. Sam—" John began.

"I know, you could tell me to mind my business and you'd be within your rights. I hope you're not going to."

John was silent.

"I wish I were a sermon preacher. A doctor rarely has time to say things roundabout. John, I don't know why you're doing this, but—don't. Don't start out in life by trying to push people around. People like Freeman and Payn, who've made their way in spite of their weaknesses, won't allow themselves to be pushed. You haven't lived long enough to find that out. They'll push back. Have you considered that?"

"Dr. Sam," John said, "I don't know what in hell you're talking about. Are you going to examine my wrist or aren't you?"

Dr. Samson Dark looked down at John for a long moment. Then he walked over to the door, unlocked it, and quietly left.

When Dr. Dark strode back into the living room that night after having left to go to bed only a few minutes before, Ellery did not have to look around to see the Christmas package in his hand.

"I just found this on my bureau."

As Ellery took the package, he wondered what role the physician had played during the day to earn the dubious nightly honor. But the doctor's fleshy lips were clamped together, and Ellery knew it would be useless to question him.

He took the package to the refectory table and in silence removed the green and red wrappings. There was the usual Santa tag with the typewritten "John Sebastian." He noted automatically that the same typewriter was still being used.

The white box was one of the smallest of the series. The typewritten card, however, displayed one of the longer verses:

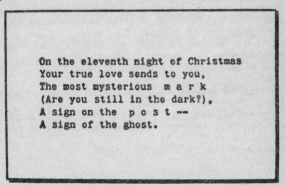

On the eleventh night of Christmas
Your true love sends to you,
The most mysterious m a r k
(Are you still in the dark?),
A sign on the p o s t --
A sign of the ghost.

The reverse of the card was blank.

The "gift" was a little signpost. It consisted of a wooden upright stained brown, to the top of which a tiny brass bracket had been tacked. From the bracket hung a little oblong wooden "sign" with jagged ends, in the rustic mode, also brown-stained. On the sign was painted a crude *X*.

"Well, this makes a tidy little nest out of it," John said. "Do you suppose it's complete now, or will there be a mailbox tomorrow night?"

"I say it's complete," Mrs. Brown hissed. "Don't ask me why. I *feel* it."

"I say it's spinach," said Marius Carlo, "and I say to hell with it. John, how about pouring me one for the Ostermoor?"

"*X*," Mr. Gardiner said thoughtfully. "The Greek letter *chi*, initial letter of *Christos*. The symbol of Christ, as in Xmas."

Ellery looked up. "You know, I hadn't thought of that, Mr. Gardiner. But I don't believe that's what was meant. 'A sign of the ghost,' the message says."

"The Holy Ghost?" Dan Freeman suggested.

"Blasphemy," the Episcopal minister muttered. "This entire thing is an abomination."

"No," Ellery said to Freeman.

"Then what ghost?" Rusty cried.

"In the Era of Jackass Brandy, Hijack and the Concrete Kimono," Ellery said, "*X* usually marks the spot, and the ghost that results hovers over a slab in the nearest morgue. This is about as subtle as a Chicago shakedown."

"Lovely," John said. "What it all adds up to is that I'm to be killed in the house."

"Don't *say* things like that, John!" Rusty screamed. Arthur Craig went to her, glaring at his ward.

"You're all wrong, Mr. Queen," Olivette Brown said passionately. " 'A sign of the ghost' refers to the *sender*. And the ghost's sign is *X*, the unknown. Someone who has crossed over is trying to make contact with John. There are ghosts who either have no identity or have lost it, and they're doomed to be chained to the world of matter until they find it ..."

She went on and on, while the others listened with exasperation.

Ellery did not listen at all. He was thinking: 19 individual "gifts" now in 11 boxes. Tomorrow night the twelfth—and last—box.

What would that make the final tally?

Chapter XIV ✠ Twelfth Night: Sunday
January 5, 1930 . . .

In Which Olivette Brown Converses with a Ghost, Mr. Queen Is Struck by Lightning, and on John Sebastian Is Bestowed the Last Gift

SUNDAY WAS ONE of those dreadful days that seem to drag their feet from birth. People wandered from room to room, threw themselves from chair to chair. The Sunday newspapers were read and re-read, even the fat automotive section inspired by the New York Automobile Show. Mayor Jimmy

Walker's announcement that he would donate the amount of his pay rise for the next four years to charity was sniffed at, mouthed, and torn to bits. Val Warren read aloud, with emotion, the obituary of Kenneth Hawks, Mary Astor's husband, who with ten others had been killed while filming an airplane scene off Santa Monica on Friday. The literary-minded conducted a roundtable on some publishing landmarks of the season—J. B. Priestley's *The Good Companions*, John Steinbeck's *Cup of Gold*, Henry Handel Richardson's *Ultima Thule*, Donn Byrne's last novel, *Field of Honor*. Dan Freeman ruefully recounted the curious pre-publishing history of Remarque's *All Quiet on the Western Front*. But when Ellery brought up William Bolitho's *Twelve Against the Gods*, the round-table abruptly splintered into kindling. In that house, on that day, "twelve" was a bad word.

In spite of the sunshine, no one ventured outdoors except old Mr. Gardiner, who left the house before anyone was up and did not return until late afternoon. When he was asked where he had been all day, the clergyman replied, "With Christ manifesting Himself to the Gentiles," and went quietly up to his room.

The dark promise of the evening lay over the house, holding everyone fast. It was too much for the Irish girl, Mabel, who had a weeping spell in midafternoon on the astonished chest of Sergeant Devoe.

Ellen Craig came up with a suggestion.

"As long as this is Twelfth Night and tomorrow probably everyone will leave," Ellen said, "why don't we celebrate it the way people did in the Middle Ages? They had lots of fun on Twelfth Night, feasting, playing games, making merry. What do you think?"

"*Bravo,*" Ellery said, forbearing to point out that the Feasts of the Epiphany of medieval times were probably survivals of the Roman Saturnalia. "Who'll do what?"

In the end a program of sorts was drawn up.

At the festive board, Mr. Gardiner's grace referred to the Marriage at Cana and wound up in a supplication to turn "the bitter water of this house" into the sweet wine of goodness and joy. This pointed prayer did not serve to elevate anyone's spirits, and Mrs. Janssen's feast was begun in silence. John did not improve matters when he observed, loudly enough for Mrs. Janssen to overhear across the butler's pantry, that the roast of lamb was underdone; and the remainder of the dinner was eaten to a symphony of stifled sobs and nose blowings from the culinary sector, interspersed by frantic shushes from Mabel and Felton. Then, while clearing the table preparatory to serving the dessert, Mabel tipped her lofted tray and slid a nearly full glass of burgundy neatly onto the head of Roland Payn, baptizing his white hair a beautiful purplish red and sending runnels of the same lush hue down his handsome cheeks and shirt front into his lap. Whereupon Mabel dropped the tray and fled to the kitchen, adding the wails of her anguish to Mrs. Janssen's, and the feast broke up in confusion, Ellen and Rusty hastening to soothe the distressed females in the kitchen while Arthur Craig assisted his spluttering attorney upstairs.

Ellery took this opportunity to scout the living room. There was no Christmas package. He was still wondering when and where the twelfth package would be found, and by whom, when the company assembled for the Twelfth Night program.

Marius had ducked into the music room, and through the archway came a surprisingly naïve music that sounded like Purcell. To this melodic accompaniment everyone was seated.

Ellery raised his hand and the music stopped.

"As your Master of Revels, ladies and gentlemen," Ellery said solemnly, "I choose that most popular of all lines, the line of least resistance. There will be no speech from me." Ellen cheered—rather too heartily, he thought. "Instead, we shall proceed at once to the business of the evening.

"Our opening entertainment, in defiance of the time-honored vaudeville tradition, will be neither acrobats nor Japanese jugglers. In fact, I don't know what the devil it is. My friends, I give you Mr. Arthur Benjamin Craig."

The piano produced a chord, and from the library marched their host. He was carrying a corrugated carton. This he deposited on the refectory table, bowed gravely to Ellery, Ellery bowed back and sat down, and Craig cleared his throat.

Sergeant Devoe looked on from the hall archway, and Mrs. Janssen, Mabel and Felton—the women still sniffling —peered in from beyond the half-open swinging door to the dining room.

"Fellow-members of the John Sebastian Admiration Society," Craig began, one hand impressively on the carton, "tomorrow being January the sixth, The House of Freeman will publish *The Food of Love* in a trade edition as modest though sterling as its author."

Cries of "Hear, hear!" interrupted him. John was grinning, and everyone else was smiling except Freeman and Payn, who sat listening without expression. Craig held up his hand quickly.

"In my dual connection with our young hero—both as his unofficial father and the printer of said trade edition—I could not allow this historic occasion to slip by without a token of my personal dedication to the event.

"In consequence," Craig went on oratorically, "I have summoned the considerable resources of my press and of the various fine craftsmen with whom I have been associated these many years to the task of producing"—Craig flipped open the carton and lifted out a book—"this special edition of *The Food of Love,* limited to twelve copies, numbered in sequence, one for each member of this company."

A murmur went up at the beauty of the volume.

"The volume is a duodecimo, to maintain a pleasing proportion with its slimness. A special rag paper has been used, manufactured for me in England. The text has been composed in the delicate, uneccentric type which I had Chartrain design for The House of Freeman's exclusive use in the printing of poetry classics. Each sheet is printed in two colors, the text in black and the rules and decorations in mallow red, a color of medium saturation and brilliance. The endpaper design and the title page are a labor of friendship by the well-known artist Boris Akst. The sheets have been folded, gathered and sewn by hand, and then bound in full crushed levant. It is a book I'm proud to have produced, John, and I present these copies to your friends and mine in the hope that you will all find as much pleasure in the owning as I did in the making."

And, beaming, Craig handed one of the beautiful books to John and distributed ten others to the company. The one that was left over the bearded printer clutched firmly to his chest.

"Naturally, I didn't overlook myself!"

John was enormously touched. He sat there with the book in his lap, blinking at it.

Among the general exclamations of admiration came a clamor for John's autograph. Over his protests that he could write only with great difficulty because of his sprained wrist, John was seized by Rusty and Ellen, marched over to the table, and seated with a thump. Mr. Gardiner produced his fountain pen, Valentina ran to the library for blotters, and the table became the scene of an impromptu autographing party. Everyone was demanding a personal inscription as well as a signature, and John frowned and cogitated and wrote each inscription in a painful and distorted scrawl on the insert-page containing the limited-edition legend.

Ellery drifted over to the chair on which John had left his own copy of the book, picked the book up and casually glanced at its insert-page. The copy was numbered 12. A line from some unremembered Victorian author sprang into his head: "Fate laughs at probabilities."

He noticed as he brought his own copy over to the table that both Freeman and Payn were hanging back. But they were trapped by the necessities of the occasion, and before it was too late each man presented his copy for the young poet's attentions, smiling with difficulty.

"I didn't realize, when the program for tonight's entertainment was drawn up," the Master of Revels announced, "what

141

beautiful balance exists between the then unknown opening number by Mr. Craig and the second number, which I now introduce: Readings from *The Food of Love*, by the Poet Himself."

And Ellery sat down while the Poet clasped his hands above his head prize-ring fashion, and was applauded and cheered. Then, handling his leather-bound copy of the verses as if it were something out of the workshop of Benvenuto Cellini, John began to read.

He read well, with rhythm, texture and color, and what he was reading, Ellery thought, was very fine indeed. Being of the poet's own Fitzgeraldian generation, Ellery did not share Mr. Gardiner's view that the verses were brittle and merely clever; to him they sounded crisp and witty, with a delightful cynicism and a disregard of traditional form that might have been spawned among the young American expatriates of the French Riviera and the cafés of the Left Bank. He joined the applause at the conclusion with honest appreciation.

"The next entertainment is a Musical Interlude offered by that ineffable impresario of the ivories, that peerless pianistic prodigy, our consummate composer and violent virtuoso— Maestro Marius Carlo!"

Sergeant Devoe and Felton were enlisted as stagehands and dragged the piano through the archway from the music room. Marius bowed, flipped imaginary tails out of his way, and seated himself on the piano stool.

"In this era when every man is his own distiller," Marius began, flexing his fingers above the keyboard, "harvesting the materials of his domiciliary brew from his immediate environment—the farmhand from the bottom of his silo, the coal miner from his underground still, the Californian from his rotted cactus—it struck me that as a composer I might well do likewise.

"In short, in view of what Mr. Queen has referred to recently as the 'twelveness' of this holiday, I have been working on a composition, utilizing the Schönberg twelve-tone system, which is inspired by a dramatic entertainment from the pen of Bill Shakespeare entitled *Twelfth Night*, so-called not because it had anything to do with the plot but because it was meant to be acted at the Twelfth Night festivities of Elizabeth's court. Do I hear huzzas?"

He heard huzzas.

"The first movement is entitled *Shipwreck in Illyria*. Silence, please," And Marius elevated his hands, paused and then brought them down in a crash of sound so dissonant that Mabel, in the dining room doorway, uttered a yip of dismay, blushed crimson, and fled.

For twenty minutes the young composer wrenched and tore at the piano keys, accompanying his playing with a cheerful libretto that left his audience as mystified as they

142

were deafened. The applause at the end was violent with relief.

"Our next artist," Ellery announced when the piano had been rolled back to the music room, "is Miss Valentina Warren, who will favor us—I'm told—with two Thespian interpretations, but of what, deponent knoweth not. Miss Warren?"

Valentina was a surprise, at least at first. Ellery had expected something heavy—from Sophocles, say, a Jocastan speech to Oedipus, or an imitation of Blanche Yurka in *The Wild Duck.* Instead, Valentina asked them to transport themselves in imagination across the Hudson River to Hoboken and Christopher Morley's repertory theater, and launched into a hilarious monologue from the nineteenth century "drayma," *After Dark, or Neither Maid, Wife nor Widow.* Everyone hissed and hollered, including Ellery; but then, for an encore, the young actress unfortunately chose to become Nina Leeds, heroine of Eugene O'Neill's *Strange Interlude,* doing very badly a long scene in the stream-of-consciousness vein. If there was a false note in the applause that followed Valentina's bow, no one seemed to detect it but Ellery. Certainly Valentina did not.

Ellen Craig produced an easel, some sheets of drawing paper and a box of charcoal sticks, and amused the company by a series of quick caricatures of unexpected wickedness. (The one she did of Ellery was especially devastating— a vulturine face on a long snoopy neck that nevertheless managed to convey a likeness.)

Mr. Gardiner read bravely from the Song of Solomon, not neglecting to interpret it as an allegory of the union between Christ and His Church; Rusty Brown came onstage with a roll of wire and a pair of pliers and proceeded to contrive some delightful bird and animal "free forms," as she called them; and even Dr. Samson Dark performed, bringing down the house with an uncanny nasal imitation of Rudy Vallee singing the Maine "Stein Song."

"And now," Ellery said, as the doctor sat down swabbing his Falstaffian cheeks, "we come to the *pièce de résistance,* the epiphany of our entertainment, a guaranteed genuine séance conducted by the celebrated spiritist, our own Madam Olivette Brown."

Mr. Gardiner immediately rose, pleaded an indisposition, begged to be excused and left the room. But a moment later he came back, remarking grimly that on reconsideration one who had devoted his long lifetime to the world of the spirit might perhaps prove useful in dealing with Mrs. Brown's friends from the other side, if only to exorcise them. And the old clergyman reseated himself and folded his arms, ready for the Devil himself.

143

Olivette Brown paid no attention. She was too busy supervising the setting of her stage.

At last they were seated about the big round table Mrs. Brown had commandeered, in the all-but-darkness she had arranged for, hand gripping neighbor's hand, in silence; and the séance began.

At first there were suppressed giggles from the girls and a caustic murmur from Marius, but gradually these died away and an almost palpable stillness settled. As their eyes accommodated to the faint illumination, they could see Olivette Brown sitting stiffly erect and staring over their heads into the shadows of the room.

She sat that way for a very long time, so long and in such rigidity that they found themselves straining their ears. A singing tension invaded the area of the table.

And suddenly Rusty's mother fell back in her chair and began to moan. The sound was hair-raising after the silence, and hands tightened around the table.

The moaning died. She sat quiet now, slumped over, eyes wide, face a white mask in the glimmer.

And then she commenced to speak in a flatly dreamlike voice quite unlike the sharp nasality of her normal voice.

"I am in a great vaulted place, dark and yet not dark, bright and yet not bright, enclosing me and yet stretching infinitely in all directions ... It is like a place in a dream, but clearer, much clearer ..."

She went on and on in this vein, describing and not describing, so that they had an uneasy sense of what she was "seeing" without the least awareness of form or color or dimensions.

Suddenly she said, "He is coming, he . . . I see the gray shimmer of him . . . He is coming closer, closer." The flat tones sharpened and rose. "Someone I know, someone I recognize ... Death. He is dead, a spirit ... I know him, I know him ... Closer ... Who is he? Who are you, who are you?" Then she uttered a shriek that brought their hearts into their throats. *"John! It's John!"* and she fell forward on the table, striking her forehead with a sickening thump.

The séance shattered. Ellery leaped for the light switch and reached it simultaneously with Sergeant Devoe. When he turned around, Dr. Dark was easing Olivette Brown back in her chair and Rusty was patting her mother's waxy cheeks frantically.

"I don't know why I let her do this. She's always so upset afterward. Goodness knows I don't believe in any of it, but she seems to induce a kind of self-hypnosis . . . Mother. *Mother.*"

"Let me," Dr. Dark said. "Arthur, get that chair over here. I want to stretch her out and get her head lower than her feet. She's fainted, that's all. Though she'll have a lump

144

on her forehead . . . Will someone please open the windows wide? We'll need plenty of fresh air."

While the doctor was reviving Mrs. Brown, Ellery walked over to John, who was standing to one side by himself, a peculiar expression on his face.

"That climactic shriek of hers must have given you a turn, John. How does it feel to meet your shade before the event?"

John said coolly, "Interesting. A lot more interesting than you know."

"What do you mean?"

John shook his head, smiling. He was watching Rusty's mother closely.

The moment she opened her eyes, John stepped forward.

"Mother Brown, how did you know?"

"What?" she said faintly. "Oh, John. My head hurts. What happened?"

"You went into a trance, mother," Rusty said, "and you said something about seeing somebody come toward you, a ghost or something, a dead man, and then you called him John and fainted."

"I did?" her mother said. "John—dead? How silly." She felt her head. "I don't remember. I never remember anything afterward."

"How did you know?" John repeated.

"Oh, stop being so cryptic," Rusty said crossly. "How did mother know what?"

"Only one other person knows," John said to Mrs. Brown. "Someone, by the way, not present. The only one in this room who knows is myself. So again I ask you, Mother Brown: How did *you* know?"

She looked up at him blearily. "I wish my head would stop hurting. I can't seem to make sense out of anything you're saying."

"Stop it, John," Craig said sharply. "Mrs. Brown is in no condition to be badgered."

"Right, Arthur," John replied, still smiling. "I'm sorry, Mother Brown. Why don't you go upstairs and rest a while? As a matter of fact, it might be a good idea if we all did—freshen up, or lie down or something for an hour or so. We'll be up half the night tonight." At their puzzled looks, John grinned. "Why wait for daylight? At the witching hour I reverse Cinderella and turn into a prince, remember? So right after midnight, when I've just turned twenty-five, I'm going to ask Mr. Payn to do the formal reading of my father's will, converting me from a pumpkin to a royal coach, then Mr. Gardiner will marry Rusty and me for better or for worse—"

"You make it sound so romantic," Rusty sniffed.

He kissed her. "And finally, I'll unveil that big surprise I promised you."

"By George, I'd forgotten about that!" Craig said. Ellery thought, By George, so had I. "John, what the dickens have you been hiding up your sleeve?"

"You'll find out after the ceremony, Arthur, like the rest of 'em! Shall we get together down here at fifteen minutes to midnight?"

Ellery lingered in the living room after the others dispersed. He wandered about, poking in corners.

"You looking for that twelfth box, Mr. Queen?" It was Sergeant Devoe, watching him from the hall.

"In a vague sort of way, Sergeant. Everyone else seems to have forgotten about it."

"Not me. I've been on the lookout for it all night." The sergeant shook his head. "It's not down here."

"Parked in a bedroom again, I suppose."

But ten minutes later they were still waiting for someone to come running downstairs with a box.

"Suppose we've had it?" Sergeant Devoe grinned. "Though it doesn't seem right, somehow, him stopping at eleven."

Ellery did not return the grin. "It will pop up before midnight, Sergeant—I'm very much afraid." And he picked up his copy of John's book and went upstairs.

Ox.	Nail.	Water.	Head.
House.	Fence.	Fish.	Tooth.
Camel.	Hand.	Eye.	Mark (or Cross?).
Door.	Palm.	Mouth.	Post . . .
Window.	Whip.	Monkey.	

19 items in 11 packages or nights.

Ellery kept patrolling his bedroom, smoking furiously.

There would be one more tonight to complete the series of 12. That meant at least another item. A minimum of 20, then.

His thoughts kept coming back to the number 20.

Was that the clue? 20? 20 . . .

He went back to the little writing table where he had listed the 19 articles. Ox . . . House . . . Camel . . . But he shook his head. He had been over the list a hundred times, searching for a common denominator. The longer he searched the surer he was that a connection existed. And the less attainable it seemed.

20 . . .

The number teased him. There was something about the number 20 he had forgotten . . . had once known . . . read somewhere . . . Twenty Questions—the game! No, no. To interpret a series of 20 things in terms of a guessing game characterized it but advanced nothing. It couldn't be that. 20 . . .

Then he remembered.

146

The grouping of numbers by fives came from the five fingers of each of man's hands and the five toes of each of his feet. The three major scales of the quinary system were therefore the scale of five, the scale of ten, and the scale of 20. Grouping of objects by 20's still survived in the English *score* and the French notation system—*quatre-vingts*, meaning 80, was literally "four 20's." In tropical countries the scale of 20 in counting was once in considerable vogue, because in a hot climate men went about barefooted and so had not only their fingers but their toes always before them. Some native Mexicans still counted to "man finished" and then began over again. One purported evidence that Greenlanders might have had a tropical origin was that their system of counting was based on the scale of 20.

20 . . . and 12. The notational system?

Ellery stared droopily at his list. It was all true, all interesting, and all irrelevant. He could see no remotest application to the objects John had been receiving.

He rapped the dottle out of his pipe and dropped dispiritedly into a chair. Brain-weary, he reached for the gift edition of John's book of verses and opened it.

And sat up with a convulsion of joy, as if he had been granted divine revelation.

He had chanced to open to the title page. And there it was . . . there it was, darting from the page through his eyes to a forgotten treasury of his brain, opening it with the speed of light.

Avidly Ellery examined the memory, prodded it, probed, dissected, his scalpel exposing it in all its beautiful simplicity. He felt humiliation. Why hadn't he seen it long ago? There was nothing esoteric or fantastic about it.

That's my trouble, he conceded. I always ignore the obvious in favor of the abstruse.

It was so clear. Ox, house, camel, door . . . All 20. Yes, 20 was the number. He had been right about that intuitively.

As he mulled the memory over, it suddenly came to Ellery that a knowledge of the still unreceived twentieth object was his for the digging. He ran his mental eye down the list.

And his heart skipped, and he went cold.

The twelfth gift, the twentieth item, had to be . . .

He dropped the gift book, glanced wildly about, then dashed from the room.

Sergeant Devoe was loitering on the landing.

"What's up, Mr. Queen?"

"John's bedroom!"

The sergeant, for all his bulk, managed to reach the door of John's room at the same moment as Ellery. Devoe's shoulder crashed against it and it burst open.

Doors opened all along the hall. People came running.

147

The Food of Love

BY
JOHN SEBASTIAN

"If music be the food of love, play on . . ."
— TWELFTH NIGHT

THE ABC PRESS
NEW YORK 1930

Ellery went slowly into John's room. Sergeant Devoe straddled the doorway, swallowing hard.

Rusty screamed, once.

John's back was to the doorway. He was in his shirt-sleeves in a chair at his writing desk, head resting on the desk top,

148

left arm outstretched alongside, bandaged right hand dangling.

The back of his white shirt, just under the shoulder blades left of center, sported a bright red flower whose petals had run slightly.

From the middle of the flower protruded the handle of a knife.

"Sergeant. Let Dr. Dark come in."

The stout doctor stepped into the bedroom, all color drained from his heavy face.

"Try not to get your fingerprints on the desk or his clothes, Doctor."

After a time Dr. Dark straightened. He seemed confused and frightened. "John is dead."

"Please go back now. Sergeant, phone Lieutenant Luria. I'll remain here. No, Mr. Craig, *no*. You can do more by staying with Rusty. It might be easier on everyone, in fact, if I keep the door shut till the lieutenant gets here."

In the corridor, Mr. Gardiner was praying.

Alone with the body, Ellery tried to adjust his thoughts.

Just too late, probably.

He placed the back of his hand against John's neck, cheek, ear. Still warm. As in life. Except for the knife sticking out of his back, John might have been asleep.

If only I'd seen the meaning of the gifts, five, ten, fifteen minutes earlier, Ellery thought.

Then, for the first time, he noticed the card. John's face was lying on it, as if he had been reading it at the moment the knife sank into his back. Ellery wrapped a handkerchief around his fingers, grasped the edge of the card and pulled. He pulled only until the typing lay exposed. He did not pick the card up.

It was exactly like the 11 that had preceded it—white and oblong and with a message in verse:

```
On the twelfth night of Christmas
Your true love sends to you,
This fatal d a g g e r  —  this jeweled
    knife —
This finishing stroke to end your life.
```

Dagger. That was the twentieth object. As he should have foreseen.

So much was clear now. "Finishing stroke" ... Yes. Yes, that followed.

The trouble was, Ellery reflected wryly, it followed too clearly.

It followed so clearly that a man would have to be an imbecile to accept it at its face value.

Chapter XV ✠ ... Into Epiphany: January 6, 1930 ...

In Which Young Mr. Queen Declines the Gambit, the Dead Becomes Quick, Much Is Answered, but More Remains Shrouded in Mystery

WHEN SERGEANT DEVOE returned to the bedroom Ellery left him with the corpse and hurried downstairs.

They were all in the living room but Mr. Gardiner, Rusty Brown and her mother.

"I've given Rusty a sedative and she's lying down in her room," Dr. Dark muttered. "Mrs. Brown and the Reverend are with her."

Ellery nodded. All faces were dazed.

"The knife," he said. "I suppose you all got a glimpse of it. It's an antique dagger of some sort with a handle set in semi-precious stones. Looks old. Does it come from the house here, Mr. Craig?"

Craig shook his head. He looked old, too. He was erect in a chair away from the others, his lips clamped tight above the beard as if he were holding himself in by main strength.

"Doesn't anyone recognize it?"

No one replied.

Ellery shrugged. "Well, that's Luria's job. The point that concerns us is that it was the last gift." And he repeated the verse on the card. "Number twenty, completing the series."

And Ellery was silent. For why should he tell them that he knew now what the gifts meant? He could not follow through. He could not say to them that the clues in the verses, their significance as a group—the whole pattern of the case—added up to a meaning so specific it could point the finger of guilt at only one of them. He could not acknowledge the lack of alternative. He could not say, "It condemns that person and hangs him."

For to accept the one and only conclusion was to make of

the person indicated a complete idiot. And that was impossible, Ellery told himself morosely, the nature of the crime being such that only a very bright mind could have conceived it. The two didn't mix. Would someone capable of laying down such a clever trail have done it for the sole purpose of making the trail lead directly to himself? Because that was precisely where the clues went.

Inconceivable. So he had to be silent.

There had been three victims in the case from the beginning, Ellery saw—John, and the person indicated by the clues, and himself. John's death had always been the desideratum. The role assigned to Ellery had been to follow the clues like an obedient hound, to allow himself to be led by the nose up the garden path in order that he might arrive at the apparently incontrovertible conclusion. *He was to have pinned John's death on the wrong one.*

The whole elaborate structure of the mysterious Christmas boxes, their contents, the versified clues had only one purpose: to frame an innocent person for John's murder. The frame-up was clever on another count. Ellery had reason to believe that that innocent person had, theoretically, a powerful motive for such a murder. With the clues pointing in his direction, and a made-to-order motive, the murder frame-up was overwhelming.

No, Ellery told himself, he could only refuse to play the framer's game . . . to decline the role assigned him. The person indicated by the gift-clues was not the one who had plunged the dagger into John's back. The person who in actuality had gathered the gifts, composed the verses, and left the Christmas packages, was. Perhaps, in keeping silent, Ellery thought, he would force the framer's hand . . .

Lieutenant Luria and a detail of specialists arrived, dispelling the general apathy. The lieutenant said very little; the expression on his face spoke for him. He went directly upstairs.

Luria was savage. He insisted on clearing the upper floor, so that the two Browns and Mr. Gardiner were forced to vacate Rusty's room. Then the coroner's physician, Dr. Tennant, came, delaying the trooper further. They were compelled to wait in the living room—the fuzzy-minded, the grief-laden, the guilt-ridden all bound together by a common misery. Freeman, the publisher, and Payn, the lawyer, looked positively ill. Ellery knew what was going through their heads. If Lieutenant Luria should find out what John had been trying to do to them . . .

The three servants were herded into the room, where they quarantined themselves in a far corner.

Ellery himself lost track of time. He crouched in a chair as the others were crouching, nibbling at his nails and wondering what was going on upstairs.

The wait was endless.

Some time during infinity a cheerful voice said from the archway, "Quarter to twelve on the dot. What are all those cars doing outside? Hi, everybody."

A curious thing happened.

Fourteen bodies jerked as one. Fourteen heads swiveled as if pulled by the same string. Fourteen pairs of eyes widened in horrified disbelief.

Rusty struggled to her feet. She tried to speak, pawed at her throat.

Her mother screeched, "His ghost! His ghost!"

Then all six women toppled over in a faint.

The tall figure in the archway had a bandage on his right hand.

It was John.

It was John.

It was John, and he walked into the living room quite as a living man does. If he was a ghost, it was a puzzled one. He hurried to Rusty and picked her up and placed her on a settee and began to chafe her hands, looking around uneasily as he did so, as if he had wandered into a strange dimension in space-time, where even familiar things were distorted.

"What's the matter?" John asked oddly. "Why are you all looking at me this way?"

"John." His guardian wet his lips. "John?"

"I don't understand," John said. "I've been out walking in the woods, taking stock of myself before the big leap. I said I'd be here at eleven forty-five, and here I am. Who made that unfunny crack about a ghost? Anyone would think I was dead, or something."

"You are," Marius Carlo snarled.

"What?"

"I mean you were. I mean—"

"Who are you?" Craig's beard was wobbling.

"What's come over you people?" John cried. "Is this supposed to be a last-minute rib, Arthur? What kind of question is that?—who am I!"

"Are you John, or . . . who?"

"I'm Little Boy Blue," John said angrily. "Now how about pitching in with these women? Or are they all putting on an act, too? Rusty, snap out of it. Wake up!" He began slapping her.

"*By God.*" It was Lieutenant Luria, in the archway. His rugged face was bloodless. He was utterly unnerved.

"Wait," Ellery said. "Wait." He had never been so shaken in his life. But now that the first shock was over, some vestiges of sense began to ooze up in his brain. It was certainly John—the same body, the same face, the same Byronic curl, the same voice, the same clothes, the same

152

bandage on the same hand. *And this was what he had been searching for—a duplicate John.* He made himself cling to the thought. "If you're John ... who's that upstairs in your room?"

A light sprang into John's dark eyes. "In my room."

"Yes, in your room," Lieutenant Luria croaked. "There's a dead man up there who couldn't look more like you if it was you lying in his place. Who is he, Sebastian?"

The light had gone out. "Dead man?" John repeated. *"Dead?"*

"With a knife in his back."

John put his hands to his face and began to cry.

Later, when they took him upstairs and confronted him with the body, even John's sobbing collapse and the changes wrought on the corpse by violent death could not materially alter the astounding resemblance between the two. All Ellery could think of in the confusion was a scrap of speech from the mouth of some character in *Twefth Night:* "One face, one voice, one habit, and two persons ... An apple, cleft in two, is not more twin ..."

It explained many things that had mystified him, certainly. But then it was an explanation that he had long ago worked out in theory—identical twins. Nevertheless, despite the corroboration before his eyes, Ellery still labored to understand. The twin ... the twin had died twenty-five years ago at the age of two weeks. Had Sergeant Velie's information been wrong? Ellery could not believe it. The infant's death was too well documented and attested. No, the twin had been buried for a quarter of a century. And yet, here he was—a corpse, it was true, but a fresh corpse, in the cooling flesh of a twenty-five-year-old man. An impossibility. Therefore the dead man, exact resemblance notwithstanding, was not John's twin.

But if he was not John's twin, who could he be?

The answer flashed into Ellery's brain simultaneously with the question. The instant it came to him he was berating himself for his stupidity, it was so obvious.

He was John's triplet.

"My mother gave birth to triplet boys that night," John said wearily when sanity had been re-established and they were all back in the living room. "I came first. During the second one's birth my mother died, and that was the brother who died two weeks later and was buried in Mount Kidron Cemetery. The third one Dr. Hall had to take from my mother's dead body." John's head jerked ceilingward. "That was the brother ... upstairs."

"But what I want to know—" Luria began.

"Let me tell this my own way, Lieutenant," John said. "You can ask your questions later.

153

"I'd better explain first how it happened that nobody knew of the third brother's existence. Dr. Hall and his wife couldn't have children. They wanted one desperately. Then my father wrecked his car outside their house, injuring my mother and bringing her to premature labor, and fate gave the Halls a once-in-a-lifetime opportunity.

"They were bitter over their economic struggles and barrenness, and here was a rich woman having a multiple birth. My father stayed in the parlor and at no time entered the bedroom. Then mother died during the second delivery and Dr. Hall took the third baby from her dead body. It didn't seem fair to the Halls—three motherless children belonging to a man who'd have to hire strangers to bring them up, and here *they* were, wanting a child, not having the means to get one . . . and being the only people in the world with the knowledge that a third baby had just been born. The Halls discussed it in whispers over my mother's body and couldn't decide whether to tell my father about the third one or not."

John scowled. "When Dr. Hall went out to father to tell him his wife had died giving birth to the second child, the decision was taken out of his hands. To the doctor's amazement, my father refused to accept the *second* baby, saying he wanted nothing to do with it. He was so conscience-stricken over having caused my mother's death by his pig-headedness that he unconsciously transferred his guilt to the baby she happened to be having when she died. Dr. Hall crossed the bridge; he said nothing about the third one, and he asked for the second one too. My father agreed, said he'd see that it was provided for, and left."

"Oh, John," Rusty murmured; but Ellery noticed that she was sitting a little apart from him, as if she still could not reconcile his living proximity with the dead replica upstairs.

"The Halls were both scared and elated. In saying nothing about the third baby and keeping it Dr. Hall could have had his medical license taken away, and both he and his wife could have gone to prison. But they did have the two babies, one of them with my father's consent. It was a tangle they didn't quite know how to straighten out. Then, a week later, Dr. Hall read of my father's death. He investigated and found out that father had died without providing for the second son as he had promised, or taking any of the legal steps Dr. Hall had requested in his own and the baby's protection. The doctor decided to risk registering all three births at the Mount Kidron city hall, in case it should ever be necessary to document the births and establish the other two children's paternity and legal co-heirship with the known child. Within another week, to complicate things further, the second child died of pneumonia. The Halls had him buried in Mount Kidron and moved out to Idaho with the third child, being careful to leave no clue to where they were going. At no time did they let anyone in Mount Kidron know of my brother's existence—even the doctor Dr. Hall called in during the second baby's pneumonia and death didn't know about him. Mrs. Hall kept him hidden, and when they moved to Idaho they actually smuggled him out of town in a basket of laundry."

John got up and poured himself a long drink of whisky. He tossed it down and made no attempt to return to the seat beside Rusty, as if he had felt and was hurt by her withdrawal.

"So they brought John up out West, and until he was fourteen he thought he was their son—"

"John?" Ellery said. "Why do you call him John?"

"Because that's his name. Was, I mean. Before they left Mount Kidron, in talking between themselves about the triplets, the Halls got to calling them by numbers—One, Two, Three. I was One to them, the baby that died was Two and ... the brother upstairs was Three. In fact, when Dr. Hall registered the births, that's the way he did it—Son One, Son Two, Son Three. Then when Two died, and they had to give Three a name, Dr. Hall found out that I'd been named John, after my father. He decided to call my brother John III, with some vague idea that if he had the same Christian name as I it would be another tie to the Sebastian estate. So he's—he was John III, and I suppose that makes me John I."

John went over to the fireplace and stared into the flames. "He showed up at my flat in the Village back in September. I was absolutely floored. I'd never had the slightest inkling that I had a triplet brother in existence."

Arthur Craig said feebly, "This is—this is astounding."

"You can imagine how I felt, Arthur. His fantastic resemblance to me alone confirmed his story, but he had documentary proof with him, too—originals of the three birth certificates, which I'll produce for you, Lieutenant; a sworn statement by Dr. Hall, and one by Mrs. Hall drawn up before she died in 1921; and certain other papers that made the possibility of a swindle out of the question. Naturally, I accepted him with open arms. You know, Ellen, how I grew up wishing I'd had a brother. I could have used one!"

"Yes," Ellen murmured. "You certainly could."

"Well, John told me the whole story, and how when the Halls told him the truth about himself they kept pounding away that he was as much entitled to my father's estate as I was, and that when I came into it—Dr. Hall had made it his business to find out the terms of father's will—their John was to show up and demand his share. John grew up with that as his objective. He'd had to lead a pretty hard life, because the Halls were always poor—either Hall wasn't a very good doctor or he didn't have a bedside manner or something; anyway, he only just managed to scrabble along

—and John III had to educate himself and work like a hound-dog to make out. You can imagine what a heel I felt when I learned all this. I'd led the life of Riley. I assured my brother he'd get his half of the estate without any fuss or mess."

"Of course, of course," Craig groaned. "But why didn't you tell me any of this, John?"

"I was going to, Arthur. But then I thought what a lark it would be if my brother and I kept it a secret for a few months. You remember how long ago we started planning this party—back in early November; and it struck me what a topper it would make on January sixth, when I came into the estate and had my poems published and married Rusty, if I were to spring John III on all of you."

John turned away again. "Well, John thought it was a rare idea, so we went out and bought him a duplicate of every article of clothing I own, I briefed him on everyone I knew, and for months in New York he lived with me secretly and we changed places with each other, trying the stunt out. It worked like a charm. He even took my place with you on a date one night, Rusty, as the acid test. We figured if we could fool you, we'd fool anybody."

"How right you were," Rusty said in a calm voice. "And how completely I was taken in ... I wonder which night it was."

"And me?" Craig asked heavily. "You fooled me, too, John? I mean, passed your brother off—"

"Well, sure, Arthur. I wanted to surprise you, too. Remember the Thanksgiving weekend? He was up here with me then. I don't know why you're both looking at me this way," John snapped. "All right, maybe it does sound infantile now, but it seemed like fun at the time. Anyway, I brought the duplicate wardrobe up here, smuggled John III in when I came up for Christmas—"

"And started having your fun," Ellery said. "Such as the Santa Claus bit on Christmas morning?"

John smiled faintly. "That's right. That was John III, in a costume we bought in New York. The idea was to mystify everybody and sort of keep the party jazzed up. John hid in my room throughout; I smuggled food up to him, or he raided the fridge late at night. We slept in that oversize bed of mine, and all he had to do if anyone was coming was duck into one of those big closets. We were careful to dress exactly alike, and to be at different places at any given time. That's why you never found him during a search. Actually, you 'found' John III a dozen times these past twelve days, only you thought he was I. We had a real wingding."

"Er, John." Dan Freeman coughed. "A week ago Monday one of you had a talk with me here in the living room, a talk of a rather personal nature. Was that you?"

156

John shook his head. "It must have been my brother. Sometimes the spirit of the thing got the better of him and he'd start cutting up on his own. Why, Mr. Freeman? What was it about?"

The publisher murmured, "Nothing, nothing important John," and sank back.

"And, John," Roland Payn asked. "Last Thursday I, ah, had a similarly personal conversation in my bedroom with . . . was that your brother, too?"

"It must have been."

"He didn't mention anything about it to you?"

"No, Mr. Payn."

And Payn sank back and reached for his drink with a shaking hand.

"That brawl in the summerhouse," Marius Carlo said suddenly. "That's why you—or he—didn't remember anything about it. It was the other one!" He gulped down half a Scotch and soda.

"That one was fixed," John smiled. "We were in that together."

"And the talk I had in the stable—?" Val Warren's nostrils fluttered. "I don't even want to know which one of you *that* was. Of all the detestable tricks!"

Rusty said coldly, "I agree with you, Val."

"All right, all right," John said. "It was all a mistake. I know it now."

"And that business of the nightly Christmas packages and verses," Ellery murmured. "Was that part of your little game of musical chairs, too, John?"

"Good God, no," John said irritably. "Neither of us had anything to do with *that*. We kicked that one around night after night, in bed. I still don't know what it was all about."

"Except that it wound up with your brother's getting the last present in his back," Lieutenant Luria said.

They all started, including John. They had forgotten Luria was there.

"Yes," John muttered. "Some joke."

"You don't know who stabbed him?"

"No, Lieutenant. I wish I did."

"Now, tell me this." Luria came forward a step. "That old man found on the library floor, also stabbed in the back— which one of you smuggled *him* into the house? You or your brother?"

"What do you mean?" John stammered. "I don't know anything about him. I've told you that a dozen times."

"I know what you told me. But I'm asking you *now*, Sebastian. You didn't smuggle him into the house?"

"No!"

"You don't know how he got in here?"

"Certainly not!"

157

"You don't even know who he was?"

"Not a glimmer!"

"Well, maybe I can help you out. We just got the confirmation this evening; I was about to leave for here when Devoe's call came. Would you like to know that little guy's name?"

John was all ruddy. "See here, Lieutenant, I'm not in the mood for any more games. Certainly I'd like to know his name! Who was he?"

"Dr. Cornelius F. Hall."

"It was my brother who must have sneaked him into the house," John I whispered. "No one else here knew Hall. And he didn't tell me! He didn't let on once. Now I know why he looked so green around the gills after I let him take my place down here that day so he could have a look at the old man's body. Why didn't he tell me? He must have been scared . . ."

"Or guilty," Luria said dryly. "If nobody else here knew Hall, then nobody else would have any reason to plant a shiv in Hall's back, would he? That all adds up to your brother as Hall's killer. What's your opinion?"

"I don't know," John said dazedly. "It doesn't seem possible. What reason could he have had? He always spoke of Dr. Hall in the most affectionate way."

"Yes," Luria said. "And then again maybe old Hall decided he'd like a cut of your brother's share—or maybe that was their idea all along—and your bother welshed and knocked him off. Seem likely to you, Sebastian?"

"I don't *know*," John said again. "That would make him out some kind of monster. I can't believe it."

"Lieutenant," Ellery said.

"Yes, Queen?"

"If John III murdered Dr. Hall, who murdered John III?"

"Now there," Lieutenant Luria said, "there's where you've got me, pal. I'm just an ordinary dick trying to make sense out of a madhouse. Nothing adds up! Nothing!" He turned away, to whirl suddenly. "And another thing, Sebastian. You say you and your brother were having yourselves a high old time around here, driving everybody nuts, and then a mysterious old bird nobody seemed to know got himself carved up on the library rug . . . and you two *still* kept playing games? You expect me to believe two innocent men wouldn't have dropped that kindergarten stuff then and there?"

"We talked about dropping it, Lieutenant," John said feebly. "We discussed just that. But my brother seemed to feel we ought to follow through, at least till we found out what the score was . . . the nightly boxes, the murder . . ."

"Your brother," Luria said. "Funny how every time one of you did something nasty or suspicious, it turns out it was your brother. To hear *you* tell it."

158

"I resent that, Luria!" John shouted. "Next thing I know you'll be accusing me of killing my brother!"

"That's not such a screwy notion," the lieutenant said, unmoved. "Why not? You could have been putting on an act for little old John III when you found out he was cutting himself in for half of your father's millions—according to your own account, putting on acts is a talent you have. So you string him along, get him up here on the hokey excuse of doing a double act for the benefit of the guests, and when you're good and ready you let him have it."

"Why would I do that?" John yelled. "If I'd wanted to kill my brother, I'd have lured him up some dark alley in New York or pushed him off a dock somewhere. The last thing I'd have done was bring him to this house!"

"What's your answer to that, Lieutenant?" Ellery asked amiably.

Luria threw up his hands.

"As a matter of fact," John went on, in a sort of fever, "it just struck me ... Why would *anyone* here murder my brother? Nobody in this house knew he existed. Don't you see?" John cried. "*I'm* the one these gifts and verses have been aimed at—I'm the one who's been threatened since this holiday began. Whoever sneaked into my room tonight saw my brother sitting there looking just like me, dressed in clothes exactly like mine, and stuck that dagger into what he thought was *my* back!"

Lieutenant Luria was startled. He glanced at Ellery.

"Now that," Ellery ruminated, "that makes sense to me, Lieutenant. I think John's hit a vital point. But it also suggests a curious possibility."

"What's that?"

Ellery turned to John Sebastian. "You say you're John—the John that Mr. Craig raised, the John that Rusty fell in love with, the John who wrote the poetry Mr. Freeman is publishing, the John we've all known—John I."

"Yes?"

"And you say the dead man upstairs is your triplet—the brother raised by Dr. Hall in Idaho, who came to New York a few months ago and revealed himself to you—John III."

"So what?"

"So what I'd like to know," Ellery asked good-humoredly, "is the following: Why can't it be just the other way around?"

John looked puzzled. "What?"

"So far I've seen and heard nothing from you to prove you're John I except your unsupported allegation that it's so. I therefore ask you: How do we know the dead man isn't John I? *How do we know you're not John III?*"

Mouths were open all about the room.

John shut his mouth long enough to gasp, "You're balmy!"

159

"I've thought often in this case that that might help," Ellery nodded. "But in the absence of corroborative evidence it makes an interesting speculation, John, delusional or not, don't you think? You see the kind of game you and your brother started.

"Because if in fact you are John III, then you did have a motive to kill the brother upstairs, a strongly understandable one. You've told us yourself how bitter John III has been all these years over having been deprived of the goodies left by your father. Such a mood might well have nourished the conviction that, since the accepted brother had had the exclusive enjoyment of the father's property for twenty-five years, it was now as a matter of simple equity the deprived one's turn to enjoy it exclusively . . . not to divide the principal of the estate with his brother, you see, but to take it all for himself. And so John III murders John I . . . and thereafter claims to *be* John I, who wasn't bitter at all."

And Ellery asked in a sort of sadness, "Can you tell us anything, John, that would indicate what I have just said to be the vaporings of a disordered mind?"

Chapter XVI ✚ . . . And Thereafter

In Which There Is Much Ado About Nothing Trivial,
Love's Labor Is Lost, and All Is Not Well
in the Tragedy of Errors

JOHN SPUTTERED, "Well, but of course I can prove I'm me —I! Of all the nincompooperies . . ." He glanced about wildly, caught sight of his own right hand, and held it up in triumph. "Here! This will prove it beyond the shadow of a ghost of a doubt. I sprained my wrist Friday, didn't I? Who's got a scissors? Dr. Sam, take these bandages off!"

Dr. Dark rose and in silence removed the bandages, John glaring all the while at Ellery with resentful pride, like an offended racehorse. And there it was—an iodine-painted, badly swollen wrist.

"Is that the wrist you treated, Dr. Sam?" John demanded.

"It certainly is," Dr. Dark glanced at Ellery and added hastily, "I mean, it certainly looks like the same one."

"Oh, for God's sake," John groaned. "Look, this *is* a sprained wrist, isn't it?"

"I would say so . . ."

"And *I* sprained my wrist Friday! Lieutenant, you take a look at my brother's wrist, I mean under the bandage. You'll find the dressing is a fake. His right wrist is perfectly all right."

"That's a little something I was saving," Lieutenant Luria muttered. "Dr. Tennant's removed the bandage. No sign of a recent sprain, he says—no swelling, and there's no iodine on it, like on yours."

"There you are." John's look at Ellery was killing. "Satisfied?"

"Well, no," Ellery said. "And I'll tell you why, John. You say you're John I—right?"

"Right!"

"And you say that you, John I, were the one who went galloping in the snow Friday, fell and sprained your wrist—right?"

"Right-*o!*"

"And now you produce a sprained wrist, while the wrist of your brother upstairs shows no sprain—still correct?"

"To the fourth decimal point!"

"Well, what have you proved? The thing to be proved—that you're John I—still remains a matter of your statement to that effect. Don't you see that the question is, not which one of you sprained his wrist, but whether the man who did is John I or John III? All you've actually proved is that you were the brother who was thrown from the horse. We still don't know who *you* are."

John sat down abruptly. But then he looked up. "Fingerprints. Fingerprints don't lie! Dr. Sam, my brother and I wouldn't have the same prints, would we?"

"No. The fingerprints of identical twins or triplets are similar, but there are readily detectable differences."

"All right," John snapped. "Take my prints, take his prints and—"

"And what?" Ellery asked sadly, "Compare them? Very well, they'd show distinctive characteristics. But the question would remain. Which set of prints belonged to John I and which to John III?"

"But in my rooms in New York—" John faltered "—my room upstairs . . ."

"Would show prints of both," Ellery nodded, "with no way of telling which was whose, because you've told us you and your brother lived together for months in the New York flat, and you've both certainly been handling the same things in this house since you arrived for the holiday. Were you ever arrested on a criminal charge?"

"Certainly not," John said indignantly.

"Was your brother?"

"Not that I know of."

"Ever had your fingerprints taken by a government agency? By anyone, for that matter? For any reason?"

"No."

161

"Had your brother?"

John mumbled. "He never mentioned—"

"Those documents you say your brother brought with him, birth certificates and so on—does any of them show a set of prints—infant handprints, for example, or footprints?"

John shook his head.

Dr. Dark shook his in unison. "They didn't take prints of newborn babies in 1905, Mr. Queen."

Ellery sighed. "Then fingerprints aren't going to get us anywhere. If we could only strike a frame of reference ... Operations! Ever undergo surgery, John?

"No."

"Yes!" Dr. Dark said. "I took out John's tonsils myself— I mean our John's—when he was five! Lieutenant, do you mind—?"

"If you can tell me which is which, Doctor," Luria said wearily, "you have my permission to turn him inside out."

Dr. Dark hastened to John, unclipping a pencil flashlight from his vest. "Open your mouth and stick your tongue out." He depressed John's tongue with the flash, and relief broadened his face. "No tonsils. This is our John, all right!"

"Thank God," Arthur Craig said, wiping his face.

"Time," Ellery said.

"Now what?" John shouted.

"Lieutenant, is the coroner's physician still working upstairs?"

"He's through, but he hasn't left yet."

"Ask him if the corpse has his tonsils."

Luria said something distinctly not nice and dashed out. He was back in three minutes.

"No tonsils, either."

The general nail-biting resumed.

"Are there any operation scars or birthmarks and so on on the body, Lieutenant—does Tennant say?"

"None he could spot on superficial examination."

"Any such marks on you, John?"

John muttered, "No such luck."

"Back where we started from." Ellery mused deeply. "Of course! Teeth. Your dentist—I mean John I's dentist in the East here and/or John III's back in Idaho—can clear this up in five minutes."

"No dental work," John said hollowly, "aside from a prophylaxis once in a while. Unless my brother—"

"No dental work, either," the lieutenant said, just as hollowly. "Tennant looked him in the mouth."

"It figures," Dr. Dark said with a scowl. "My John has had exceptionally strong and healthy teeth from babyhood. It's not surprising that his triplet has, too, because tooth structure in identical multiples is similar."

162

"And blood type," Ellery muttered, "would be identical, too, I suppose."

"Yes."

"Bone structure, skull measurements?"

"So similar that even if a record clearly ascribable to John III exists in Idaho or elsewhere, you still couldn't be sure which is which. On this end, as far as I know, my John's never even had occasion to be X-rayed."

There was a silence. It was broken, surprisingly, by Dan Z. Freeman.

"If I may offer a suggestion ... Next to fingerprints, one of the most obvious ways of differentiating identical individuals would be by handwriting. Isn't it true, Doctor, that the influence of entirely different environments would cause marked chirographic differences?"

"I would think so, Mr. Freeman, though we don't know much about the effect of different environments on identicals."

"Well, then, why not compare handwritings? Plenty of authentic specimens of each brother's handscript must exist from before the time they met," the publisher said. "All this John has to do—"

"Is write with a sprained wrist, as he wrote in that unrecognizable scrawl in those books?" Ellery shook his head. "With one brother unable to write because of rigor mortis and the other because of rigor vitae, so to speak, a handwriting comparison test isn't likely to yield a satisfactory result, at least not for some time. And a determination tonight is what I'm yearning for. For a lot of reasons, the chief one of which is named Rusty Brown."

"It's just as well this way, Ellery," Rusty said. "The way I feel now—"

"Yes?" John flashed at her. "What about the way you feel now, Rusty? I suppose you don't believe me, either!"

"The Sebastian boys set out to make a fool of me once and succeeded—remember your saying that so proudly a while ago?" Rusty flared back. "I neither believe nor disbelieve. I just don't *know*. Until I do—"

John said through his teeth, "You mean you've changed your mind? You're calling off the wedding?"

"I didn't *say* that. And I'm *not* going to discuss such personal matters in front of a roomful of people. Anyway, I'm all at sea. I don't know what to think. Let me alone!" And Rusty burst into tears and rushed from the room.

"Let her alone!" Olivette Brown screamed, and she followed.

"You ... stand-in!" Val Warren screamed, and *sh*e followed.

Mr. Gardiner followed, too, but without saying anything.

Lieutenant Luria glared at each in passing with a frightful

impotence. Ellery tapped him on the shoulder. "Simmer down, Lieutenant. You're hung up till the sprained wrist recovers, and there's nothing you can do about it." And he glanced over at John, who was icily pouring himself a huge whisky. "It's going to be interesting to see how fast it does recover, John. If you're Number One Boy, as you claim, it will be the fastest sprain recovery on record. But if you're John III in John I's clothing, it wouldn't surprise me if you suddenly had a rash of accidents, each of which somehow managed to immobilize your right hand."

"You and I, Mr. Queen," John said, "are *fini, kaput*. I hereby give you notice that I have severed diplomatic relations. Go peddle your brain-teasers elsewhere. Here's mud in your eye, and I hope it's permanent!" And he downed six ounces of whisky without winking.

Ellery looked philosophical. "However, Lieutenant, sooner or later the identity mixup will be settled. And then—"

"I know," Luria said, "then my troubles just start. You know what I think about this case, Queen?"

Ellery glanced over at Ellen, sitting stiff as an embalmer near her uncle. "Can you say it in front of a lady?"

Luria roared, "*Goddamittohellno!*" and stamped out.

They were detained in the Craig house for another thirty-six hours. Teams of police took turns questioning them, over and over, until harried suspects and questioners alike were brown-brained with fag. Luria drove them all, including himself, remorselessly. But in the end, looking hangdog, the lieutenant had to let them all go.

Ellen said her farewells to Ellery as he sat, empty-souled, behind the wheel of the Duesenberg in the Craig driveway. He had offered to drive her back to Wellesley, but she had declined the offer.

"I'm sorry it's been such a washout, Ellery," Ellen remarked.

"I know just what you mean."

Whereupon Ellen smiled like Mona Lisa and said, "Do you?"

Ellery was halfway to Manhattan before he figured out what Ellen had been talking about.

As it developed, no one had to wait for the surviving brother's wrist to heal in order to determine his numerical identity. In a case as queer as the average Scotch label, the dilemma was dehorned by two barbers 2000 miles apart. The one-eyed barber of Missoula, Montana, site of Montana State University, spoke with authority on the subject of John III; and the mustachioed barber with the eleven children, who ran the five-steps-down tonsorial parlor on MacDougal Street in Greenwich Village, New York, rendered like testimony *in re* John I.

The initial credit was ascribed to the survivor himself (Ellery read all this in his daily newspaper, like anyone else) in unconscious collaboration was a pretty trained nurse named Winifred ("Winnie") Winkle who happened to be on duty in the Emergency Room of the Upper Westchester Hospital in Guildenstern, New York, when the patient was carried in.

What happened was that the living John Sebastian—after the red-eyed departure of John (I) Sebastian's fiancée, Rusty Brown, from the Craig premises—retired to his room (the body of his brother having been removed to the morgue), clutching a full quart of Maryland Panther Whisky (which had somehow got mixed up with Arthur Benjamin Craig's impeccable liquor supply), worked up a full charge, and in attempting (as he was to explain afterward to Lieutenant Luria in the hospital) to duplicate the New Year's Eve feat in Cleveland of the Fokker trimotor which had set a new speed record for commercial airplanes of 203 m.p.h., did misadventurously fly down an entire flight of stairs, making a one-point landing (on his head) at the junction of the newel post and the hallway floor.

On-the-spot first aid having been administered by Sergeant Stanley ("Zbyszko") Devoe and Mr. Arthur Craig, the Alderwood Icarus was rushed to Upper Westchester Hospital, nine miles from Alderwood, where he arrived looking more like a freshly butchered steer (in Sergeant Devoe's phrase to newsmen later) than a human being. An intern made the first medical examination, determined that the cause of bleeding was a severe gash in the scalp, and ordered Nurse Winkle to shave off the patient's hair in the area of the wound while he prepared sutures. By this time Dr. Samson Dark of Alderwood had arrived and, independently, Lieutenant Luria. It was while Dr. Dark was taking over from the intern that Lieutenant Luria heard Nurse Winkle make the sprightly remark, "Oooh, he's not going to like it, having this ugly birthmark show!"

The rest is history. The patient, on recovering consciousness with nothing worse than a split-head hangover and some aching bones, and being informed by Lieutenant Luria of the birthmark on his head, swore with what energy he could muster that he had never been aware of same, having had naturally thick hair all his life and not ever having been given to lingering narcissistically over his reflection in mirrors. Dr. Dark, his lifelong physician, and Mr. Craig, his lifelong guardian, also disclaimed knowledge of it, neither having ever had occasion to examine the patient's scalp at nose length, man *or* boy. Lieutenant Luria made a hurried phone call to the coroner's physician, Dr. Tennant, and a hurried drive to the morgue, where Dr. Tennant hurriedly joined him. Dr. Tennant commandeered the remains of John (I or III) Sebastian, examined the head in the area indicated by the lieutenant, and proclaimed to the lieutenant triumphantly, "This one has *no* birthmark!"

The singularity of the birthmark on the living John's scalp, when in identical triplets it might have been expected that the triplet's scalp would exhibit the same mark, and a closer examination of the mark itself when the dressings were removed, inspired Dr. Samson Dark to suggest that it was no true *naevus*, but probably a forceps mark inflicted by the delivering physician during the patient's birth.

The next chapter was written by Faustino Quancchi, the many-blessed barber of Greenwich Village, whom Lieutenant Luria sought out in a burst of inspiration. Mr. Quancchi had been John I's barber since the Sebastian heir had taken up residence in the Village in 1925. Yes, Quancchi he has cut Mr. Sebastian's hair since four years, *personalmente*. Birthamark on head? Yes, Quancchi see birthmark since first time Mr. Sebastian come sit in chair. Where ona head? Justa here (illustrating with a hairy forefinger on Lieutenant Luria's skull). What it looka like? So big. Thesa shape (illustrating with stub pencil on margin of the *Graphic*.)

Ergo, the living John was John I.

Success did not go to Lieutenant Luria's head. It should not be written against his record, sorry as it is, that he erred on the side of overconfidence. Lieutenant Luria caused official inquiries to be made in the State of Idaho. The trail led to the west slope of the Continental Divide, to M.S.U. in Missoula, Montana where John III had spent four years of his life. Campus barbers were shown John III's picture in his M.S.U. yearbook. Barber Clarence Rodney Pick, who had lost his left eye in the Argonne Forest, remembered John III well; the sonofagun almost got my younger sister Marybell in trouble. He used me to get next to my sister, always came to my chair for haircuts. Till I found out what the bastard was after and then I said to him I said the next time you come to my chair you defiler of Montana womanhood I'll slit your goddam Idaho throat. He went over to Wormser's butcher shop for his haircuts after that. Birthmark on his scalp? Hell no. Least I never noticed any and I'd have noticed anything about that young bastard. Don't let my one eye fool you buddy I got forty-forty vision in it hahaha!

Ergo, approached either positively or negatively, the dead John was John III.

Subsequent handwriting comparison tests of authenticated John I-John III specimens, when the survivor's wrist had dwindled to normal, proved beyond question that, at least in respect to his identity, the living John had told the truth.

It seemed a momentous victory for the forces of law and order at the time; but when enthusiasms cooled it was seen that sorting John I out from John III benefited no one but

John I. It certainly did not benefit Lieutenant Luria or, when Lieutenant Luria was peremptorily transferred to another post, his successor or their superiors. The mystery of who had buried a dagger in old Dr. Cornelius F. Hall on Arthur Craig's library floor vied for impenetrability honors with the mystery of who had performed the same disservice for John (III) Sebastian in the bedroom upstairs ten days later. There were simply no clues. Not only was significant *res gestae* evidence lacking, even theories died of indigestion.

In due course John (I) Sebastian came into his inheritance (this, too, Ellery learned from the papers). There was no legal difficulty, whatever. For he was the veritable and authentic John (I) Sebastian, the "My only son, John" specified in his father's will; and against the granite of this fact the life and death of his brother might have been a passing goose feather. (As Attorney Payn pointed out to Arthur Craig in a private conversation, even if John I had murdered John III, and this could be proved, John I's right to inherit would in no wise be compromised. John III had never had any rights under his father's will, hence he could not be deprived of same. Indeed, insofar as his father's will *or* his father were concerned, Mr. Payn remarked with savage relish [he had long since decided, as had Mr. Freeman, that the blackmailer had been John III], John III might just as well have never been born at all.)

A sad side-effect of the catastrophe, one which Ellery followed sympathetically, was the fate of John Sebastian's romance with Yolanda (Rusty) Brown. It was climax in reverse; a nullity. Miss Brown, accompanied by her mother, went to California, on "a new-ideas trip" of unannounced duration. Before her departure she and John Sebastian had a twelve-minute conversation behind a locked door. When she emerged, pale but proud-chinned, reporters noticed that the diamond "friendship ring" which had illuminated the fourth finger of Miss Brown's left hand was no longer there. Although Miss Brown refused comment (as did Mr. Sebastian), the press drew a fair bow and opined that the pair were no longer affianced; and when Miss Brown entrained for Los Angeles still Miss Brown, it was reasonably clear that no Brown-Sebastian nuptials would ever take place.

They were right.

As for the dual murder case (it was assumed that the murder of Dr. Hall and the murder of John III were connected, although in the pathless jungle of this case no one would have been astonished had it proved otherwise), no solution was ever officially offered, no one was ever arrested for either or both, and it—or they—remained in the "Open" file until the file moldered.

It is officially unsolved to this day.

To Mr. Ellery Queen—young Mr. Queen—the aftermath

of the Sebastian case constituted one of the blackest periods of his life.

Into this darkness not even the fatherly light of the Inspector's love was able to penetrate. Ellery paced night and day, or stared at walls. He dallied with his food, grew emaciated and forlorn. His friends knew him not.

The light of Inspector Queen's professional experience made no impression, either. Son and father discussed the case interminably—the frame-up, the possible framer, the ways in which he might be arrived at. But they arrived nowhere.

Eventually the darkness lifted—from young Mr. Queen's spirit, at least—and other cases came along to engage his interest and talent for seeing twos and putting them together. He solved them. He wrote his books. He even became famous. But he never forgot how he had failed in his second—really his first—murder case. Long after the details faded from his memory, the fact of that failure remained—like a ringworm routed but not destroyed—itching under his skin.

BOOK THREE

CHALLENGE TO THE READER

In Which the Reader's Attention is Respectfully Requested

The current vogue in detective literature is all for the practice of placing the reader in the position of chief sleuth . . . At this point . . . the interpolation of a challenge to the reader . . . [is pertinent] . . . The alert student of mystery tales, now being in possession of all the . . . facts, should at this stage of the story have reached definite conclusions . . . The solution—or enough of it to point unerringly to the guilty character—may be reached by a series of logical deductions and psychological observations . . .

—*The Roman Hat Mystery*

Chapter XVII ✢ 27 Years Later: Summer 1957

In Which Mr. Queen Is Seized with a Serious Attack of Nostalgia and Suffers Himself to Be Fatally Tempted to Resuscitate the Past

BY MANHATTAN standards it was a perfect midsummer day, with the temperature at 72 degrees midmorning, a humidity of 33 percent, and the barometer at 30.05 and steady—warm and dry and breezy-fresh, with pigeons fluttering about the front windows and boys playing stickball on West 87th Street to the frosty tinkle of a Good Humor man, the Park beckoning a few blocks east, the rivers calling east and west, the beaches murmuring lecherously north and south . . . just the sort of day, Ellery thought, whipped up by a malicious Mother Nature to plague the whole race of spread-seated, typewriter-shackled, apartment-bound idiots who insisted on being writers.

He had been toiling for almost two hours now at his beautiful electric typewriter, and all he had to show was a sheet of yellow paper dirtied with five and a half lines of less than deathless prose containing 53 words, 21 of which he had gone back and Xed out.

No energy, Ellery thought, drooping. I'm vitamin-poor, a man with a built-in tranquilizer. Give me a harp and I'm happy. Thirty novels under my belt—what do I want with thirty-one? Weren't nine symphonies enough for Beethoven?

With some alarm he realized that he was getting old. This was such an overwhelming thought that he immediately typed two and a half lines more, disdaining to X out so much as a typographic error. But then the futility of it all hit him again, he drooped again, and he found himself wishing it were noon so that he might decently make himself a Bloody Mary.

At this point the telephone rang. He leaped on it.

"Ellery Queen speaking!"

The voice was male, bass and vibrato with emotion. "Mr. Queen, I bet you'll never guess who this is."

Ellery sighed. This was the one telephonic approach that was calculated to depress him in times of high receptivity. "I never bet, friend, let alone guess. Who is this?"

"Stanley Devoe," the voice said. Then it said into the silence, hopefully, "Devoe? Remember?"

"Devoe, Devoe. No," Ellery said, "I can't say I do. Where do I know you from?"

"From away back. Maybe you'd remember Sergeant Devoe?"

"Sergeant De . . . *Sergeant* Devoe!" Ellery shouted. "Hello, Sergeant! How could I ever forget you? Grown any?"

"Backwards about an inch."

"Sergeant Devoe. I'll be double-dyed-in-Danbury. How are you?"

"Getting on, getting on. And you?"

"Ditto, ditto," Ellery said glumly. "How in the world did you happen to call me up, Sergeant?"

"I'm not a sergeant any more, Mr. Queen."

"Lieutenant? Captain?"

"Chief."

"Chief! Well. Chief of what?"

"I retired from the troopers a few years back and there was this opening for a chief of police job up here—"

"Where is up here?"

"Alderwood."

"Alderwood!" Memories were popping up from long-buried brain cells like corn from a hot grid. "What ever happened to Chief Brickell?"

"Brickell?" Chief Devoe chuckled. "Doesn't time mean

170

anything to you writer guys? Alderwood's had two police chiefs since Brickell. Old Brick died back in 'Thirty-seven."

"Old Brick dead for twenty years." Ellery had known Old Brick for just about five hours, but he felt terrible. "Well, well. Sergeant Devoe." And now he couldn't think of anything to say.

Devoe was quiet, too. But then he said, "Tell you why I called. You remember that cockeyed case, Mr. Queen—those two murders over in the old Craig place?"

"Yes?" Ellery's nostrils began to quiver.

"You know, it was never solved."

"I know."

"Well, the last week or so I've been having one of the storerooms in the basement here at police headquarters cleaned out of a mess of old junk—"

"Police headquarters. That used to be one cubbyhole in the city hall."

"We've got our own building now. Well, this stuff is not only the accumulated junk of the twenty-two years since the building was put up, but also some that was transferred from the old city hall. Anyway, this morning we ran across a crate, and what do you think it was marked? Sebastian Case."

"Crate?"

"The whole damn file on the case."

"Well." Something was stirring deep inside, something distinctly not pleasant. "What's it doing in Alderwood? That was a county investigation."

"I know. Nobody seems to know how it got here. But it's here, and I was going to have it burned with the rest of the trash when all of a sudden I said to myself, Hey, I'll bet Ellery Queen would like to have this. Would you?"

Ellery was silent.

"Mr. Queen?"

"I think I would," Ellery said slowly. "It's all there? Those Christmas boxes, the cards . . . ?"

"The whole kit and caboodle of the screwball stuff. Say, I'm glad I thought of it." Chief Devoe sounded pleased with himself. "Okay, Mr. Queen, I'll ship it to you Railway Express."

"No, no, don't go to that trouble," Ellery said, quickly this time. "I might take a drive and pick it up myself. Yes, I think I'll do that—today, in fact. Would today be all right for you, Chief?"

"Are you kidding? My whole department's a-rockin' and a-rollin' just knowing I'm on the phone with you."

"All four of 'em, eh?" Ellery chuckled.

"Four? I've got thirty-two men working out of this building, besides the office staff."

"Oh," Ellery said humbly.

171

"I guess you'll find a whole lot changed. Including me. Don't expect to see that skinny kid trouper you used to know." Stanley Devoe guffawed. "I've kind of put on a little weight since back in 'Thirty . . ."

Chief Devoe weighed 300 pounds. It took Ellery's total powers of imagination to see through the layers of lard to the beautiful figure of the Sergeant Devoe he had known. The face was all but unrecognizable.

"Changed some, huh, Mr. Queen?" Devoe said wistfully.

"Haven't we all?"

"I'd know you any place. You've kept in condition."

Not where it counts, Ellery thought . . . Everything was changed everywhere. He had driven his '57 convertible into a strange city up to an aging marble building of WPA vintage, with parking meters, 30-minute time limits, and business buildings towering in every direction. None of it had any more relation to the Alderwood he had visited in 1929 than a TV color set had to Mrs. Janssen's old crystal radio.

It was an uncomfortable experience. Chief Devoe felt it, too. They chatted in his fine big office for a while—about his career, the growth of Alderwood, juvenile delinquency, radioactive fallout, the hopeless task of civil defense, the Thruway, the Earth Satellite—even about Lieutenant Luria who, according to Devoe, had resigned from the state trooper organization a few years after the Sebastian fiasco and had gone into the insurance business somewhere in the Midwest. But it was a nervous sort of conversation, with no roots anywhere, and after the third awkward silence Devoe got ponderously to his feet and suggested that they visit the basement. Ellery could have hugged him.

"You know, I'm getting a real bang out of this," the huge man said, leading the way down a flight of concrete steps. "You're a pretty famous guy, Mr. Queen. I'll bet there's not one of your books I haven't read."

"I'll bet, even though I never do."

"What? You name it, I've got it home."

"The Twelfth Night Mystery."

"Twelfth—? Oh! Say, I never did at that. You did one on the Sebastian case?"

"You never read it," Ellery said grimly, "because I never wrote it."

"Couldn't figure out the solution, hey?" Devoe laughed. When he laughed his whole mountainous body quaked. Ellery felt a little sick.

"Something like that."

Devoe gave him a queerly sharp look. "Well, here it is."

The wooden lid had been wrenched off. Devoe switched on an overhead bulb, and Ellery peered.

There it was again, the fossil remains of his youthful failure, in a perfect state of preservation. As if the last twenty-seven years had never been. The little sandalwood ox ... the toy house ... the jeweled dagger ... And there was the stack of white cards. A shred of desiccated rubber band was stuck to the top one; someone had tied a piece of string around them to hold them together ... And the little black

Ellery replaced the dusty little relic in the crate with book.

Black book?

The diary!

Ellery snatched it from the crate. It was plastered with He had completely forgotten about his diary.

dust. He opened it eagerly. A youthful script sprang out at And here it was.

him ... His own handwriting, over a quarter of a century old. Lieutenant Luria had confiscated the diary and it had never been returned to him.

tenderness.

"Could one of your people put this in the trunk of my car, Chief?"

"Right away."

"I can't begin to tell you what this means to me."

"Sure, Mr. Queen. I understand." And for a moment Ellery had the warmest feeling that the big man really did, and for the only time that afternoon he felt close to Devoe.

On impulse he drove through the unfamiliar streets toward the old Craig property. He passed it twice without recognizing it. The third time he checked with a street sign to make sure he was in the right location. He was. The Craig house was gone. The woods beyond were gone too. So were the lordly lawns. On the site stretched dozens and dozens of identical little houses disguised with yellow or red or purple trim, like jukeboxes, each with a tiny garage in the rear, each with a postage stamp of lawn and a small play-yard fore and aft, a TV antenna above, and one miserable tree to a lot.

Ellery backed around and drove agedly back to New York.

Inspector Queen surfaced out of a drowning sleep, wondering what had awakened him. Blearily he peered at the radial hands of his watch. Twenty past four. Somebody had said something ...

Somebody was still saying something.

There it was again, a loud clear tenor, intense, full of self-loathing and triumphant.

"I'll be damned. I'll be *damned*."

A light shone somewhere in the apartment.

The old man crawled out of bed. He wore no pajama top.

173

Yawning and rubbing his damp, skinny torso, he padded across the invisible living room to Ellery's study, the source of the light.

"You out of your mind, son?" The Inspector yawned again. "Haven't you been to bed yet?"

Ellery was in his stockinged feet, still wearing his trousers and shirt. He was seated Indian-fashion on top of his desk staring down at the floor, on which he had laid out in a satisfying circle the contents of the Alderwood crate. The black diary lay open on the desk beside him.

"Dad, I've got it."

"Aren't you a bit on in years to be playing house?" His father sat down on the leather couch and reached for a cigaret. The couch felt cool and he leaned back. "Got what?"

"The answer to the Sebastian riddle."

"Sebastian?" The old man puffed, frowning. "Sebastian. It doesn't click. Who's Sebastian?"

"It was a long time ago, Dad." Ellery had a refreshed aura about him, as if he had just come from a dip in a mountain lake. At the same time there was a sadness in him, a sad wisdom the Inspector found puzzling.

The old man stared.

"You remember," Ellery said softly. "Alderwood. That poetry-writing kid who lived in Greenwich Village. This was back in 'Twenty-nine. You and Velie dug some background out for me—"

The Inspector slapped his ropy shank. "Sure! Are these—?" He looked at the circle of objects intently. "But that's ancient history, Ellery. Where did you dig these up?"

Ellery told him, and picked up the black book. "I've spent most of the night re-reading my diary. You know, I was pretty young."

"That's bad?"

"That's good, but it had its disadvantages. I must have been insufferable. So cocky and know-it all. Did I get into your hair much?"

"I was a lot younger then myself," Inspector Queen grinned. He tamped out the cigaret and said, "You've cracked the case? After all these years?"

"Yes." Ellery locked his arms about his knees and rocked. "I was the Brain. My powers were absolute, and when they collided with the facts it was the facts that suffered. "That's why I never saw the truth in the Sebastian case. Dad, I had it right in my hands. I turned it over, sniffed it, examined it inside and out. And I never really saw it."

"Want to tell me about it?" his father said.

"No, Dad, you go on back to sleep. I'm sorry I woke you."

"Want to tell me about it?" the old man repeated.

So Ellery told him.

This time it was the Inspector who said, over and over, "I'm damned. I'll be *damned*."

Chapter XVIII ✠ The Next Day

*In Which, As Briefly As Possible, Some Long
Histories Are Unfolded of Persons Living
and Dead, and Ellery Plans a Journey*

IN THE REGULAR course of author-publisher relations, Ellery had seen Dan Z. Freeman with reasonable frequency for almost three decades, but today, as the publisher rose from his desk in greeting, it struck Ellery that he had not been seeing Freeman at all. It's like the Einsteinian illustration of relativity, he thought: two trains running along on parallel tracks in the same direction at the same speed, and a passenger in either would swear that both were standing still. There was no frame of reference until one looked out the opposite window and saw the landscape flying by.

The old diary had given him a frame of reference in its twenty-seven-year-old impressions about the people of the house party, including Freeman. He now saw an elderly man with a few fine straws of gray clinging to the rim of his scalp; the brown eyes that had been beautiful were still beautiful, but they lay imbedded in worn showcases of flesh like old jewels in a museum; there was a stoop to the slender shoulders, a settling of shape, a slowdown of gesture that were almost painful to observe.

Ellery wondered uneasily how he must look to Freeman.

"No, it's not about our mutual interest in best sellers, Dan," Ellery said with a smile. "Not this time. First, because the new book is crawling on its hands and knees through a burning desert; second, because I've had a rather remarkable experience. Remember our stay in Arthur Craig's house over the Christmas-New Year holiday in the winter of 'Twenty-nine-Thirty?"

The publisher sat still. It was a momentary freezing, like the stoppage of a film; then motion was restored, and he murmured, "What on earth reminded you of that, Ellery? I haven't thought about it in years."

"Neither had I, really," Ellery said. "But something happened yesterday that recalled those two weeks to me forcibly, and I began wondering. You know my mind, Dan. Let a question creep into it, and I start thrashing about. I suddenly find myself with a great curiosity about the people who were with us in the Craig house over that holiday. Silly, I suppose, but I'll be fairly useless until my curiosity is appeased. Have you any idea what's happened to them?"

His publisher gave him a searching look. Then Freeman depressed one of the levers of his interoffice communicator, murmured, "No calls or interruptions, Harriet," and talked for over an hour.

John Sebastian had waited only until the legal formalities were satisfied and he took possession of his legacy, then he had quit the United States. The young millionaire had bought a villa in the south of France, near Cannes, and he had never returned. In the beginning there were stories of princely parties, fabulous women, unsavory escapades; but apparently this had been a passing phase. He settled down to a quiet life, entertaining a few friends on rare occasions, for the most part writing poetry, raising finches and building an art collection through agents in Paris, London and New York. So far as Freeman knew, John had never married.

"Yes, he published his poetry," Freeman said, "but not through me. Not in this country at all, in fact, but in Paris. Three or four slim volumes in French. After the war I heard that John was still living in his villa, unscathed. I've been told told he collaborated with the Nazis, but how true that is I can't say. Certainly he hasn't been molested by the French since the war. As far as I know, he's still there. I haven't had a word from him for ten years or more."

Ellen Craig?

"At the time, I thought you two were working up to something," the publisher laughed. "You didn't keep in touch?"

Ellery had reddened. "For a few months. After Ellen graduated from Wellesley we lost sight of each other. I did hear somewhere that she'd married —"

"Ellen married a bright young fellow in the State Department," Freeman said. "You know the life—from one embassy to another at two to three year intervals, tight little islands of home in a sea of unfamiliar people and surroundings. She has five children, all grown. The last I heard she and her husband were somewhere in Africa. I saw her two years ago, when her husband was back in the States brushing up on African affairs preparatory to his transfer. She's very stout and discreet, a typical diplomat's wife."

That's that, Ellery thought; and he asked about Rusty Brown. According to Freeman, Rusty had closed her Madison Avenue shop during the depression, her "Rusty Brown's Creations" vogue over. He had had no idea what had happened to her until, years afterward, on a visit to Hollywood in connection with some literary properties, he had run into her at a Beverly Hills party. She was a very successful interior decorator in Los Angeles. She had gone through four husbands, had never had any children, and had struck Freeman as a desperately unhappy woman. As far as he knew, she was still on the Coast. He had no idea what had happened to her mother. Rusty had not mentioned her, and Freeman had not asked.

"She doesn't call herself Rusty any more, by the way," the publisher said with a smile. "It's Yolanda, period."

The Reverend Mr. Gardiner was another of the group Freeman had no information about. "It's hardly likely he's still alive. He'd have to be over a hundred."

Dr. Samson Dark had died of coronary thrombosis in 1935.

Roland Payn was dead, too. He had committed suicide in the late '30's, for a reason no one had been able to determine. He had left no note, and only a few minutes before he shot himself at his desk he had been discussing a will case with a client with his usual suavity.

"I remember talking over Payn's death years later with his son, the literary critic. Wendell had no faintest idea of his father's reason for taking his life. The subject was painful to him, and I dropped it."

"But you knew why," Ellery said.

"I didn't *know*."

"A woman, of course."

Freeman shrugged. "It's not unlikely. Payn was one of those plausible hypocrites who lead an impeccable life in broad daylight, but who at night crawl into the woodwork. It was probably a sex mess of some sort. He couldn't face exposure and took the easy way out."

Valentina Warren had married Marius Carlo. It had been a stormy marriage, and it wound up in a noisy divorce suit. Neither had remarried, and neither had got anywhere professionally. Valentina had graduated from ingénue parts to character roles; the mainstay of her income was still summer stock; occasionally she appeared on Broadway in a small role, or played a TV dramatic show. Marius ran a shabby music school in Chicago. He was living with an aged ballet dancer to whom he was quite devoted. Freeman had visited them only the winter before in connection with a book on music Carlo had been trying to get him to publish.

"Need I mention that his title was 'Unisonorous Chants in the Eight Church Modes'?" Freeman said sadly. "The text was equally formidable. They live in a barnlike studio apartment in the Loop that looks like something Dali threw together at the end of an extended binge. Positively the dirtiest place I've ever been in, too."

Incredibly, Arthur Craig was still alive.

"But he must be ninety or more," Ellery protested.

"He's a tenacious old fellow. Clings to life like a barnacle."

Shortly before John Sebastian decamped from the United

177

States, Craig had decided to go out of business and had offered his press to Freeman for sale. Freeman had purchased it for his elder son, who at the time was an apprentice at Craig's press. For some years the printing establishment was run for the Freemans by an old employe of Craig's until the time when young Freeman should be qualified to take over. Now, with Freeman's son in full charge, and the publisher keeping a sentimental eye on it, it was still the fine press Craig had made it, turning out limited and gift editions of standard works with imagination, craftsmanship and taste.

At the same time that he sold his press, Craig had sold his Alderwood estate, liquidated his other holdings, and left the East. He had settled in San Francisco and was still living there. Freeman wrote him an occasional letter, and for old times' sake sent him samples of the press's output, but Craig never answered the letters or acknowledged the books.

"He's become rather odd in his old age," the publisher said. "Lives in a horrible shack, cooks his own meals, dresses like a hermit and so on, even though he must have a considerable income from what he realized when he sold out here in the East. In fact, he's become a miser; the last time I saw Ellen she told me he writes her dunning letters regularly, and she's actually been sending him money for years! I used to drop in on him when business took me to San Francisco, but the last time I visited him he so distressed me that, frankly, I've stopped doing it."

Ellery said abruptly, "Then you have his address."

"Certainly. I still write him."

"May I have it?"

Freeman looked surprised. He spoke to his secretary, and she came in a moment later with an address.

"You're going to write him, too, Ellery?"

"I'm going to pay him a visit."

"What on earth for?" Freeman cried.

"I owe the old gent an explanation that's some twenty-seven years overdue." Ellery rose. "Thanks, Dan."

He took the 11:30 plane for San Francisco that same night.

Chapter XIX ✠ **The Day After That . . .**

*In Which Mr. Queen, to Make His Point, Journeys
Through Space More Than 2500 Miles and
Through Time More Than 3000 Years*

ARTHUR CRAIG'S HOUSE was not far from the waterfront—a scabby yellow-brown frame cottage on a scrubby little elevation scored with broken steps, and squeezed in between two monster warehouses. It could only have been a relic of the days when these were mud flats and there had been an unobstructed view of the Bay. How it had escaped being demolished, how it had managed to survive the growth of the city—how it had got into Craig's possession—Ellery never found out.

Still, if you accepted its shabbiness, it had its points. The crustacean smell of the Embarcadero was in the old man's nostrils night and day, and if he descended his broken steps and got clear of the overprotective warehouses he had a view of Telegraph Hill. The cry of distant gulls was pleasant, and ships of all sizes and descriptions were to be seen at their wharves for the price of a short walk. A man who asked for little in the way of material things might live his old age out here in something like content.

There was a crazy little porch before the cottage which had long since lost its railing, and on this precarious perch— a pipe dangling from his toothless jaws, moving himself gently back and forth in a lopsided strawback chair—sat Arthur Benjamin Craig.

Physically, he was quite unrecognizable. The great frame Ellery remembered had melted and run into itself, to harden again as a knobby and misshapen smaller mass. The hand reaching for the bulldog pipe was now a shriveled claw, blotched brown where it was not purple-gray; the jaws clamping together when the claw came away with the pipe settled into the likeness of a bird's bill. Even the face was birdlike, its skin feathered and ruffled by time, out of which two lidless eyes peered brightly. The skull was a shining old bone. The lusty beard was no more.

As Ellery mounted the ankletrap steps he found himself recasting his impressions with rapidity. Dilapidated derelicts do not shave. At first glance the old man's garment might seem a collection of rags; but it was simply an ancient suit from the prime of his life which had been torn and mended and retorn and mended again, and it was quite respectably clean. Had his body not shrunken so, had he filled the suit out, it would not have seemed the costume of a hermit at all.

Ellery paused before the porch. It had once had an approach of three steps, judging by its height above the ground, but the steps were missing. He must be agile enough still, Ellery thought, to be able to get on and off his porch without snapping a leg.

"Mr. Craig?" Ellery said.

The bright eyes took him in very calmly, from head to toe.

"I know you," Arthur Craig said suddenly. Ellery was astonished at the quality of the voice. It was brittle, but sharply aware, without a note of senility.

179

"Yes, you do, Mr. Craig," Ellery said with a smile. "But it was a very long time ago."

"When?" The question crackled.

"Christmas of 1929."

The old man's face broke into myriad wrinkles, he slapped his thigh, he began to cackle.

"You're Ellery Queen," he gasped, wiping his eyes.

"That's right, sir. May I come up?"

"Yes, yes!" The nonagenarian jumped out of the rocker like a bird, shaking off Ellery's protests. "No, you sit down here. I'll squat on the edge of the porch." He proceeded to do so. "I used to do this when I was a boy, dangling my legs over my father's porch, which didn't have steps any more than this one. I didn't mind it then, and I don't mind it now. So you've come all this way to see old Craig? I take it you flew? Don't care for flying myself. Too chancy. I knew you'd look me up some day. I don't see anybody from the old days. I used to see Dan Freeman, but he's stopped coming—doesn't approve of my way of life." And the old man slapped his thigh again. He did not ask Ellery into his house, and Ellery gathered that his garrulousness was at least partly deliberate, to cover up his failure to do so. "It was Dan gave you my address, I suppose?"

"Yes, Mr. Craig. Why do you say you knew I'd look you up some day?"

The old man swiveled to rest his back against the cracked pillar, drawing his left leg up and swinging the other over the edge of the porch. He reached for a box of stove matches, selected one carefully, scratched it on the porch floor, applied it to his pipe, and puffed with great deliberation until he was seated in a shroud of smoke, like some ancient Indian.

"Because you never finished that business back in Alderwood," he mumbled, puffing vigorously, "that's why. You're like me. Hate a shoddy job. Can't stand slovenly craftsmanship. Especially your own." He snatched the pipe from his lips and cocked an inquisitive eye at Ellery. "Seems to me you took an almighty long time to solve that problem."

"Well, I haven't been working on it continuously," Ellery said with a grin. He was beginning to enjoy himself; it had turned out quite differently from what he had anticipated. "In fact, I gave it hardly a thought for over a quarter of a century. But yesterday . . ."

So Ellery told Arthur B. Craig how he had happened to come back to the case.

"There it was, all spread out on my study floor. The twelve cards, the twenty gifts." He paused to light a cigaret. "You know, Mr. Craig, I discovered the meaning of the gifts back in Alderwood."

180

"You did, hey?" The old man seemed surprised. "As I recollect, you didn't say anything about *that*."

"No," Ellery said. "No, I didn't."

"Why not?"

"Because I was expected to say something about it. Someone was trying to frame someone else for John's murder, and I was supposed to fall for the frame. But let's begin at alpha instead of omega, shall we, Mr. Craig?"

"Neatly put." The toothless mouth curved in a grin. "So it was all a frame-up, was it? You go right ahead, Mr. Queen. I've been waiting for this twenty-eight years come Epiphany."

Ellery smiled at the sly sally. "For a long time I tangled myself up in numerical speculations. The number twelve gave me a really bad time. Twelve people in the house party, the twelve days and nights of Christmas, the twelve signs of the zodiac, the twelve nightly gifts, and so on—some of them clearly coincidences, others clearly planned. I was certain the number twelve was significant. Of course, I was meant to be held up by that. It was the obstacle placed in my path to make the winning of the goal sweeter. And, of course, the number twelve was nothing but a red herring. A whale of a red herring, you might say.

"But the number twenty was a different school of fish." Ellery leaned over to tap his ash onto the ground. "It was the number of the individual *gifts*, or at least of the emphasized words in the verses. That number was associated with concrete concepts—an aggregation of twenty *things*, ox, house, camel, whip, what have you. Could it be a series? In what sort of context did twenty things appear serially? Series meant *order*, a first followed by a second followed by a third and so on. I studied the objects. Ox—first. House—second. Camel—third. Door—fourth . . . right through to a twentieth *different* object. I almost grasped it a number of times, but always I stumbled over that number twenty. I couldn't think of an orderly series of twenty consecutive different things. When I did crack it, I saw why I'd been frustrated. The number twenty was another red herring. It had its meaning, but not for our time. In our time—in the culture dictating my thought processes—it's a different number altogether."

"Is it, now!" the old man said in a kind of glee.

"The discovery came by accident, on the night of January fifth. I went upstairs to my room, taking with me my gift copy of John's book of poems. I happened to open to the title page. And there it was. The key, the key that unlocked the door. And beyond that door lay the answer."

"What answer?" the old man demanded.

"The alphabet," Ellery said.

181

"The alphabet." The old man shaped the syllables almost with affection. "How basic."

"Yes, the exact word, Mr. Craig," Ellery said. "For the alphabet as the ancient Phoenicians bequeathed it to us *began as a collection of pictures of concrete familiar objects*, objects basic to the lives of primitive people—food, shelter, transportation, parts of the human body and so forth. All I had to do was think of the concept 'alphabet' to realize instantly that that was what the concrete familiar objects of the gift packages were intended to convey. And to hell with numbers. We think of the alphabet as consisting of twenty-six letters. Well, it does, but it wasn't twenty-six in thirteen hundred to one thousand B.C., when the Phoenician alphabet was in the process of formulation. It consisted then of twenty-two 'pictures,' twenty of which have come down to us, the other six stemming from later sources.

"Was it actually the basic Phoenician alphabet I was being teased with? It most certainly was. The ox—or more strictly speaking the ox head, which has come to us upside down—was the basic food-object the Phoenicians chose for the first letter of their alphabet, *alef*, or *A*. The second gift was a house; a house—*beth*, meaning *B*—is the original picturization of the second letter of our alphabet. The third gift was a camel—and the Phoenician camel, *gimel* or *gamel*, became our letter *C*. *D* came from door, *E* from window, *F* from hook or nail. There was no *G* as a separate letter until the third century B.C.—until then the *C* character served for the *G* sound, too. Our *H* came from the Phoenician *cheth*, meaning fence—and it was a fence that John received immediately after the nail or hook. *I*, hand; *J*, which was a Roman elongation of *I* to give it a consonant instead of a vowel value, didn't become a separate letter until the sixteenth century—so John received no *J*-object; *K*, palm; *L*, whip; *M*, water; *N*, fish; *O*, eye; *P*, mouth; *Q*, monkey; *R*, head; *S*, tooth; *T*, mark or cross; *U*, *V* and *W* came later; *X*, post; *Y* we got from the Greeks; and finally *Z*, derived—grimly enough—from *zayin*, meaning dagger . . . the 'finishing stroke' that finished the life of John's triplet. Twenty objects, coinciding precisely with the twenty basic sources of the Phoenician alphabet."

"Yes?" the old man said eagerly. "And this meant to you —?"

"Obviously," Ellery said, "that the mind that had conceived the whole macabre stunt had a working knowledge of alphabet sources. Other events had indicated that the gift-leaver must have been one of the people in the house; and what were they? A dilettante poet, a jewelry and textile designer, an amateur student of the occult, a Protestant minister, a lawyer, a medical doctor, an actress, a musician, a young college girl—and a book publisher and a printer . . . I omit

Mrs. Janssen, Mabel and Felton as too absurd for serious consideration.

"It was clear at once that the choice lay between Mr. Freeman and yourself. And that really wasn't a choice. A publisher is connected with language editorially and commercially. But a printer is connected with it technically. And you weren't merely a printer; you were a book designer, a craftsman in superb presswork, necessarily with a broad working knowledge of typography and the typographic art. There was no doubt in my mind that the Phoenician-alphabet basis of the gift series pointed the finger at you, Mr. Craig, as the sender of the gifts and the planner of John's murder."

"I see," the old man said thoughtfully. "And you didn't believe that."

"No, because I was equally certain that no man would devise a series of elaborate clues whose only effect was to point to himself as the villain of the piece. So I chose not to name you to the police, John, or your guests, Mr. Craig. If you were being framed, I wasn't going to play the framer's game.

"The big question," Ellery said, "the question that confronted me that January night in 1930, and that has bothered me on and off during the more than twenty-seven years since, was: Who framed you, Mr. Craig?"

The old man squinted at him through the tobacco smoke. "And now you know, eh?"

Ellery nodded.

"And now I know."

Chapter XX ✠ . . . Continued and Concluded

*In Which Mr. Queen Confesses to the Folly of His
Youth, and Brings the Story of the Twelve
Nights, Albeit Belatedly, to Its End*

"I KNOW," Ellery went on, "from just having synthesized three clues which, on that Epiphany eve so many years ago, I failed to think through.

"The first was a group of odd little drawings. Do you recall how, on the backs of some of the white cards, Mr. Craig, the creator and typist of the verses had penciled some primitive-looking pictures? They didn't appear on every card, or even on most of them—just on four of the twelve. Their very random character was indicative more of involuntary than voluntary design—as if, in the case of those four cards,

183

the typist, perhaps deep in thought, had played with a pencil—in a word, doodled.

"If that was so, the pictures might be significant, an important clue to the versifier-typist-framer-murderer-doodler's *unconscious* self, in contradistinction to the verses and other creations of his consciousness. Unfortunately, the little drawings told me nothing. They merely appeared to be ultrasimplified picturizations of the particular objects with which the typewritten verses of those cards were concerned."

The old man was listening sharply, almost critically.

"Yes, yes?" he said. "Go on, Mr. Queen."

Ellery took a sheet of paper from his pocket and unfolded it. "I copied these from the original cards the other night, Mr. Craig. Perhaps they'll refresh your recollection." He leaned forward with the paper. "Look at them."

The claw seized the paper. On it appeared:

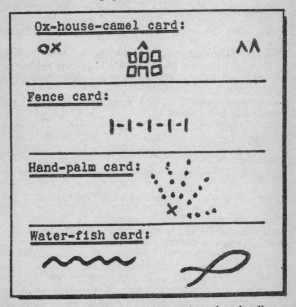

"We all recognized at the time that the doodles were representations of the subject matter of the card on which they appeared," Ellery said. "The card introducing the ox, the house and the camel bore on its reverse a doodled 'o x'; a doodled little house made up of a pitched roof, five windows and a door; and the most recognizable feature of a camel, its humps. The card introducing the fence bore on its back a doodled fencelike drawing. The card introducing the hand and the palm—a most interesting one, by the way—bore on its back a sort of stenciled-effect hand, composed of five out-spread fingers, with a crossmark where the palm would be. And the card introducing the water and the fish illustrated on the back a squiggle that could only have meant water, and a very simple fish-abstraction.

"Did they tell me anything about the doodler?" Ellery shook his head. "Not until about thirty-six hours ago. What do they tell you about him, Mr. Craig?"

The old man was staring at the drawings in amazement.

"Incredible," he exclaimed. "I've only just seen it."

"Yes, the unconscious mind is tricky," Ellery nodded. "The hand that drew the originals of these little pictures was consciously if idly drawing the subject matter of the cards involved, *but in an unconscious technique that gave him away.* The proof that it was unconscious and unrealized is that he permitted the cards with the doodles on them to go through. Had he thought they might give him away, he had only to tear them up and type duplicate cards with blank backs.

"And what was this unconscious technique that gave him away, and that it took me over twenty-seven years to see?" Ellery said. "Why, simply that every last element of these drawings—every circle, square, line, dot crossmark and so on in them—is identified with a certain system of signs, an actual code used in a specific phase of editorial and print-ing work—proofreading. If a proofreader going over a manuscript or a set of galleys finds a digit or number in the text which he thinks ought to be spelled out in letters, he'll mark a little 'o' in the margin as a code sign meaning 'spell out.' If he comes across broken or imperfect type in a galley, he marks a small 'x' in the margin, and the typographer knows what to look for. Thus the 'o' and 'x' of 'ox.'

"Alone, of course, they could be the merest coincidences. But take the 'house.' It's composed of seven elements. The little square used for five of them is the proofreader's mark meaning 'em-quad space,' or 'indent one em.' The little door-like sign is a proofreader's mark meaning 'move in direction indicated.' The little peaked sign is a caret, meaning 'insert at this point.' The two little peaks the doodler used to represent camel humps are simply two carets side by side.

"The representational 'fence'? Made up of vertical lines and short horizontals. The vertical line has at least two specific meanings to the proofreader and typographer; the horizontal lines are, of course, simply indicated hyphens.

"The dots composing the fingers of the 'hand'? Dots under words are a proofreader's way of saying, 'retain words I have crossed out,' the word 'stet' usually being written in the margin in addition: the 'x' of the palm is the broken-type sign again.

"The squiggle of 'water'? This mark placed under text means 'reset to bold-face type,' And the fish-abstraction is one of the several ways of indicating 'delete.'

"Where *every* element employed, without exception, is a part of the sign language of proofreading, there can be no doubt at all that the doodler had an intimate knowledge of same, so intimate that he employed them unconsciously. Do you agree, Mr. Craig?"

"Absolutely." The old man was fascinated.

"That was my delayed-clue Number One." Ellery lit another cigaret. "Number Two was equally interesting.

"You'll recall that the key words of the verses on each card were spaced out—for example, the word 'house,' instead of being typed 'h, o, u, s, e,' was typed 'h, space, o, space, u, space, s, space, e.' Oh, I saw what it meant, all right. I pointed out the very first night that it was obviously intended to emphasize the word so that it would stand out in the verse. What I didn't see until the other night was that this *method* of emphasizing—by letter-spacing—was another unconscious giveaway on the part of the typist.

"For what would the average person do who wanted to stress a typewritten word? He would underline it, or in the case of printed matter, italicize. Yet as long ago as 1931 a famous British artist, engraver and type designer, Eric Gill, was urging in print the universal adoption of what only typographic purists had been employing up to that time— the use of letter-spacing to emphasize single words instead of italicizing or underlining. The practice still hasn't been adopted universally—*but many typographic purists continue to letter-space for emphasis.*"

"True, that's true," the old man muttered.

"Two clues so uncompromising made the conclusion all but inescapable," Ellery went on. "But the other night I found still a third clue that I'd overlooked during that Christmas holiday, and this one clinched it.

"Remember, Mr. Craig, the last line of the last card John received, the card on which I found John III lying with a dagger in his back? That line read: 'This finishing stroke to end your life.'

"Perhaps it sounds far-fetched, but not when you recall how devious the unconscious mind so often is in its operation. 'Finishing stroke' happens to be the definition—deriving originally from the ancient Ionian city of Kolophon, whose famous cavalry troop was supposed invariably to put 'the finishing stroke' to a battle—of the modern bibliographer's word 'colophon'—which, as I hardly have to tell you, sir, is an inscription placed at the very end of a book containing facts relevant to its production ... names of printer, author, illustrator, place and date of publication, and so on.

"How the typist-framer-murderer's unconscious betrayed him there! It made him, in murdering the brother he thought was the original John and so winding up *his* production, employ the definition of a printer's term meaning the identical thing!"

Ellery flipped his cigaret away with a gesture as final as his subject. "And there it was. Who in the group had such an intimate knowledge of proofreader's marks that he would unconsciously use them as drawing elements? Who in the group would employ by habit the emphasis-device of letter-spacing used only by the most finicky of purists in the typographic profession? Who in the group would be most likely to use the precise printer's meaning of the word 'colophon'? Who but the one person in the group who was a professional typographer and printer—a man so deeply grounded in his trade that he had raised it, as someone once said, to a profession? Mr. Craig, you typed those cards. You drew those doodles. You sent those 'gifts.' You plunged the finishing dagger-stroke into the back of the man you thought was your ward. *You framed yourself for the crime.*"

The old man was silent. He sat clutching his pipe, which had gone out, swinging his right leg over the side of the porch, jaws working as he ruminated.

And then he said, almost slyly, "I framed myself, you say. And you have just said that no intelligent man would build an elaborate structure of clues that had no other effect than to point to himself as the criminal. You told me yourself that it was on that very point you decided I was the innocent victim of a frame-up."

"In January of 1930, Mr. Craig," Ellery said, nodding, "I was very young, and it does sound logical, doesn't it? Yes, no one would believe that an intelligent man would point suspicion to himself. But it's taken me over a quarter of a century to learn that an intelligent man might point suspicion to himself for the very reason that no one would believe it."

The old man cackled so long and so hard that he wound up choking and gasping. Ellery got up and patted his back gently. When Craig stopped choking, Ellery sat down again.

"You're clever, my boy, clever," the old man wheezed.

"You were a great deal cleverer, Mr. Craig. You'd read my book, you'd undoubtedly pumped John dry about me—you dug until you found out what my cleverness was made of, then you planned accordingly. You offered me the obvious, certain I would reject it, and you were right. It was a masterly double bluff that took me in completely. I can only offer you my belated admiration."

"But what a risk I took, eh?" the old man chortled. "Foolish, wasn't it, to take such a risk? Eh?"

"No," Ellery said, "because you ran a far greater risk. You wanted to kill John. But if you killed him directly, even if

187

you left no clues to yourself in the commission of the crime, you would stand out as the most prominent suspect. For you had a powerful motive for wanting John dead before the sixth of January, 1930. And there was no conceivable way in which you could conceal that motive. According to his father's will, *if John died before his twenty-fifth birthday you, Arthur Benjamin Craig, inherited the Sebastian estate.* The only way you could hope to draw attention *away* from that motive was to draw attention dramatically *to* someone else. If I could be convinced that you were being framed for the murder, I would accept your motive as something the framer merely took advantage of. I would pass over it—as I did."

"Still, it wasn't in character, wouldn't you say?" And now a tinge of bitterness colored the old voice. "Why would I, a wealthy man, want the Sebastian estate, too? Did I ever strike you as that grasping a man, Mr. Queen?"

"No, Mr. Craig," Ellery said, "but this was Christmas of 1929. Only two months before, on October the twenty-ninth, the stock market had collapsed with the biggest bang in its history. You must have been caught in the crash, like hundreds of thousands of others. But I don't believe you're the type of man who would have committed murder merely to recoup his own monetary losses. You were the administrator of John Senior's estate; you had been handling its assets, investing in its interests, for almost twenty-five years. I suggest that it was principally the estate's funds that you had unwisely gambled away on the market on the dangerous margins dangled as bait in those days—and for that you could have gone to prison. The only way you could cover up your maladministration of the estate was by getting rid of John before he could legally come into it. Then the gutted estate would pass to you, and nobody'd be the wiser ... The alternative was not to kill John, but to confess to him that he was inheriting little or nothing, and to throw yourself on his mercy. I think you had reason to doubt John's mercifulness, Mr. Craig. I myself sensed the hard streak in him. You knew he would probably not only make you liquidate everything you owned and turn it over to him, but send you to prison in the bargain. And to keep from going to prison you were willing to commit murder."

"Yes," the old man mumbled, "and it all went wrong anyway ... I'd lost every cent of the estate. I planned the whole thing in the last two months after the crash—got the gifts together, typed the verses on a machine I had hidden at my plant—got everything ready for you, to the last detail ... And then, when I did the killing, I found out I'd killed the wrong man."

His voice had sunk to a whining whisper.

"I'd no idea John had a triplet brother alive. I didn't know a thing about the multiple birth ... I didn't know John had

188

his brother hidden in my house ... By the time I found out what I'd done—that John was still alive—it was too late. When John walked in that night at fifteen minutes to midnight, in the midst of everybody, with the police in the house, I had no chance to correct my mistake. Fifteen minutes later it was midnight, he was legally twenty-five years old, he had legally inherited his father's estate ... I was ruined."

"So you liquidated everything you owned," Ellery said, "your press, your house, all your property and holdings and you scraped together enough to hand over to John the equivalent of his father's estate, without him or anyone else suspecting that it was your own wealth you were turning over to him, not his. Isn't that it, Mr. Craig? Isn't that why you're living here in this shack—on Ellen's charity?"

"Yes," the old man said with dignity, "I broke myself and I've been a pauper ever since. For a few years out here I managed to make a living at my old trade. But then they said I was too old ... Ellen thinks I'm a cracked miser, worth a fortune. God bless her, she sends me money anyway. If not for her, I'd have starved long ago."

His head sank to his breast. Ellery said nothing. A long time later, when he saw that the old man had forgotten him, he said gently, "Mr. Craig."

The head jerked. "Eh?"

"Mr. Craig, you also killed Dr. Hall, didn't you?"

"What? Oh. Hall? Yes. Yes, I did."

"I admit I haven't been able to figure out why you killed Hall, when you didn't know anything about the triplets."

"That was a mixup, a bad mixup ... It was the other John —the one you called John III—who smuggled him into the house, but I didn't know that. The first I knew of him, I found him in my library, waiting for me. He said he was the doctor who had delivered John in 1905. He didn't mention any other John. He must have known about the surprise the boys were planning and maybe promised not to let on.

"Anyway, he kept talking about 'John,' and I thought he meant my John, when all the time he meant his John. Dr. Hall had got suspicious of me; he'd nosed around and somehow learned that the estate was wiped out in the crash. He'd devoted years of his life to seeing that his John got half of the estate, and he was furious with me. He threatened me, said he'd expose me then and there, send me to jail unless I made up the losses. My plans were set, I'd already made up my mind to kill John the night of January fifth—and here this Hall was going to spoil everything before I even got started. So I saw I had to kill him, too. And I did.

"If I'd been able to sneak his body out of the house," Arthur Craig said, "and dump it somewhere, I'd have done it. But with so many people running around in the place, I knew I'd be seen by somebody. So I did what I could—I removed every clue I could find to his identity, or possible identification, burned them all in the fireplace, and hoped for the best."

There was no glee in the old man now. His head sank to his breast again, but this time it came up quickly.

"Now you know it all, Mr. Queen," he said. "What are you going to do with me?"

"I don't know." Ellery fumbled for another cigaret, stared at it. But then he looked the aged man in the eye. "Or perhaps I do, Mr. Craig. These crimes were committed twenty-seven years ago. My solution of the case may be very clever, as you say, but it's also—from a legal standpoint—very futile, too. There's no evidence in the legal definition on which to base an arrest and trial. And even if there were . . . How old are you, sir?"

"I'll be ninety-two my next birthday."

"Ninety-two." Ellery rose. "I think, Mr. Craig, I'll bid you good day."

The old man stared. Then his shaking fingers went to some cavern in his clothes, came out with an ancient tobacco pouch, and he began to refill his bulldog. Ellery hopped off the porch and began to negotiate the broken steps.

"Wait," Arthur B. Craig said. "Wait a minute, there."

Ellery stopped. "Yes?"

"I've got a peculiar type of mind," the old man said. He was feeling around for his matches. "Active, you might say. And curious. Like yours, in fact."

"Yes?" Ellery said again, smiling faintly.

The old man found his matches, struck one and puffed deeply.

"Now along about an hour or so ago, Mr. Queen, you were talking about how you first came to realize what those twenty things I'd been leaving for John must mean. You said you opened your copy of that limited edition of John's poetry I'd printed up, and that something you saw on the title page gave you the key to the fact that the twenty objects stood for letters of the alphabet. I'm trying to remember what could have been on that page that would tell you a thing like that." Arthur Benjamin Craig asked, "What was it, Mr. Queen?"

"Why, the name of your printing firm, which I assume you took from your own initials," Ellery said. "The ABC Press."